THE WORLD WE SAW BURNING

First published by Charco Press 2025
Charco Press Ltd., Office 59, 44-46 Morningside Road, Edinburgh
EH10 4BF

Copyright © Renato Cisneros 2023
Published in agreement with Casanovas & Lynch Literary Agency

First published in Spanish as *El mundo que vimos arder* (Lima: Alfaguara)
English translation copyright © Fionn Petch 2025

A CIP catalogue record for this book is available
from the British Library.

ISBN: 9781917260084
e-book: 9781917260091

www.charcopress.com

Copy-edited by Tim Gutteridge
Cover designed by Pablo Font
Typeset by Laura Jones-Rivera
Proofread by Fiona Mackintosh

2 4 6 8 10 9 7 5 3 1

Renato Cisneros

THE WORLD WE SAW BURNING

Translated by
Fionn Petch

CHARCO PRESS

*To all those who left
the place they were born in.*

*It's a terrible thing to discover that you carry
inside the thing you hate the most.*

George Stevens

*I have Dutch, nigger, and English in me, /
and either I'm nobody, or I'm a nation.*

Derek Walcott

*The past is a foreign country.
They do things differently there.*

L.P. Hartley

1

Today it's been a year since Erika and I got divorced. I wish I could say it's only just occurred to me, but the truth is I've been pondering it since the early hours. I didn't think the memory of that day would remain so clear, yet twelve months later I can still reconstruct it with ease. We got divorced on a Tuesday, on a lacklustre summer afternoon. Half of Madrid was away on holiday, meaning the city was abandoned to that unreal calm of mid-July. The judge read out a dozen clauses full of incomprehensible terminology, and when the moment arrived for us to sign, Erika and I avoided each other's gaze. She scribbled on every page, expressionless. I spent a few minutes pretending to read the ruling, but I couldn't take my eyes off the expression *by mutual agreement*. We left the court and returned to the apartment on foot; walking in silence for eleven blocks downhill in the heat. That night I slept, or tried to, on the sofa-bed in the living room, and the following morning I took a direct flight to Lima. I planned to stay for two months. Erika said she'd use the time to pack up her things and move to Berlin, to her parents' house. Before saying goodbye, as I was shutting my suitcase and spinning the numbers on the lock (*0-5-1-0*, referring to the fifth of October, our anniversary; I hadn't got round to changing it), she told me that in Germany she'd start over, *from scratch*. The remark upset me; I felt it was premeditated, as if she wanted to erase or diminish our five years of marriage. *From scratch.* Those were her words, and the determination with which she uttered them suggested that, right there, she was already commencing this new chapter in her life in which I no longer had any function to perform, no role to play.

I confess that to this day I still find her decision not only sudden but somewhat inexplicable. In the preceding weeks, I had noticed a certain evasiveness in her behaviour, and even wondered if she was suffering from depression, as her mood had fluctuated similarly in the past. In any case, I was not concerned, trusting that we would return to normal within a few days. That didn't happen. The malaise became a crisis that I – that we – were unable to get a grip on, let alone halt. Now I have reason to think that Erika blamed me for everything that frustrated her: our precarious financial situation, the few opportunities for advancement in her job (one she had taken at my insistence) and, above all, the failure to get pregnant. Strangely, she didn't cite any of these causes on the day in question. With hard-edged German pragmatism, she limited herself to saying that she needed to rethink her life and that, after so many years together, she no longer loved me. Not one word more. The news took me unawares, of course. I had neither the instinct nor the courage to point out that just two evenings earlier we had drunk several glasses of wine together – on her initiative – and made love in a somewhat hasty, but I thought satisfactory, manner, which gave me the misguided impression that perhaps she was on the road to recovery.

Everything went downhill over the following days. Erika's volubility increased, and with it, my hopes that she would reconsider rapidly faded. One fine day I found myself with the dreamlike impression that I was attending the wake of a still-warm body whose countenance, as the hours passed, increasingly resembled my own. It was a premonition. There was nothing more to do.

That is why I left for Lima: I wanted to take my distance, to absorb the blow, to think as little as possible about the separation. It didn't work, of course. I spent the whole period on the receiving end of repeated condolences, awkward questions, unfortunate conjectures, unsolicited advice and − worst of all − I had to dodge insufferable enquiries from my family about what I was going to do with my life now. My parents and siblings talked to me like a child who had been orphaned and lost everything from one day to the next. I can't blame them. That's kind of how I felt: lost, rudderless. I guess it showed.

2

A day before my return to Madrid from Lima, I sat down to make plans and define goals. The first of these was to clear out the apartment I had shared with Erika. Flat 3B, number 76 on Calle de Ferraz, in a nice area near the Parque del Oeste, the Teleférico, and the Temple of Debod. I invited her to move in together eight months after we met, nine before we married. Vacating that apartment wasn't going to be easy. It wasn't simply a matter of packing up clothes and books, taking posters off the wall, checking the accounts and giving notice to the owner. However much care Erika might have taken in removing all traces of her presence there, I was sure I would come across indelible signs of those glorious days we spent cooking together after making love, or passionately debating on the tiny balcony the films we'd seen at the Renoir cinema, or sitting listening to music, smoking, drinking a glass of wine and making plans for the future. Sometimes planning the future meant speculating about the names and features our children would have. Erika told everyone she wanted to have two or three, and people were struck by my enthusiasm for this family project. No, it wasn't going to be easy to return so soon to that particular trench without taking a false step.

I decided not to complicate things and rented another flat I found online. Everyone in Lima thought I was crazy to be spending my savings on maintaining two apartments in Madrid. No one understood that it was a question of my mental wellbeing: I too wanted to rethink my life, not to remain stagnant, but to start over – like Erika – *from scratch*. And it was important to do so in Madrid, the city that has seen in succession the greatest joys and the most instructive disappointments of my adult life. In any case, the new place would just be a provisional refuge, a hideaway for working, eating and sleeping for a few months, without worrying about the wounds or reminiscences that disturbed my peace. I chose a bright, one-bedroom flat in the Malasaña district, on Calle de la Palma. The day I moved in, as soon as I crossed the threshold I knew I'd done the right thing.

3

'Good evening, allow me,' said the taxi driver as he took my suitcase and placed it in the boot of the car. I tried to guess where he was from by his accent: Peruvian, Ecuadorian, Bolivian? When he asked where we were going and referred to me as *maestro*, I knew right away. Peruvian. Only in Peru do people use *maestro* without distinction to address a colleague, a garage mechanic, a janitor, a waiter or just about anyone we want to treat in an amiable manner. My phone was out of battery, but I'd memorised the address of the new apartment: 59, Calle de la Palma. I relayed this to the driver and we set off. Retaining useful information was one of Erika's qualities. My forgetfulness with such things always annoyed her; she said I had selective amnesia. In the final stage of the marriage, just to prove her wrong, I effortlessly learned by heart countless shared codes, PINs, passwords, phone numbers and addresses. All of which are now useless, but I am stuck with them.

'Is here alright for you? This your place?' asked the driver as we pulled up in front of the building. I didn't know how to reply. Was it my place? I told him that yes, it was.

The new flat was smaller than it had looked online, but at least it was fully equipped. I hung my jacket on the coat rack, left my suitcase in the corridor and explored the rooms without noticing the details that Erika would never have missed, such as the thickness of the curtains, the texture of the bath towels, the number of sockets, the location of the fuse box and of the user manuals for the appliances. Instead, my attention was drawn to the titles of the few books on the shelves, how comfortable the mattress was, and the pictures on the walls, in particular one showing a lit candle over a Chinese proverb that left me in two minds: 'It is better to light a candle than to curse the darkness'. I washed, changed my shirt, opened the glass door onto the balcony and leaned on the railing. For a few minutes I observed the symmetrical segments of the pavement, the colour of the leaves that even at this time of day were an intense green, the chunky metal and concrete balconies on the far side of the street, the brightly lit stores, the rowdy bars, the terraces crowded with people enjoying a life that, from above, with no expectations of any kind for the coming period, I could only classify as enviable, carefree, and wholly alien to me.

4

In all these months I've been unable to get out of my head what Antonio told me that day. That's the name of the taxi driver. Antonio. It was a story woven from a series of coincidences. Erika, of course, would deny this, she'd say there are no coincidences but rather *synchronies*. For her, all events, from the most trifling to the most significant, have an explanation behind them, an explanation that might be ordinary, metaphysical, divine or supernatural but which is always expressed in that most fraudulent of adages: *everything happens for a reason*. It drove her crazy to hear me talking about chance or inertia. Some of our dumbest and most ridiculous arguments were about this. If a friend or relative died, Erika would immediately check the calendar, establish numerological correlations and try to decipher the *meaning* of this death, as if there were always loose threads in the cosmos waiting to be tied off by an unknown hand. I used to call her out on it, at first mocking her esoteric sixth sense and her fortune-telling deductions a little, then telling her in earnest that misfortune exists, that sometimes people just die and there's nothing more to it, but she persisted. A couple of times she made serious decisions under the influence of such superstitions, like when she turned down an attractive job offer in London just because Pascal, the dog we had at the time – in reality, her dog – fell ill and she, instead of resolving the issue by taking the animal to the vet, took the illness as a 'sign' that it was not a good moment to be making 'traumatic' changes. Perhaps, I now think, our break-up was also preceded or marked by some such indication. I don't know, I didn't see it, I didn't realise.

Yet even if Erika's impenetrable theories had some anchor in reality, they don't apply to Antonio's story nor to the chance events that brought it to my ears that day, the day I returned to Madrid. First, the delayed flight: the plane from Lima landed half an hour later than scheduled due to congestion in the skies. Second, a series of casual incidents: my decision – or the lack of urgency behind my decision – not to use the toilet in the airport, my rejection of the temptation to buy cigarettes or booze in the duty free, the unusual promptness with which my bags appeared on the carousel, the green light on passing customs control. The concatenation of these capricious circumstances progressively altered the course of the day and how it subsequently unfolded. It was pure luck. Or mere chance. On top of that, on exiting Barajas airport there were only three people ahead of me in the queue for taxis; if just one of them had arrived after me, or had changed their minds, or if the proper order of cars had not been followed, as so often happens, then Antonio would have left with a different passenger and most likely would not have got caught up in the traffic accident that delayed our journey and prolonged our conversation. If just one of the links had been missing from this chain of events, then Antonio's story would not be written down today. At least not here. Not by me.

5

'It's a bright day,' I remarked. I'm not one for opening conversations in taxis, but the man's accent had awoken my curiosity.

'Yes, we've been having good weather. You live here, in Madrid?'

'Yes, I do,' I said, and went straight to the point. 'You're Peruvian, aren't you?'

'That's right, maestro. You too?'

'Yes. We're compatriots,' I smiled.

'Which city are you from?'

'Lima.'

'Ah, me too. Which part?' he asked. In the rear-view mirror his eyes met mine, enquiring. His right eye appeared smaller than the left.

'Miraflores,' I replied. 'How about you?'

'Rímac.'

We fell silent. Another taxi overtook us.

'Do you know Rímac?'

'Sure,' I lied.

Another silence.

Despite the heat both inside and outside the car the man was wearing a polo neck sweater that came up to his chin. There was a faint smell of aftershave. I asked how many years he'd been living in Spain. 'Oh, it's going to be twenty-five soon,' he replied, as if surprised at the answer to his mental sums.

'Have they gone fast?'

'Very fast – or very slow, depending on how you look at it.'

'You haven't picked up the accent,' I remarked.

'Not really, the only words that have stuck are the bad ones, you know, *hostia, cojones, joder*, but I only use them when I'm complaining about the traffic. The few times I've insulted somebody face to face it's almost always come out in pure Peruvian – although one time I told another driver that *I shat on his dead fucking ancestors,* the way they do in this country. I couldn't quite believe I'd said it.'

We both laughed.

'Did you ever think about going back?'

'To Peru? My missus wanted to, but our daughter was born, and then our son, and we ended up staying. Now they've nearly finished school… it's not so easy to move. In any case, life is good here, things work, nobody bothers you, no one gets on your case, you feel safe. When my kids were little we took them to Lima more often. They went to visit their cousins, their grandparents, but after a while they wanted to come back. It was the same with me: after a couple of weeks I was ready to return to Madrid, get in the car, get to work. It's been a while now since we've been. You're just back from there, right?'

'Yeah. I was over for two months. It felt eternal. Like an overdose of Peruvianness.'

'And how are things there?' he wanted to know. 'I try to keep up with the news online, but it always seems the same, like nothing ever changes.'

'That's just it. Everything's changed, but nothing changes. To give you an example, in Lima there are more parks, which is great, but one half is covered in rubbish and the other has been invaded and occupied. And let's not even talk about the muggings and the killings. You can smell the violence as soon as you step onto the street.'

'I saw that the recent elections caused a big ruckus. The guy who won is a left-wing teacher, is that right?'

'Yes, the one who always wears a hat.'

'That's the one. Is it true he's a terrorist?'

6

My trip to Lima had coincided with the second round of the presidential elections. The left-wing candidate won by such a tight margin that his rival at the other end of the political spectrum used flimsy pretexts to cry fraud. It was self-evident that, whoever won, the country would be damned and divided. And so it came to pass. The capital was swamped in a wave of hysteria, recriminations and widespread tension. It was impossible to emerge from that dense crossfire unscathed. But nor was it possible to remain silent. At the request of a Spanish online newspaper I wrote two long articles on the electoral process and the resulting mess that Peruvian society found itself in. When they went live, I shared them on social media. Some of my oldest friends in Lima, with whom I believed I shared unbreakable bonds of affection, publicly denounced my position and, with an arrogance that perhaps should not have surprised me, and yet did, called my motives into question. They found it impertinent for a Peruvian to express his opinion on Peru when living elsewhere. The saddest thing of all was not the fact that I stopped speaking to them, but that I no longer felt any need to speak to them again. They weren't the only ones: other people I knew from my youth, from school or university, my first jobs, my first dates, also flung their political grievances in my direction, with that unpleasant superiority so particular to a certain class in Lima. Their messages pullulated with prejudices, assumptions and terrible spelling. I saw no point in replying to these provocations. In most cases, I deleted their contact information with a steady hand, as if slicing off somebody's head with a single blow; considering that after all they were mere distant shadows, names that had held a certain importance in their day but to which I was no longer connected by enduring bonds. If I had to pick one of the many unfriendly remarks I received over those months, I'd choose the message from an anonymous user whose unintentionally rhyming attempt to insult me only drew a guffaw in response: 'No one likes you in Peru, in Spain nobody knows you!'

7

'Is there a solution for Peru, maestro? What do you reckon?'

I didn't know what to say.

'A solution? I don't think so.'

'Will the new government last? They barely scraped in.'

'The victory of the left has made a lot of people very nervous,' I said, cautiously. 'Starting with themselves.'

'In the end they all steal, whether they're right or left.'

'I couldn't agree more. The only consolation is that corrupt presidents tend to end up in jail nowadays,' I noted.

'Or kill themselves, like García.'

'Or flee the country, like Toledo.'

'And what about Fujimori? Is he still in prison or did they let him out again?'

'He's still inside and I don't think he's getting out any time soon.'

'When I came to Madrid, in the mid-nineties, just a few months after the coup, *El Chino* was untouchable. Him and his advisor, Montesinos, old Uncle Vladi.'

'So was it because of the coup that you left?'

'What happened was that a cousin of mine worked in the police, and he told me about stuff you never saw in the news. Bad things, by the government, the military. My missus was studying accountancy at San Marcos and you'll know yourself how the terrorists had infiltrated the place, there were whole faculties taken over by Sendero Luminoso. The rector couldn't lift a finger. One day the army went in and they took away a bunch of students to different barracks. My cousin said the army tortured them to make them confess they were terrorists, regardless of the truth. Some of those kids were never seen again. Their families went to the university to protest, but it was all in vain, no one listened to them. Any day now they'll take me for a Maoist, my wife would tell me.'

'And did they?'

'Not her, but some of the other students. Do you remember the massacre of Barrios Altos?'

'Of course, at the end of '91.'

'We were worried when we saw the reports on the TV and in the papers, because my mother-in-law worked three blocks from Jirón Huanta, where it had all kicked off. The government imposed a state of emergency and had the whole area locked down. The soldiers would stop my mother-in-law in the street and ask for her papers every day.'

'It was a really screwed-up time, I don't know how we lived through it.'

'It wasn't living, it was surviving. On curfew nights, if you didn't have a safe-conduct, you had to be home before ten. Even in Callao we shut ourselves up early.'

'Didn't you say you were from Rímac?'

'I moved to Rímac, but I'm from Callao. A Chalaco born and bred, me. I grew up in the middle of the shanty-towns. Do you know them?'

'Yes,' I said.

This time I wasn't lying. In my early days as a journalist, I was sent to the slums of Callao to cover the seizure of a drug shipment involving a congressman. At the end of the assignment, my boss asked me to return to the newspaper by taxi because the press cars were allocated to other assignments. At the first corner I stopped to look for one, a man appeared out of the blue and put me in a headlock, said he had been released from Lurigancho prison forty-eight hours earlier and threatened to stick a shard of glass in my abdomen if I didn't give him everything I had on me. I didn't resist. He even took my sneakers; in exchange he left me a pair of worn-out loafers, two sizes too big.

'I lived at the corner of Arica and Loreto. Don't know if you've been out that way. That area was really rough. I've seen my childhood friends stabbed to death there.'

'Because of drugs? Or revenge?'

'Sometimes for drugs, sometimes for alcohol, over a woman, or just because someone took a dislike to you and sent their sicarios to do you in. At the age of seven or eight the lads were already heading down the wrong path, learning to nick stuff. By the age of twelve they were forming gangs. No one cared if they wound up in the slammer. They all knew that if you went inside, you came out tougher for it. I don't know what it's like these days, but that barrio was hell then. After nine at night the streets were a free-for-all and the cops would show up once in a blue moon. My missus lived close by, on the second block on Apurímac. Once we started going steady we swore we'd get out of there, so as soon as we were able we left for Rímac, which was a quieter neighbourhood.'

'And things were better there?'

'Things were going well until she began her studies at San Marcos. Not long after, the university was declared a red zone, and all the students and professors were placed under suspicion. I'd go to pick her up and the soldiers would come up to me while I waited. "So, you a terrorist then, you piece of shit?" they'd hassle you. If you didn't answer, it'd be worse, they'd stick their rifle in your ribs. Then one day they started to follow us, they'd come to the neighbourhood, ring the doorbell in the middle of the night, call us on the phone and hang up, tell our neighbours to be careful of us because we were with Sendero. Just imagine!'

'So that's why you decided to come...'

'Right. My sister-in-law was already here, near Alcobendas. She told us there were opportunities on building sites. We didn't think twice. My wife came over first, then me. No visas, no papers. Gradually we were able to regularise our situation. Now it's all above board, she has a contract, I have my taxi licence from the city, our kids go to state schools.'

'And they can grow up in peace, right? That security we never had.'

'So much so that they don't believe me when I tell them these stories about Lima. They think I'm making it all up. They don't know fear, they don't know what it's like to live with fear inside.'

'I can understand why you didn't want to go back.'

'Look, maestro, I'll be sincere. Peru's never given me anything. Nothing. Maybe I'll go back when I'm old, but now – what for? Everything's still a mess.'

The car rolled along the highway at a steady speed. It was twilight, and the outline of the city ahead was still just about visible.

'How about yourself, how long have you been living here, then?' he asked me.

'It'll be nine years, soon.'

'Have you got your nationality yet?'

'I've just applied. I'm taking the exam next month.'

'It took me two years.'

'So you're already Spanish.'

We grinned at each other in the rear-view mirror.

'You're a subject of the Spanish crown?,' I said ironically. 'You pay your taxes, you use public services, your kids were born here, they go to school here...'

'We'll always be foreigners here, maestro,' he replied with a scornful expression. 'The European passport only means they don't give you nasty looks in the airport.'

8

The first time Erika travelled to Peru she was astonished by Cusco, Arequipa and Puno. She loved Iquitos, too. Of Lima, she only liked Barranco, the sea views from the Malecón Armendáriz, a few buildings in the old town. The second time, though, visiting with me and my family, we had such a good time we even began to discuss the possibility of buying something close to Miraflores with a view to living there in the future. She was the one to suggest it, fascinated by the 'energies of the sea'; seeing her so at ease, unable to pour cold water on her ideas, I left the possibility open. Happily, the notion gradually evaporated. Would we have been happier living in Lima? I doubt it. For years I felt stupidly proud of having been born there. When I was growing up, not coming from the capital was a sign of inferiority. I'd been ashamed to admit that my father was from Huánuco, from the sierra. If I could avoid mentioning it, I did so without shame. Or perhaps, with shame. I remember a family holiday to his village, Paucarbamba (officially known as Amarilis, the Spanish name I preferred to use), where we spent two weeks in the country house of a family he'd long been friendly with, the Trinidads. For a fortnight my sisters and I went everywhere with their three children, who were a few years older than us. They taught us to milk cows, herd goats, ride donkeys, run at almost two thousand metres above sea level, and spot animal shapes in the forms of the mountains: a puma, a condor, a snake. They took us on expeditions to clear, glacier-fed lakes, showed us mummies of children with terrifying expressions, and a cemetery of giant, ancient stones with hieroglyphic inscriptions that we couldn't decide whether to ascribe to the Incas or to aliens. We learned to dance in the fashion of Los Negritos, wearing leather masks, and to eat chicken stew until we were fit to burst. We had the time of our lives. Then one Sunday we said goodbye to the Trinidad family, to the farm, to the blue sky, to the countryside, and we headed back to Lima aboard an interprovincial sleeper bus that belched thick black clouds from its exhaust. Two days later, in Spanish class, the teacher asked us to recount what we'd done in our holidays. The girl sitting in front of me, Camila Chávez, spoke about her trip to Miami, to Universal Studios park in Orlando, and raised her left arm to show off the phosphorescent waterproof watch she'd won at an attraction whose name I don't recall. As she chattered away like a parrot, my head filled with images of Paucarbamba and the rosy cheeks of the Trinidad kids. By the time I realised the teacher's attention had turned to me, despite the brilliant memories I had, I timidly muttered: 'We didn't go anywhere for the holidays.' I grabbed my pencil and started doodling on my notebook. I never said a word to my sisters, let alone to my parents. They would have been appalled. A rumour had once reached them that in school I used a different name on my exam papers. I denied it outright: I could never admit to them how uncomfortable the Andean echoes of both my surnames made me.

With the years of economic growth in Peru — between 2004 and 2006 — those around me embarked on a phase of extraordinary frivolity. Most pathetic of all was how easy it was to fall in with the spirit of the time. I found it very easy to behave just as someone with my education, my appearance and my habits was expected to. My attitude, like that of the rest of them, turned arrogant, dismissive. It exhausted me to be so predictable, so efficient at satisfying expectations, pursuing ideals and defending positions that weren't strictly my own. Rather than coming to Spain, I think I fled Peru. Or Lima, at least. More precisely, I fled the person I was in that city, the one who interacted so mechanically. I left so as not to be that person any more. Was that not the definitive step I had always longed to take, without ever finding the right excuse to do so? Wasn't I the one who, as a child, had driven my older and younger sisters to despair, telling them I was going to run away from home forever? That drive to escape had always been there; the question is how I could last so long without giving it free rein. Perhaps at bottom I was held back by the knowledge that the day I left would mark a dividing line and there would be no turning back.

As I listened to Antonio in the taxi telling me about the 1990s I thought of how, even as two Peruvians from Lima, there were things we would never share. He abandoned Peru because he felt they were on his heels. He saw his future, his life under threat. He travelled without documents, without money, without even knowing where he would end up. The only thing he carried with him together with his uncertainty was the wit to hold his breath when the cops passed by. More than a decision to migrate, his was a forced exile. I left Peru when I could just as well have stayed: nothing I had achieved there was under threat. Indeed, the country was still reaping the benefits of the economic upturn at the start of the millennium, and the stock market experts were optimistic about the growth of reserves in the medium term. Working three jobs, I could afford to indulge myself, even enjoy a certain amount of ease. When I came to Spain, I did so without a hitch, with a student visa, a national insurance number, an address to go to. The only apprehension I brought with me was a question that has remained unanswerable over the years: should I go back? Perhaps that is the only thing that unites Antonio and me: neither of us has been able to disengage completely from Peru, from that enduring sense of unease that is Peru. Putting an ocean between us is not enough. Distance makes the past hazy, but doesn't erase it. In the long term, you realise that the life you began outside of your country doesn't replace the previous one: it is an extension of it in a different geography. They are different lives, but bound one to the other in simultaneous coexistence. The new life is a lengthy insomnia on which you uncertainly embark, while the previous life, the life you lived and cut short, wanders in parallel, in the distance, like a hypothetical headless ghost, a worthless shadow, a soul in torment that never ceases to roam.

ONE

The New York banker Gordon Clifford entered the life of Matías Giurato Roeder on just three occasions, but each of these three proved decisive to the events that determined his fate.

The first time was on June 28, 1939, shortly after departing the port of Salaverry, south of Trujillo, in northern Peru, on board the Grace Line steamship *Santa Bárbara* that was making a stopover on its regular voyage from Valparaíso via the Panama Canal to New York, where Gordon Clifford lived and to which Matías was emigrating. As the ship drew away from the pier, the nineteen-year-old gazed at the coast where he had been born and sensed, without any feeling of homesickness, that it would be a long time before he would again look upon that beach washed by a sullen sea, with its grey-blue gulls and upturned boats, along which he had walked so many times with his mother. The peak of Cerro Carretas, so imposing from the city, had become little more than a small hill, a bulge of sandy earth that would soon be hidden by the horizon.

It was a chance meeting: twenty minutes before boarding, on a café table in the port, Matías found a leather portfolio and pipe that both bore the same set of initials stamped in gold: *G. C. H.* The absentminded banker, taking advantage of the layover, had gone ashore to explore the stalls set up on the broad pier, bought some souvenirs and sat down to drink a coffee. Hurrying back on board, his hands full, he left his pipe and portfolio behind. Matías tried to give them to the waiter, but he waved him away. Instead, as soon as he boarded the ship he handed them to the first crew member he encountered. An hour later, just as he was beginning to familiarise himself with the ropey third-class cabins, this same crew member brought him an anonymous invitation to take up one of the spacious first-class compartments. 'It must be a misunderstanding,' Matías ventured. The sailor repeated the offer and this time the young Giurato accepted without hesitation. Although he had agreed with his parents that in New York he would lodge with his Uncle Enrico (in fact a distant cousin of his father, who Matías couldn't even recall), his real intention was to get by without papers in the United States until he saved enough cash to sail on for Hamburg. There, he would seek out his mother's family, who he had got to know through the letters, photographs and postcards that his grandfather, Karsten Roeder, sent four or five times a year to the mansion on the Chiclín estate, where Matías enjoyed a life that was all-too-peaceful, or perhaps all-too-trivial. It was for this reason that, climbing the stairs two at a time, passing the control room and feeling the growl of the *Santa Bárbara*'s engines as it sailed the open sea at full throttle, he had a presentiment that this chance invitation to first class was a rare good omen for the uncertain voyage he had just embarked on.

Gordon Clifford was waiting for Matías in a private booth of the ship's main bar. He greeted him with aplomb, asked if he spoke English or Spanish, invited him to sit down and, having formally thanked him for returning the leather portfolio and wooden pipe, asked him to choose one of the carpeted cabins close to his own for the duration of the voyage. He assured Matías that he would be much more comfortable, and Matías – who was already feeling perfectly comfortable just being there, in the company of this man who treated him with respect – accepted with an elusive gesture that hid his astonishment. He repeated the gesture a minute later, as he accepted the glass of gin Clifford served him despite it not yet being midday, and despite the fact that, as much for his disposition as his age, he was not in the least bit keen on drinking. As he cautiously sipped the transparent, citrusy liquor, a fleeting image of his father Massimo Giurato entered his mind, and he reflected that they had never shared a single drink together, despite the fondness for alcohol for which Massimo was famous throughout Trujillo. On more than one night Matías, at his mother's urging, had had to seek him out in the crowded downtown bars whose names he knew by heart, the Chicago Club, the Tokio, the Trieste, the 606 on Calle Gamarra, and hear the owners implore him to take his father away, immediately, without bothering to settle his bill, before he regained consciousness and continued to harass the customers with his insufferable drunken outbursts. Yet it was not because of his alcoholic tendencies that Matías hated the man who was his father, but for reasons which, at this moment, savouring his glass of gin, he had no desire to ponder.

Clifford told him that, although he had spent years sailing to and from Valparaíso, it was the first time he had gone ashore at Salaverry. 'And I almost lost my papers and my favourite pipe for my pains,' he added, with a sudden burst of laughter that rather alarmed Matías. Clifford went on to tell him about his work, trying to make it sound appealing to him as he ran through the abstract world of stock market investments, bank loans, bond issues, share purchases, earnings yields and capital losses, without producing the desired positive effect on the young man. Switching track, Clifford did his best to present a more easy-going side, recounting that his wife was Chilean (hence his fluent Spanish), that he had no children, and that he enjoyed the itinerant nature of his work because it took him away from the hectic and sometimes overwhelming pace of New York. He told him that, despite the economic recession in the United States, New York continued to grow, change and welcome migrants from different countries who, if they were smart, quickly found a place for themselves. Imbued with confidence at this last remark, Matías briefly set out his plans, and didn't hesitate to ask the banker's advice on what steps he should take once he reached North American soil.

Over the following days and weeks, in their encounters in the main bar, the English dining room, the salons, the terraces, and on their daytime and nocturnal strolls around the deck of the liner that soon became routine, their mutual cordiality deepened. Matías was drawn to Clifford's cultured character but didn't want to seek to please him; the banker, meanwhile, was impressed by the young man's idealism and the audacity of crossing the ocean to reach Germany at a moment when, in June 1939, following the occupation of Austria and Czechoslovakia, and the arrest and confinement of Jews and Gypsies, the country had already embarked on a bloody episode in Europe that threatened to spread to the whole world.

What Matías most valued in Clifford, however, was the frank interest he showed in him, something not even his revered mother, Edith Roeder, afforded him – despite the love she felt for him as her only son, or indeed perhaps because of her incorrigible tendency to overprotect him. He was not shy about answering Clifford's keen questions about his day-to-day life in Trujillo. Matías told him of his upbringing with the stern Marist priests at the seminary school, of the times he would sneak out with a couple of friends to slip into the Chinese theatre and catch the last few minutes of the films showing at the matinees, or crawl under the canvas of the travelling circus tents pitched near the centre of town and throw food to the starving caged horses that would later prance onto the stage; of how they would creep into the backyard of the rooms on Calle del Arco or Jirón Sosiego, where they would listen to the feigned gasps of the prostitutes as they attended to those men who, once they had been seen to, would leave with a light step, wipe a sleeve over their faces and return relieved to their lacklustre lives. Matías saw Massimo Giurato, his father, emerge from those shacks not once but multiple times, his brown hair unkempt, his shirt tails untucked, swaying from the alcohol, but he did not discuss it with his friends at the time and nor did he now with Gordon Clifford. Instead, he focused on the years after secondary school, years he devoted – or wasted, his father said – to watching Mexican movies at the theatre on Jirón Junín, attending tedious scientific lectures at the Athenaeum, learning to swim at the public baths on Calle Pizarro, practising his rifle shooting at the Gun Club, and memorising irregular verbs in the private English classes his mother paid for at the Larco Herrera library. And he told him about the letters from his grandfather Karsten, which arrived with blue and red stamps that he carefully steamed off to add to his collection; letters in which his grandfather spoke of the good life to be had in Hamburg and took pride in recounting chapters from its history, going back as far as the invasion of Napoleon; letters that his mother translated painstakingly from German so that he could familiarise himself with the language and the constellation of relatives that one day – he was sure – he would meet in person: great-grandma Helga and grandma Ingeborg; aunts Ilse, Christa and Elke; uncles Klaus, Rainer and Helmut; cousins Günter, Angelika, Wolfgang and the other Roeders mentioned in these missives, which described their interests, mannerisms, obsessions, physical peculiarities or sentimental attitudes. Aunt Elke was love-struck but stubborn; Aunt Ilse painted still lifes and saved coins in a pottery piggy bank she guarded zealously; Aunt Christa was stubborn with maths, inconstant with sports, and fussy about vegetables; Uncle Rainer had a complex about his mismatched legs, his receding gums, his tiny ears; Uncle Klaus was prone to giving orders and telling the children racy jokes; Grandma Ingeborg could not go a day without saying *es geht um die Wurst*, 'it's time for sausage', an expression meaning 'now or never'; Cousin Günter was torn between becoming a magician, a doctor or a race car driver, while Cousin Wolfgang – who every morning got first dibs on the newspapers, but for the entertainment and puzzles pages, not the politics – was counting down the months until he could apply to architecture school. Thanks to this correspondence he knew that his grandfather Karsten had worked for over twenty years at the Blohm & Voss shipyard in Hamburg, where he continued to go even once retired, since he was 'bored out of his mind' in the house, the terraced flat in the penultimate building on Bernhard-Nocht-Strasse in the Sankt Pauli district, behind the fishermen's market, some five hundred metres from the waterfront. Matías had calculated this distance on the three maps of the city that his grandfather had drawn with cartographic rigour so that 'you won't get lost the day you come to visit us'.

The grandson conscientiously studied these maps until he had learned by heart the names of the places old Karsten had highlighted in dense circles of red ink because they would be the first sites they would visit together on this long-awaited future journey: St. Nicholas' Church, the Astra cinema, Dammtor Station, the Atlantic Hotel, the shops of Altona, the Hagenbeck Zoo and – depending on what age Matías had reached by the time of his visit – the invigorating side streets of the Reeperbahn. On other occasions the letters included unexpected family heirlooms, which Matías treasured: a faded portrait of a heavily bearded ancestor in whose features he sought his own, notes or coins in old Imperial Marks, great-grandmother Helga's recipes for desserts made from red berries, cornflour and red wine, or purely decorative objects like a beautiful Kienzle pocket watch with the hands set forever to a time – twenty-five minutes past four – that Matías tried in vain to find meaning in; or that Wieden petrol lighter, laminated in silver and embossed with the red cross of Saint James, which he always carried in his pocket, even though he didn't smoke.

On one occasion, when he was seven or eight years old, his grandfather sent him a box containing thirty pieces of plywood and, on a separate piece of paper, the instructions for gluing them together. The result was a magnificent biplane with two sets of rigid wings, one above the other, a two-bladed propeller, a slender tail formed of three braces, and the cockpit hole, with drawings of the controls. It was an exact replica, explained old Karsten in the letter, of the Albatros in which Manfred von Richthofen – the legendary Red Baron, the greatest German pilot of the First World War – had shot down over eighty planes of the Triple Entente powers. In Matías' hand, the little plane flew over the sugarcane fields of Chiclín for whole afternoons, performing daring pirouettes that ended abruptly when the engine was hit by an imaginary enemy projectile, forcing the only crew member, the Red Baron ('the Lead Baron', Matías called him), to parachute into a dark imaginary jungle while the craft plunged to the ground at great speed and smashed to smithereens against the rocks. Eventually, placed on a shelf from where it proudly displayed the dents and scratches of its ruined fuselage, the wooden biplane would cease to be just a toy and become the symbol of the single desire that had grown within Matías over the years until he knew he could not put it off any longer: to take flight.

In his letters, whether to avoid alarming his daughter or disappointing his grandson, old Karsten avoided relating just how worrying the situation had become in Hamburg – in the whole of Germany really – since the Nazis took power. As a supporter of the Communist Party (though not only for this reason) the grandfather was a bitter critic of the Reich; from the outset he had been wary of its segregationist rhetoric, and rejected its violent methods, with which he was well acquainted. Years before, one night in August 1930, in the Am Stadtpark beer hall in the Winterhude district, in the middle of a Nazi party election meeting, about ninety individuals burst into the premises with obvious intentions of sabotaging the meeting. They claimed to be Red Front members, a faction of the Communist Party, and called themselves the Iron Fists. Half of them occupied the empty seats and the rest the back of the hall, blocking the access to the auditorium. Up on the podium, speakers from the National Socialist Workers' Party had spent the past hour spouting openly anti-Semitic, anti-Marxist, anti-Liberal diatribes. When the unexpected visitors made their appearance, the current speaker interrupted his flow to ask if their presence was peaceful or not. A beer jug flew past his ear and shattered against the wall, eloquently settling the matter. From his position, old Karsten regretted having missed. No one had time to complain, however, as the brawl broke out immediately. Communists and Nazis set to using the nearest objects as weapons, from brooms, knives and broken glass to the hall's weighty seats. Many fled the pandemonium, but others, indeed the majority, joined with the Nazis to kick the intruders out onto the street. In the midst of the uproar, a pair of old men beat each other to a bloody pulp, ending up on the floor, their yellow beards marbled with blood. Although the Communists outnumbered them, their opponents prevailed with their strength and aggressiveness. Seeing the way things were going, the Iron Fists sounded the retreat, while continuing to yell slogans that the Nazis drowned out with ever-louder cheers of victory. Old Karsten would never forget the ferocity of those crimson faces nor the violence of their scorn and abuse: he heard them claim their win was thanks to their stronger ideology, their fiercer courage, that they would pitilessly fight the 'misfits who infect Germany'. They seemed to be in raptures, possessed by a disdain which, far from dissipating, was to gain furious hordes of followers as the months and years went by. But Matías' grandfather recounted none of this in his letters. He underestimated Hitler, reducing him to the caricature of an outlandish dictator. He said nothing of the dissolution of political parties or the attacks on political opponents, many of whom were killed or sent to concentration camps. Nor of the closure of radio stations not aligned with Nazism, and their replacement by faithful sources of propaganda. The three newspapers that had always been read in the Roeder household, the *Hamburger Echo*, the *Hamburger Nachrichten* and the *Hamburgischer Correspondent*, suddenly disappeared from the stands. By 1934 the Nazi ascendancy over the city was impossible to hide, and nowhere was it more evident than in the person of the governor, Karl Kaufmann. When Kaufmann's face began to appear in the press, old Karsten recognised in those clouded pupils the orator of the Winterhude brewery, and once again regretted that he had missed him with the beer jug on the night of the brawl. His grandfather did not mention to Matías that books that angered the Nazis were burned in a school gymnasium. Nor that school and hospital heads were often replaced by submissive supporters of the Reich. He said nothing about the families prevented from going on holiday without the say-so of *Kraft durch Freude*, the body that supervised and standardised people's leisure time. He failed to mention that the family's apartment on Bernhard-Nocht-Strasse had received numerous 'invitations' addressed to uncles Helmut and Rainer, and aunts Christa and Elke, to 'voluntarily' join the Hitler Youth and the League of German Girls, and nor did he tell them that, although they had refrained, they spent their days biting their nails, thinking that they would soon be forced to sign up to this unabashed hotbed of Nazism. At Cousin Angelika's school, religion classes had been abolished, and the pupils were now taught about the origins of the National Socialist Workers' Party and studied biographies of Hitler in which he was portrayed as their predestined leader. The new history textbooks expounded on the myth of the 'stab in the back', according to which the German army had been undefeated on the battlefield during the First World War but had victory stolen from them by the betrayal of enemies at home. Geography textbooks emphasised the need to redraw the country's borders, to reconquer the territories lost after the signing of the Treaty of Versailles and to secure a hegemonic state. And biology textbooks underscored the notion of racial purity and the upcoming struggle for supremacy. The headmistress of Cousin Angelika's school was dismissed for refusing to implement this curriculum, which she denounced as 'retrograde'; within two days a servile loyalist was appointed to her post. And at Cousin Wolfgang's school, five teachers, denounced by their own pupils, were dismissed for making anti-Nazi remarks. Cousin Wolfgang reluctantly signed this denunciation, but two of his friends resisted and were expelled.

Old Karsten said nothing about this, and even less about the incipient persecution of intellectuals, of Gypsies, of homosexuals, of foreigners and of the disabled. Nazi fanaticism was such that even kids who liked jazz music were treated as degenerates. Uncle Klaus himself was forced to spend a period in the Moringen youth concentration camp, euphemistically described as a 'camp for the protection of youth', for gathering with friends in a garage to dance swing and listen to Earl Hines records. A neighbour had tattled to the police and they were carted off in handcuffs, accused of 'sexual promiscuity' and of 'dancing to negro music like wild animals'. Nor did he write a single word about his Jewish colleagues, the ones who worked with him in the Blohm & Voss shipyard, the Hofsteins, Greenbergs and Kleins whose rights – after the draconian 1935 Nuremberg laws had made anti-Semitism state policy – were crushed underfoot. Jewish businesses were boycotted or attacked while the local police stood by. Those who could afford a visa – Mr Greenberg among them – fled the country with their families, while the rest, including the Hofsteins and the Kleins, suffered increasingly virulent attacks that instilled fear and impotence among Hamburg's Jewish community. On November 9, 1938, which became known as Kristallnacht, the Nazis desecrated tombs and overturned hundreds of gravestones at the Altona Jewish cemetery. Throughout the city, Jews were rounded up, and there were disturbances and vandalism, mainly in the Elbe district where synagogues were ransacked and set alight. Karsten and Grandma Ingeborg took in a number of Jews who, in addition to suffering the fearful spectacle of the destruction of their stores, their only livelihood, a few days later were invited by the government to shell out exorbitant sums to repair the building frontage, and to clear the streets that the angry National Socialist mobs, led by the SA and the SS, had left strewn with glass, ruined merchandise and broken banners.

In Trujillo, some of these events were reported by the radio stations or published on the international news pages of *La Industria*, but with considerable delay and lacking in sufficient detail to enable Edith Roeder or Matías to understand the tyranny of the Reich outside of Berlin. One day, fed up with her father's evasiveness, Edith wrote to him demanding solid proof that the family was safe. In his next letter, Karsten finally mentioned the situation, though his lines were so cautious and meandering that they failed to make clear the grave outlook:

> *the Germans no longer rebel against the uselessness, yesterday's pessimism has been diluted together with the antagonisms that meant we knew who was who. What many of us found reprehensible a few years ago is now tolerated without regard for the ignominy of it, which is why it has been so easy to bring national self-esteem to its knees.*

Matías, who had often seen his mother weighed down with worry but never enraged, was startled when Edith crumpled up the letter and threw it to the ground with a distraught expression, before picking it up again and tearing it to pieces, while emitting shrieks in German that he made no effort to translate as he correctly assumed that they amounted to a fulsome rosary of curses and oaths. Matías carefully put together the torn pieces of the letter and transcribed it so he could read it himself, with the help of the dictionary, before safeguarding it in the chest where he kept everything Grandpa Karsten sent: the photos, the missives written in his illegible doctor's writing, the maps, the drawings, the gifts, and even the stamps the old man used to communicate with the Peruvian grandson he dreamed of embracing one day.

It was no surprise that Hamburg became the epicentre of German rearmament as the country prepared for 'total war', given its manufacturing capacity and suitability as a transport hub. The city's ailing economy began to recover as high unemployment rates fell. Shipbuilders received huge military contracts, and numerous businesses that had been close to bankruptcy were saved by the pressing need to build oil refineries, engine factories, dry docks for warships and submarines *en masse*. The vast injection of money to turn Hamburg into an industrial giant (which was christened Great Hamburg) silenced the complaints of even the regime's most relentless detractors. From 1937 onwards, Hitler had countless bridges and motorways built, as a result of which many members of the burgeoning working class who had once disowned him decided to give him the benefit of the doubt. While he was leader of the Nazi party, there was no city more frequently visited by the Führer than Hamburg, 'the pearl of the North'.

'Do you know Germany?' Matías asked Gordon Clifford one night on that boat, as they leant elbow to elbow on the starboard railing. The New York banker was just about to reply when a hubbub erupted on the far side of the deck. They went over to find a commotion of people all staring in astonishment at the sea, where something heavy had just broken the surface. The cries of alarm and general clamour made for an impenetrable din. There stood out from the crowd a blonde with bony arms and prominent cheekbones who was struggling to stifle a howl of shock, while a man, who was not particularly old but was completely bald, clumsily attempted to console her. The captain appeared and issued abrupt orders to halt the ship and recover the inert body slowly rotating below. After battling with the curious onlookers for a quarter of an hour, the crew finally managed to clear the deck. No one slept. The jittery passengers spent the night speculating and spreading such inconsistent rumours that by morning, accounts of the incident circulating in the mahogany-lined first-class lounges bore no relation to the whispers running through the shared bathrooms of second class, nor to the gossip inundating the narrow, stifling corridors of third class. In first, they spoke of an accidental stumble; for those in second it was a suicide; only in third was the possibility of a murder given credit. When the authorities on board discreetly let it be known that a passenger had chosen to end their life, the distortions didn't let up: in first class they said it had been a Dutch gambler pursued by his creditors; in second they theorised that he was a poor Californian actor downcast at yet another failure; and in third they asserted that the deceased was an Argentinian cabin boy driven mad by a disease caused by parasites and sandfly bites. Two days later, the identity of the dead man was finally known. He was a young Italo-Albanian named Brunetti, the lover of another passenger's wife. He had thrown himself overboard after she – the skinny blonde – had denied their relationship up to five times in front of her husband, who turned out to be the bald gentleman.

The passionate affair continued to be remarked upon for some time aboard the *Santa Bárbara*, and provided an excuse for Gordon Clifford to ask Matías to tell him how many girls he had fallen in love with. With some incredulity he received the answer: none. Clifford, meanwhile, boasted of his experience in such matters, and told him how fortunate he felt with Manuela Altamirano, his current wife, whom he had met on his trips to Valparaíso and now awaited him in New York. At that moment, Clifford was distracted by a fencing exhibition that two white-clad crew members were presenting on deck, and stood watching as the adversaries, their faces concealed behind the grilles of their protective masks, expertly measured and dodged each other, cutting through the generalised silence with the sharp whistling of their foils. Matías took advantage of the pause to ask if he wouldn't like to have children. The banker pulled deeply on his pipe, retained the smoke for three seconds before expelling it in a dense cloud and, without deviating his gaze from the swordsmen, who approached and withdrew from each other in elegant lunges, replied dryly: 'I cannot, I am sterile.' Some time later in the journey, Matías would return to the subject to confess something that had intrigued him from the outset. On the morning they embarked at Salaverry, when he found the portfolio and pipe with the banker's initials on the café table in the port, he checked the contents to try and identify its owner and found a photograph among the papers. He identified a younger Gordon Clifford posing alongside a woman he now deduced must be Manuela Altamirano; between them was a freckled boy of eight or nine, wearing a cotton shirt, braces, short trousers and boasting an impeccable parting and a smile missing the top two front teeth. It was a charming family portrait that clearly conveyed the love they all felt for each other. Matías reflected that there was no such photograph in his own house. Clifford set down his glass of gin and picked it up again three times as if to delay the question on the tip of Matías' tongue: 'Who is the child?' No sooner had he uttered these words when Clifford felt in his right eyelid a fluttering that for a moment he had cause to think was an incipient heart attack. He was angered by the directness of his young friend, yet when he sought to object he found his jaw muscles were so tense he was unable to get a word out. Matías realised his impertinence and was about to swiftly change the subject when the portly fifty-eight year old banker – who never lost his composure – rubbed his pale cheeks with his palms and adjusted his carefully tied shoelaces before breaking out in disconsolate weeping that took him by surprise. 'His name was Samuel,' he said, still agitated, stringing together the syllables with difficulty. Matías didn't know if he was ready to hear the story that would resolve the mystery of the photograph, but just as he was thinking of dissuading him, Clifford had embarked on the tale. One year after the boy's birth in Chile, the three of them had moved to New York, where, despite the impact of the Depression, they enjoyed a lengthy period of prosperity. This ended with the accident, the day after Samuel's eighth birthday. The photograph had been taken one day earlier. Stumbling over his words, Clifford told Matías about a basement, a short circuit in high-voltage wires that made contact with the willow trees growing on the street outside their house, about a broken and rusty latch handle, about a blocked door, about the endless banging from the other side of that door, about the raging heat on the walls, the eerie shadows cast by the flames, the creaking of the furniture as the fire ate away at it, the desperation with which he and Manuela called out to the neighbours for help though no one could do anything for them, his son crying as the flames began to encircle him, and the screams, the piercing, dreadful screams of Samuel, screams that would never cease to ring in his ears whether he was awake or not. By the time the firemen were able to break into the basement and put out the fire, there was nothing left of the boy. A few days later, before the presence of a bishop, Gordon and Manuela placed their son's ashes inside a casket. Manuela descended into a progressive spiral of grief, denial and delirium from which she would never emerge. She blamed herself for having insisted that the child go to play in the basement that morning. Sometimes, to disguise Samuel's absence, she would serve him food at the table or talk to him, not mentally or figuratively, but out loud, as if the boy were still alive and could hear her. The morning Gordon caught her scattering Samuel's remains in a suitcase to take him 'on a trip', he decided to commit her to a psychiatric hospital on Long Island. Matías, stupefied, dismayed, followed the account of these events which, he suddenly inferred, explained the presence of that black bracelet on the right sleeve of Clifford's jacket. The final thing the New York banker revealed to him was that he was not returning from Valparaíso having closed a business deal, as he had boastfully told him the day they met in the bar. Nothing of the sort. He was returning from carrying out the ritual that put an end, at least symbolically, to the last chapter of his ill-fated paternity: to scatter Samuel's ashes in the sea, near the seaside resort where he and his wife had fallen in love years before, and to dispose once and for all of the child's most precious objects, among them a fencing suit, a child's mask, two leather gloves and a foil.

For Matías, no pair of personalities in the world was more incompatible than his parents, Massimo Giurato and Edith Roeder. He had no idea how they had fallen in love – if that is what had happened – nor if they had really wanted to have a child, let alone how they had spent over two decades together. Although he did know their secret: a coexistence like theirs could only be explained by the constant practice of the most complete indifference. For him, his parents were two adults who wandered around the hacienda without touching or looking at each other, as if they had worked things out so as to occupy each their own plot, exchanging the minimum words necessary for the conjugal and domestic system to carry on functioning. Otherwise, it was hard not to confuse them with sleepwalkers, or worse, ghosts who mutually ignored each other despite being condemned to rattle their chains in the same corner. How had this courtship ever come about? As far as he knew – and he knew very little – his mother had left Germany as a young woman with this Italian bounder who promised her a comfortable life in northern Peru, where his Genovese family had established itself a century earlier and become large landowners. What Massimo failed to mention when wooing her was his drink problem, which would only become more chronic with the years; even less did he speak of his addiction to prostitutes, or his already complicated legal problems.

From the age of fourteen, Matías had suspected that some members of the Giurato family were wrapped up in nefarious business. An uncle on his father's side, the one nicknamed Toto – mention of whose name would have Edith leaping up from the table in the middle of lunch – was a self-declared fascist who, in both the U.S. and Argentina, had published screeds in praise of Benito Mussolini. Now he worked in Lima organising the Italian community along the guidelines conveyed by the government of Il Duce, to whom he would send gifts, ornaments and clothing adorned with Inca motifs, although they rarely reached the hands of their intended recipient. Massimo boasted about being Toto's nephew and, with the backing of his two older brothers, Giacomo and Donato, supposedly operated in Trujillo under fascist directives, though in truth their ambitions had little to do with imposing ultranationalist policies, and more with filling their pockets as they engaged in their illegal activities. Throughout the province of Ascope and the centre of Trujillo people spoke of how the Giurato brothers were responsible for robberies, protection rackets and the settling of scores. They extorted the owners of the stores along Jirón Bolívar, the hotels on Calle Ayacucho and La Merced, and other establishments on Calle Gamarra, threatening to do over their businesses if they failed to *collaborate*. If they received free shaves at the El Progreso barbers' shop, or if they lunched without spending a cent at the Fonda de Hiraoka, it was because they were drawing down the *debts* the business owners had with them. Their shameless impunity was largely due to the fact that a high percentage of their ill-gotten gains paid for the social activities of the Italian bank, whose favoured clients included the upper echelons of the police force. As a result, none of the senior officers had any interest in ordering their arrest. Nor did the victims act on their own accord: who was going to face down these three Italian goons who, with their black shirts, two-tone shoes, trilby hats and striking tailored striped jackets (which, it was said, camouflaged semi-automatic pistols, although in reality it was merely razors swiped from the barbers) were the closest the city had seen to an untouchable mafia gang? The day one local dared to lay charges against the three for the murder of her husband, Eudoro Ganoza, manager of the railway hotel, the police could no longer turn a blind eye and were forced to put them in a cell to avoid arousing suspicions. Yet in a matter of hours they were back on the streets. The strategy to keep them out of prison had its own name: Paolo Farinella – Fatboy Farinella – an Italian from Basilicata, with no wife or children, whose one job was

45

to incriminate himself whenever the Giurato brothers got into real trouble. When Ganoza's widow accused them of robbery, kidnapping and cutting her husband's throat, it was Fatboy Farinella who handed himself in to the police wearing the face of a pitiless murderer. He received a hefty sum in exchange for his silence and loyalty, but only too late did he realise that it was petty change compared to spending fourteen years rotting in a jail cell. His maths was always out when it came to these calculations. On previous occasions, he had done time for shorter periods, four years or six, but taking sole responsibility for the murder of the railway hotel manager was too much. Altogether, Fatboy Farinella, whose age could be guessed at around fifty-three, spent twenty-six of them behind bars, over half his life, and all for money that was worth significantly less once he finally emerged.

It was thanks to Farinella's self-sacrifice that the Giurato brothers continued to give the law the slip, and they remained a regular fixture of Trujillo social life. They were frequently to be seen preening themselves at the Club Central soirées, at the bullring or at cock fights, at the street fairs or zarzuela shows, though the day's end always found them back at their dive bars where they boasted of their swindling, their ability to hold their drink, until they passed out amidst the mounds of dead bottles. Matías learned of Paolo Farinella's existence and his shady role as the result of his father's indiscretion one night when, after searching long and hard, he tracked him down still drinking in a dingy chingana and set about dragging his deadweight home. He said nothing to his mother, let alone to Lizardo Carcelén, the cadaverous priest at the La Merced church who heard his confession once in a blue moon. Instead, he told the story to Gordon Clifford while aboard the ship, and added that he felt a deep resentment and shame not only with respect to his father, but to the whole Italian family he didn't see as his own, and by extension the country itself, which he had no desire to visit.

'When I turned thirteen,' he told Clifford, 'my father gave me an air rifle. One morning he took me up to a valley just outside Chiclín and showed me how to shoot at the owls and the guanacos. It was a whole ritual. First we placed the bait, then we looked for a hiding place. You had to have patience, instinct and a cool head – but above all patience. The owls were easy to hit, not like the guanacos with their tiny little heads. You had to aim at the middle of the chest, adjust your view without blinking the other eye so as not to mess up your peripheral vision, and not hesitate with the trigger; if you delay more than a second the herd smells the humans, and when guanacos take off it's next to impossible to chase them, they're as fast as tigers. We kept watch a good while, without talking, a couple of gestures were enough to know what the other was thinking. For months we shared this passion, we killed dozens of animals, but the day came that my aim was better than his. I remember it well. With a single shot, *bang!*, I took out two guanacos that were lined up one behind the other. Meanwhile he only injured one, he missed the heart. That day my father received a wake-up call. I wasn't yet fifteen and I'd already become a better hunter than he was, and instead of filling him with pride it so offended his ego that we no longer went out to shoot or fraternise around any other activity, nor did we smoke or drink together, or ask each other anything of importance. From that moment on he mistreated me. His contempt for my achievements was such that I began to wonder whether I was in fact adopted, or an unwanted child, or only wanted by my mother. I asked her directly, and she assured me that her pregnancy had the blessing of my father from the outset. Even today I find that hard to believe. I've been nothing but an obstacle to him. The man is unscrupulous, depraved, a murderer who will have to pay for his crimes, though I am not there to see it.'

At that, his mind went back to the bitter memory of those childhood mornings when Massimo, with the pretext of teaching him to swim from the banks of one of the tributaries of the Chicama river, forced him to hold his breath by plunging his head into the muddy waters for seconds on end until Matías started to flail around, and came back up with his lungs drained of oxygen. He failed to understand why his father had recourse to this sadistic method that, rather than boosting his confidence, seemed aimed at breaking his will. It was enough for Massimo to order 'get changed, we're going to the river' for resentment and nerves to become lodged in that gap between the chest and the stomach. Many years later, he would learn that this was one of the unspeakable torture methods used by the Giurato brothers to terrorise their victims: taking them to this filthy river, holding them under, leaving them half-drowned and broken until they got what they wanted.

Matías' countenance, twisted by rage, was trans-formed when Clifford asked him about his mother. 'She is a saint,' he said, 'selfless, generous like no other.' It was no exaggeration. During the floods in Trujillo caused by the El Niño current of 1923, Edith Roeder set up action committees with other pious women from the German community, the ladies Rosemberg, Clausen and Albrecht. Together they established a refuge in the cathedral, and contributed to the construction of an orphanage to house children left homeless. She did the same after the mudslide of March 1925. That summer the rains fell relentlessly for ten days and ten nights, causing incalculable damage to public buildings unable to withstand such a furious onslaught, including the Belén Hospital where patients died of pneumonia after being left exposed. In the valley the gravelly waters of the Chicama overflowed its banks, filling the irrigation canals, ruining the fragile electricity network and leaving haciendas vulnerable and without power. Families abandoned their homes, fearing the walls and roofs would fall in. Newspapers were not printed for a whole week. Prisoners escaped through the damaged walls of their cells. And in the cemeteries the landslides broke open hundreds of tombs, scattering skeletons every which way, so that afterwards, in response to the outcry of the relatives, the bones were returned to their coffins willy nilly, with no certainty that they even belonged to the same owner. Matías was captivated by these tales of terror from the days of the mudslide, especially when his mother told of the caskets that ended up floating in circles around the central square and that, weeks later, once the water level had fallen and calm had returned to the town, skulls, hip bones and femurs could still be seen scattered over the streets and avenues, yellowed by the mud or varnished by the sun, and no one claimed them or gathered them so that they ended up crushed beneath the hooves of the donkeys pulling their carts, or under the rubber tyres of the first automobiles arriving in the city.

The young Giurato couldn't wait to turn eighteen so he could leave home. It took him a whole year to put together the fare and persuade his mother that the time had come for him to see the world. He would have loved her to come with him, but no, it was unthinkable for gentle Edith Roeder to leave Massimo alone, and she had long been resigned to her life. Why didn't she shake herself out of her lethargy? the son fumed. Why didn't she leave too? What was it about Massimo that had her so under his thumb? Didn't she know he was a criminal who frequented prostitutes? Was she really unaware?

Where had the rebelliousness gone, the spirit that led her to challenge her parents back in Germany before she had even reached adulthood? Where did she lose that bravery that pushed her to leave her country, her city, her neighbourhood, her family and start over on another continent, in the north of Peru, in a distant valley with a bizarre name where the only man she knew was the goon she had chosen as a husband? What became of that anarchical streak? Was it too late to get it back? Matías was repeatedly bewildered by the paradox of his mother reacting with such strength of character, solidarity and celerity to natural disasters, while seemingly being so lacking in resolve when it came to taking the reins of her own life and correcting its course.

In counterpoint to Massimo's criminal endeavours, indeed as a way of dealing spiritually with this burden, Edith Roeder maintained in Trujillo a fervent routine, such as her weekly visits to the churches of Del Carmen, San Agustín, Santo Domingo and La Merced. Sometimes Matías would set aside his air rifle and the desire to hunt ever larger animals, and accompany his mother on this self-sacrificing pilgrimage. He liked to spy on her movements, as she knelt in the pew whispering a prayer that no doubt pleaded with God for the corrupt soul of her husband and the hazy future of her only son, before disappearing into the gloomy side aisle on her way to the confessional with its garnet-red velvet curtains where Father Lizardo Carcelén, with that air of meekness and indolence so typical of certain on-call pharmacists, administered the penitence that would serve to mitigate the agony of her venial sins. Edith so trusted Carcelén that she frequently invited him to the lavish feasts she held at the hacienda to strengthen the ties between Trujillo society and the German colony, and Carcelén was a regular, knowing that he could recruit there not only members for his flock, but generous sponsors for parish events.

On those festive evenings, the butlers multiplied, the Italian crockery was dusted off, the collection of hunting equipment and pre-Columbian pottery was exhibited, and the dogs were let loose among the cane fields so that they would not bother the visitors. The Gildemeister cousins, Werner Stein, Carlos Bickel, Herman Berendson, the Doigs and the Schneiders arrived. The uncouth Massimo Giurato made an appearance to greet them, but as soon as he could he would vanish back out onto the street, heading straight for his lock-ins and intrigues, or to bed the most sought-after prostitutes in the Sosiego. Accustomed to his rudeness, Edith didn't waste her time rebuking him for his absences. Matías, meanwhile, though little more than an adolescent inexperienced in social engagements, would talk with the visitors until after midnight, if only to see whether Hamburg came up in the conversation.

At one such dinner he heard Edmund Moeller speak, a German sculptor who five years earlier had unveiled the ostentatious twenty-five-metre tall monument in the central square of Trujillo, commemorating the centenary of independence. Edith Roeder was there on the occasion as part of a delegation from the German colony, met the artist and offered him an invitation to the big house. By then Moeller was already well known: the Peruvian government had awarded him the Order of the Sun and in Germany he had received the Grand Prize for Arts and Sciences (it was rumoured that it was directly bestowed by Hitler in Berlin). Matías paid more attention to the guests when he heard one of them say that the enormous travertine marble and bronze figures that made up the monument had been carved, cast and crated up in Hamburg, and that over the nine-year period that Moeller worked on the piece he regularly travelled from Trujillo to Germany. The next day, leaving school, the young Giurato approached the square to scrutinise the sculpture that, despite its size, he had never looked at properly before.

'And so? Did you like it?' queried Clifford, his wooden pipe hanging from his curved lips.

'I don't know. It wasn't a question of liking or disliking, so much as I was troubled by it,' came the answer.

Two days before he discovered the existence of Edmund Moeller, Matías had heard the episode about Sodom and Gomorrah from the priest who taught religion at the seminary. He was struck by the story of Lot. With the Bible wide open, the priest told his students how Lot had taken two angels into his house and that an angry mob of men had come to the door and demanded that he hand them over. They wanted to sexually abuse, humiliate and sodomise them. Lot refused and offered his two virgin daughters for the intruders to do with as they pleased, but the sacrifice was not consummated because the angels blinded the attackers. They immediately urged Lot to go with his family to a neighbouring mountain, announcing that the two cities would be reduced to ashes as punishment for the wickedness of their inhabitants. As they fled, they were warned not to look back or pause their march. The angels ascended to a high plain from where, in obedience to Yahweh's command, they mercilessly unleashed a fiery rain of brimstone on the men, women, children, animals and trees of Sodom and Gomorrah until the last vestige of life was wiped out. Lot's wife felt the flashes of hellfire behind her and, in a second of weakness, disregarding the angels' command, she turned around and was transformed forever into a pillar of salt. Of all the questions raised by this story, Matías chose the most disconcerting one: what was Lot's wife's name? His astonishment was great when he heard his mother's name emerge from the priest's mouth: 'Edith.'

That biblical text sprang to mind the day he stood before the Moeller monument. He focused on the three robust effigies of men in chains at the base; paused briefly on the bronze reliefs depicting scenes from the battles of Ayacucho and Junín, and the independence declaration in Trujillo; but was transfixed by the image crowning the ensemble. It was a bronze statue of a young man, naked apart from a cloak around his shoulders, perched on a globe set in turn on a mass of stone faceted like a diamond, and holding a torch in his right hand. Matías noted the disproportionate size of his arms compared to the rest of his body, and his pronounced ribs. The chiselled eyes of the youth appeared to be two holes, two empty sockets like those of the blind men of Sodom and Gomorrah, but Matías, focusing on the torch or the immobile flame of the torch, thought that the sculpture looked far more like the angels who had unleashed the fire decreed by God. He wondered what Edmund Moeller meant by this disturbing figure. Did it conceal a message? What was the mission of this near-naked angel who seemed undecided between illuminating the city or burning it down, guiding it to freedom or to destruction? Was his mission to save it from extermination or to annihilate it? Was this an angel fallen from heaven, expelled from paradise, exiled in some eternal limbo? To what extent was his presence an exhortation of encouragement to the living, and to what extent a metaphorical revenge of the dead? Why did his boyish features form this implicit gesture of guilt, defeat and betrayal? Why was his chin raised as if boasting of his timeless youth? Who had been Moeller's inspiration in sculpting a face so innocent yet malign? Was his blindness real or was it an allegory on the part of the sculptor to insinuate that humanity is incapable of looking either forward or behind, not to the inconceivable past nor the non-existent future and that, in the grip of unspeakable catastrophe, is condemned to inhabit a point of no return in which the world has stopped spinning forever? Matías observed the admiration with which passers-by glanced up at the statue and wondered why, where others thought they saw a hero, a prince or a saint, he saw only a monster.

Gordon Clifford so enjoyed hearing Matías talk of these things that he didn't take long to adapt to his gestures, his choice of adjectives, his fondness for indiscriminate hyperbole. Adapt, too, to the unhurried way in which he would intertwine his hands before resting his chin on them, his habit of scratching both elbows at once, the docile manner in which he crossed and uncrossed his legs, the hiccups and yawns that punctually assaulted him with the third gin. Several times during the trip he tried to guess the demons that might be tormenting his young friend. He sensed, for example, that Matías' decision to embark for a destination so far from his homeland was motivated, at least to a certain extent, by the undeniable urgency of being at once Peruvian, Italian and German – feeling like a Peruvian among Italians and a German among Peruvians. Clifford understood this affliction as he knew it so well himself. The son of a conservative Englishman from Coventry and an American of Jewish descent, the grandson of Irish emigrants on one side, Czech on the other, Gordon Clifford grew up in New York with a strong sense of living everywhere and nowhere, unable to clearly distinguish the local from the foreign, the known from the alien. He lived in a state of latent suspense rich in interpretations of roots, traditions and where such apparently basic questions as 'where am I from' or 'where do I belong' often lacked a persuasive answer. He wasn't an only child like Matías, but he did share with him a solitary childhood since his two older brothers had fled the nest while still young, leaving the rooms, courtyards and gardens of their home free for the youngest to roam in. As Matías told him of his mother's opulent dinners at the Chiclín hacienda and of his hope that one of those cosmopolitan connoisseurs would tell him something new about Hamburg, Gordon Clifford had the impulse or the need to protect the boy who reminded him so much of himself, to help him realise the far-fetched but still romantic dream of going to a Germany under the thumb of National Socialism to meet his grandfather, his uncles, his cousins, half of his family lineage. Clifford himself, when he was twenty, could have done with support like that he was about to offer. In his own day he also set up a trip to Ireland to visit his grandparents, but he had to postpone it not out of safety but because his father Hamilton Clifford had already enrolled him in a business school and young Gordon, whether to stay in his good books or because he never had the balls to refuse him, gave way to his preferences, agreeing to follow a profession that there was no doubt he was suited to, and which soon proved profitable. Yet the fact he was good at it and that he had an innate ability at dealing with tax, accounting and commercial matters in no sense signified that he enjoyed it.

As soon as Matías related his impressions of Edmund Moeller's monument in Trujillo's central square, Clifford hastened to take him on a stroll around the upper deck in order to put to him the idea that he had already been weighing for some time. There were only seventy-two hours of the voyage remaining, and they had passed every day together save for the five that Clifford spent shut up in his cabin with his lungs overwhelmed by a tropical fever, and the full day that Matías spent wandering around the port of Balboa during the lengthy stop in Panama.

Over that time their mutual goodwill had naturally grown into affection, and although they had said nothing to define it, neither of them had any doubt that they shared a friendship more truthful and promising than others of longer standing that had faded with the years or been shrivelled by ingratitude. On board the *Santa Bárbara* they had witnessed and participated in dinners, parties, anniversaries, marriage proposals, and even the captain's birthday, when he invited a select group of first-class passengers to the bridge. They had seen fights, altercations, reconciliations. But above all, they had talked without falter, pacing the deck from bow to stern, port to starboard, sharing confidences, remarking on the letters they would or would not send to their families and friends, reading them to each other as if they were poetry, not so much in order to discuss the style as to examine the degree of truth these missives conveyed. All of this, day or night, at the mercy of the sunrises, sunsets and the vast constellations that glitter in the Pacific skies on the high seas.

What Gordon Clifford proposed in good faith was to adopt him. Matías heard these words and, bewildered, scratched his elbows. Clifford explained that if he registered as his son when he entered the United States, not only would he save time and money on future paperwork in case he needed to extend his stay, but he could work legally and make a living, asserting the rights of any U.S. citizen. Matías proffered a sceptical glance. Where did this sudden philanthropy come from, he wondered. 'It costs me nothing, it is wholly disinterested on my part,' reiterated Clifford, reading his thoughts. Matías remained silent. 'Throughout my career I have noted hundreds of times how small bureaucratic gestures have a tremendous impact on people's lives, freeing them from impossible situations,' the banker added, backing up his argument with a series of complex analogies. Matías finally opened his mouth to ask whether – if he consented to the adoption – he would have to change his surname. When he heard Gordon say 'only the paternal one', he returned the banker's ambiguous grin, that studied device he used when he did not want to reveal his satisfaction. Dispensing with the Giurato name and everything it signified was a categorical victory in the battle to free himself from his father's shadow, as well as an unbeatable opportunity for reinvention.

On Friday September 1, 1939 they arrived in New York. Once the passengers had gone ashore, Matías stuck close to Clifford as they shuffled towards the port building exit. 'What if they don't let me in?' he asked, anxiously. His friend put him at ease, saying he would take care of the inquiries by the port authorities and completing the migration forms. All Matías had to do was undergo a brief medical check-up and answer the eleven questions that the customs official put to him. First of all, his full name. 'Matías Clifford Roeder,' he enunciated, sticking coolly to the script practised while aboard. Gordon placed a hand on his right shoulder to help him get through the questioning, and within minutes they found themselves outside near the station, relieved and congratulating each other on how effortlessly they had pulled it off and joking at the novelty of being father and son, at least for legal purposes. 'So, do you know where you'll go?' Clifford enquired. 'I suppose I must find Uncle Enrico,' Matías replied, dodging the question. In reality he hadn't decided on his next move. After a pause, Clifford hugged him, to avoid melodrama. He didn't offer him money or any other kind of support, since Matías had already rejected it. Besides, the adoption – it was a shock to describe it this way – was already a big incentive, the rest of the road he would have to pave on his own. Before getting into the black Pontiac that was waiting for him with its engine running, the banker left him a card with the address of his house, north of the city in the quiet village of Washingtonville. Once in the back seat, as he watched the young man wave his arms and become a slowly fading silhouette, he regretted not having invited him to spend a few weeks with him. Clifford's car was slowly swallowed up by the streets, disappearing into the columns of steam rising from the drains. Matías remained there for a brief moment, unable to do anything but stare in all directions, overwhelmed by the vast scale of the skyscrapers that swayed above him in the clouds, the advertising hoardings one on top of the other, the endless bridges stretched over the even more endless Hudson River, the gleaming steel rails of the elevated lines and, at the centre of the bay, to one side of Ellis Island, the portentous, splendid Statue of Liberty, its right arm raised in timeless gesture, at once offering a warm welcome to new arrivals in America and seeming to threaten them with expulsion if they transgressed the law in the slightest. Trujillo was so remote from all this, he thought. 'It's a different world,' he told himself. He wasn't yet able to comprehend that he too was changed, someone very different to the young lad who in the bustling port of Salaverry, with a single suitcase and a third-class ticket, had bid farewell to his mother, a few college friends and that beach with its mottled waters and grey seagulls that – he was sure now – he would never see again.

9

It's nine years since I came to live in Madrid with the perfect alibi: to study for a Masters in Creative Writing. I spent a month holed up in the apartment of a friend of a friend until I found a two-room flat of my own. Flat 3B, Number 76, Calle de Ferraz. On most mornings, twenty metres along the pavement, between a well-stocked store run by a Chinese couple and a bakery selling gluten-free pastries, I would see a myopic man in his eighties sitting on a red chair, with silver hair, a bulbous nose and a cigar clenched between his teeth. He was in the habit of talking to anyone who would listen, and sharing, or rather imposing – brooking no opposition – his memories of the Spanish Civil War. His name was Miguel. Nobody knew for sure what he had done in his youth and nobody showed any signs of wanting to find out. They saw him as a harmless old buffer, stuck in his ways. One day he addressed me with an inquisitive air, asking if I was new in the neighbourhood. I pointed to my building, saying I'd barely been there a month. 'Ah, you live at number 76?' 'Right,' I said. 'It was hit by a few bombs,' he mused, pushing his glasses up his nose, 'but it wasn't as bad as in Leganitos.' I asked him what he meant, allowing him to embark unhurriedly on an account of the events of November 1936 and early 1937, when the German and Italian bombers systematically attacked Madrid in support of the side that had risen up against the Spanish government. 'Not a building was left standing,' Miguel said, a shaking finger indicating the residential blocks along Calle de Ferraz and the adjacent streets. 'Though Leganitos was worse,' he repeated. Once I was home I googled. The old guy wasn't making it up: Nazis and fascists eagerly collaborated with Franco, lending aircraft, while enabling their pilots to gain experience and to practise the tactics and techniques they would go on to apply in the theatre of the Second World War. From that point on, every time I climbed the stairs I thought of how the explosions of the falling bombs weighing between 50 and 250 kilos would have shaken the buildings of the period. I thought about it constantly. Sometimes I'd go out on the balcony or prowl the streets and I could barely look up without imagining the Junkers and Heinkels of the Condor legion of the Third Reich, or the Capronis and Savoia-Marchettis of Mussolini's Aviazione Legionaria stampeding across the cloudless skies of Madrid. Night and day, the planes unloaded their bombs pitilessly on the city and its civilian population who, alerted by sirens, ran for cover in the metro stations or wherever they could find shelter. The bombardment had a clear, non-military objective: to sow fear among citizens, erasing their neighbourhoods, dismantling their homes, and impoverishing them until they were forced to surrender. And so, a couple of times a week when I saw Miguel sitting out on his red chair, I'd get him talking. After the bombings, he told me, all was fire, shouting, confusion, panic. The streets were filled with piles of rubble. Countless buildings were holed, through which protruded twisted beams and broken pipes; and in the avenues the bombs produced craters so deep that they exposed the rails and wagons of the Metro. Miguel bitterly recalled how there were too few rescuers to put out the fires, dig through the rubble or keep a detailed account of the dead and wounded; and he always reiterated that, even though in the street where we found ourselves, Calle de Ferraz, the tragedy had been of significant proportions, 'Leganitos was worse'. I found it overwhelming to imagine that his tales referred to the streets, neighbourhoods and squares that I walked through day after day, without a thought for their horrific past: Moncloa, the Las Letras district, Gran Vía, the banks of the Manzanares river, Plaza Pedro Zerolo and so many other sites that, eight decades before, had been disfigured by bombs, shells and mortars. My chats with Miguel might last an hour or two, but the images from his stories would remain with me the whole day, invading my thoughts and changing my mood. At the pool I would swim one length after another, back and forth over the rectangular sky-blue tiles, and suddenly I wasn't a swimmer but a bomber plane flying over a city crammed with buildings about to be turned to dust. The bubbles streamed from my nose as if they were incendiary bombs. My arms turned like the propellers of the German and Italian planes, and beneath me, on the pool floor, I saw anti-aircraft guns rotating on the circular drain grilles, while the twenty-five metre black line stretched like the runway where the aircraft landed at the conclusion of each operation.

Barely any of the Spaniards I went on to meet were aware that they lived among buildings that during the war had been partially or totally destroyed and, even when they showed interest in old Miguel's stories, none seemed eager to learn more. Perhaps the subject obsessed me because I came from a city that was also used to explosions.

The bombs of Sendero Luminoso and the MRTA didn't fall from the sky, but were planted beneath cars, inside municipal dumps, or hidden at the foot of electricity pylons so that when they exploded whole cities were left in darkness. On another scale, and with different repercussions, these bombs also killed, mutilated, and sowed chaos. At gatherings with friends, Erika would encourage me to speak of those terrible years of political violence in Peru. 'You've got to write about it,' she would say, and right away, as though acting out a practised routine, I'd push her to share the traumatic memories of her parents and grandparents of the bombing of Berlin at the end of the Second World War. Erika spoke of those attacks with real consternation, as if she'd been there, as if, despite having grown up without tragedy or privation, she felt the monstrous after-effects of that genocidal war within her. 'Did you know that, in terms of the area affected, Berlin suffered more damage than any other city?' she would always say. And then would come the same remark, the one that caused most surprise among those listening: 'Almost four times as much as Dresden.' I adored the gesticulations she would make every time she repeated it. On a wall in the hallway of the apartment, below a reproduction of an oil painting by David Hockney, we had a triptych with maps of Lima, Berlin and Madrid drawn by her, sombrely titled 'our bombed capitals'. Erika showed it to visitors, saying that these cities were closely linked by pain, and defended a thesis that I made my own from the first time I heard it: 'Bombing,' she said, 'never ends.' She argued that, however effective the reconstruction of a city that had been subject to such horror, the specific type of horror generated by deadly bombings meant that the nightmares continued to assail its inhabitants while the testimony of survivors continues to be handed down by them or their descendants.

One figure who did not come up often in Erika's conversations on the matter was her own paternal grandfather, a fervent member of the Hitler Youth in the 1930s. Nor did she say much about her father, who had openly declared himself anti-Nazi but never made any effort to hide his disgust if asked for an opinion on African and Asian immigrants seeking asylum in Germany. Both were distant figures. The grandfather I saw three or four times but don't remember talking to. I met the father on more occasions, usually at dinner parties crowded with relatives I didn't know, so our conversations were limited to the exchange of innocuous or diplomatic statements. I never knew for sure what he thought of me becoming his only daughter's husband, though I had a pretty good idea. Although he endorsed our relationship in principle, he never evinced any visible sign of emotion in our regard. The one I did make friends with was Erika's mother, Soledad, a magnificent, cultivated, open-minded woman. An Argentinian, she was delighted to have someone to speak Spanish with. 'My German is still so basic,' she would lament. It was fascinating to hear her recount her own parents' wartime flight by boat from Italy, uncertain of their destination. Once in Buenos Aires, her father made contact with anarchist trade unionists and wound up a hardcore Peronist. Whenever I saw Erika's parents, whether in person or in the photographs that spread throughout our flat, I wondered how on earth the son of a Nazi and the daughter of a communist had ever fallen in love and, even more, how they had remained together for so many years.

10

'And what do you do?' asked the taxi driver.

'At the moment I'm working freelance. In Peru I did journalism, but wound up working as a consultant.'

'Ah, so you're a journalist. Television? Any channel they show here?'

'No, no. It was mostly for newspapers, though in Peru I did get into TV and radio a bit. Here I work for Spanish outlets, writing articles, but not regularly.'

'And you can make a living from that?'

'Let's say I can pay my rent. But I have to find something steadier soon, Madrid has got so expensive.'

'Have you ever thought of teaching at the university? They pay well there, I've heard.'

'Sure, but you need to study a master's in education and I already did a master's when I got here. I don't have the energy to do another one.'

'What was the first one in?'

'Creative writing.'

An awkward silence fell.

'Tell me, maestro,' – he looked for the words – 'what is that useful for?'

I smiled without shifting my gaze from the window.

'I often ask myself the same question,' I answered, frankly.

'Are you a writer?'

'Not really. I'd say I'm more of a...'

'Frustrated writer?'

'I was going to say "amateur". "Frustrated" is a little bit...'

'Peruvian of me?' he laughed.

'I was going to say pessimistic, but maybe that's pretty much the same thing.'

'Well at least you've got time on your side. How old are you, thirty-five?'

'Appearances can be deceptive. Forty-two.'

'Pah, you're still young. I'm fifty-five.'

'Something'll come up, I'm not worried yet. If I've made it this far, I can't be doing too badly. Sometimes you get so worried about what you lack, what you don't have, that you don't value what you've got.'

'Don't dismiss driving a cab, you earn well above minimum wage. Remember me.'

'I've thought about it, believe me. Taxi driver, waiter, delivery man, even if just for a few months.'

'Here they are professions like any other. You talk to the men and women who drive taxis here and they are honourable, well-dressed folk. Not like in Peru where if you drive a cab or wait tables in a restaurant people look down on you.'

'Well, in Peru discrimination is like the national sport. You're discriminated against for what you do, for what you say, but above all for your colour.'

'Sure, but here too, eh. If you're black there's no escaping it. And I don't just mean the African guys who hang around in Plaza Mandela, but black people who were born here. For some reason Spaniards think there aren't any black people who are Spanish. There are loads!'

'Right, but…'

'And let's not even start with the Gypsies or the Muslims. In Barcelona, when an ambulance responds to an emergency call in the neighbourhoods where the Gypsies live, do you know what they do if they find someone who's already dead? They act as if they might be able to revive them so that the family doesn't think they aren't making an effort. The paramedics know they're dealing with a cadaver, but if they don't go through the motions then they get hassled. That's how sensitive things are. A passenger told me, he was a doctor. He'd experienced it.'

'I take your word for it, but I still reckon we're dealing more with xenophobia than racism. And I think it's the immigrants who pay dearly for it. I've never seen Spaniards discriminating against each other as harshly and cruelly as they do in Peru.'

'Listen, maestro, I talk with these people every day… there are guys in Salamanca who can't stand Catalans, there are Catalans who hate folk from Murcia, and there are people from Lugo who rip into anyone from Madrid. There are any number of villages barely five kilometres apart and they detest each other. It's just the same as in Peru.'

'And why do you think they hate each other?'

'Now, that I don't know. Habit, imitating their folks, their grandparents, or for any dumb reason. But the resentment is there. I see it all the time.'

'I'm pretty sure this hatred doesn't have racial connotations, though. It might be dislike, classism, political rivalry or, like you say, inherited animosity, but it's not the same racism as we see in Peru, especially in Lima, where if you're not white you've no chance of getting ahead. There, they classify, judge and exclude you based on the colour of your skin.'

'But that's how it's always been, maestro, why are you so surprised?'

'I'm surprised that things haven't changed even the slightest bit. Supposedly acts of discrimination get reported more and more often, but it's not enough. It's like a hereditary disease that...'

'...no, no, maestro, Peruvian racism isn't an illness, it's an incurable epidemic. Deadly. And everyone's infected with it.'

It was impossible for me not to feel seen. I'd caught that disease a long time ago. Perhaps it came from my mother, with her biases and contradictions. Her parents, my grandparents, were from Huaraz, a village at the foot of the cordillera. They migrated to Lima as a young couple and rented a bare apartment in a block in Mirones, where robberies were the order of the day. My mother was born a few months later and spent her early years there, in those half-built streets thronged by the poor. That was her world. That and Huaraz, where she'd return for periods and be left in the care of aunts in their seventies who wore their hair in plaits, still dressed in traditional skirts and raised guinea pigs that would disappear from the pen one day only to reappear on their dinner plates, parboiled and smothered in hot sauce. She didn't know what privilege was until much later. By the time I was born my mother was a different woman altogether: her world, her habits and ambitions had become middle class. Visiting the grandparents in that housing unit was like traveling to a different country, and for my mother a trip back in time where everything – the food, the music, the décor and the jokes – reminded her of Huaraz. Despite her Andean background, my mother harboured a racism that only emerged with certain people, such as the ones who came to do cleaning or maintenance work around the house. She treated them with contempt, and when they left she'd talk about them in terms of 'stinking cholos' or 'lazy blacks', mocking their behaviour, their manner of speech, their clothing or appearance with unpleasant gestures. She couldn't help herself. It was the same with the market stallholders when they didn't play along with her haggling. 'That's what these people are like, so ignorant, what can you do. You can take the monkey out of the jungle, but you can't take the jungle out of the monkey.' I would criticise this ill will and believed myself inoculated from it, free from her influence – that is, until the day I was driving through Lima and a minibus cut me up, forcing me to brake so sharply my wheels skidded, and I opened the window and yelled at the driver with a fury that wouldn't dissipate for an hour: 'You could have killed me, you black motherfucker!'

'Have you ever gone to the fiesta the Consulate organises for Independence Day every July 28?'

'I haven't. To be honest, I avoid them. Why, are they fun?'

'First of all they offer you a pisco sour in a plastic cup, then the Consul, his secretary or any old representative gets up on the platform to make a speech about Peru, a whole spiel about its cultural diversity, its geographical diversity, its ethnic diversity, and everyone claps, sings the anthem, dances the dances – and then two hours later with four drinks in them they're chucking the chairs around at the slightest excuse.'

'Well you know, that's Peru for you. I couldn't have put it better: the least thing will have them at each other's throats like cholos.'

That word, 'cholos', hung in the air.

'My dad was treated like a cholo, too, you know,' the taxi driver said suddenly. 'He was almost thirty years old when he arrived in Lima from the mountains, such that it was obvious from how he spoke. There was one time, when we lived in Callao, he was working selling bread, he went out with his cart and a bunch of hoodlums started making fun of him because of the way he talked. 'Go on, spit it out, peasant,' they'd say. And my dad, who couldn't keep his mouth shut, who was a troublemaker, replied by chucking stones at them, which only led to more insults and aggro. Shitty cholo, stupid cholo, why don't you go back to the hills? What didn't they say to him. They started beating him up, too. My dad returned with his shirt torn and told it all to my ma in a fury, while we gobbled up the bread he hadn't been able to sell because he'd been brawling.'

'And was he ashamed?'

'Of selling bread?'

'No, of being from the mountains, I mean.' I nearly said 'of being a cholo'.

'Not at all. On the contrary, some days he'd start talking to us in Quechua. And Sunday afternoons he'd take his chair out on the stoop, drink chicha de maní, listening to his huaynos on the radio and singing along as he got drunk. He'd weep with nostalgia.'

Right away, I thought of my own father, an affable man who spoke with an accent that I didn't notice or didn't want to notice. I thought about the Quechua words he never taught us, about the two or three times I came across him whistling huaynos as he folded his shirts the way my grandfather did, arranging them by shade and colour; and about the heavy body odour that even today he tries to conceal with lotions.

'Chicha de maní is the typical drink in Huánuco, right?' I asked.

'Of course. That's where my dad's from.'

'Mine too,' I said.

'Seriously?' he turned around in disbelief, raising his eyebrows. 'What part? My family comes from Churubamba.'

'My dad's from Amarilis.'

'Amarilis? That's in Paucarbamba, isn't it?'

'Yup, Paucarbamba.'

'That's not far from Churubamba, maybe half an hour by car.'

'A couple of hours by donkey, that's for sure.'

He laughed heartily.

'Do you know what Paucarbamba means, though?' He answered his own question: 'Plain of flowers. Pretty, right?'

'The name does the place justice,' I agreed. I wanted to say more, but wasn't sure where to start.

'Churubamba is also pretty,' he added, exhaling.

'Am I right to think that mummies were found there?' I inquired, already knowing the answer.

'Sure, the Papahuasi mummies. I think they're on display in some cabinets in the town hall.'

'That's right, we went to see them. There were lots of children that were all bound up.'

'They'd place the bodies in bags made from ropes, that's why they're so well preserved,' he explained. 'So I guess you must have tried shacta too, while you were there?'

'No, I was too young to drink liquor when we visited, but I do remember the guinea pig in hot sauce and the chicken locro.'

'That locro is my favourite.'

'You don't happen to know the Trinidad family, by any chance?'

'That surname rings a bell,' he said, pensive. 'Aren't they the owners of a hacienda up there in Paucarbamba?'

'That's it. Rodolfo and Margarita Trinidad.'

'I think my father knew them. He spent a lot of time in the area, everyone knew who he was.'

'Perhaps your father knows mine!' I exclaimed.

'If he were still alive, I'd ask him.'

I fell silent, feeling like an idiot.

'Relax, maestro, that's life,' he offered in a vain attempt to put me at ease.

'Has it been long?' I ventured, trying to make up for my lack of tact.

'The day after tomorrow it'll be ten months.'

'Was he ill?' I asked. And immediately regretted it.

'Cancer. Lymphatic cancer.'

I looked at him in the rear-view mirror. He wasn't upset, but the lines under his eyes had suddenly expanded to cover his whole face.

'I'm sorry,' I said, for want of anything else to say.

'The worst thing was being unable to bury him together with the rest of the family.'

'These things happen for a reason,' it occurred to me to utter.

I decided not to open my mouth again. Once death slips into a conversation, there's nothing more to be said. It's impossible to say anything intelligent. I could not, however, avoid imagining that circumstance, every migrant's worst nightmare: losing a relative in the country you left behind and being unable to find a plane in time to get to the funeral; or finding one and spending the longest and saddest flight of all the long, sad flights ever conceived. In either case, the blow is insurmountable. The space between the driver and me was suddenly filled with a tangible tension. I remembered that in my backpack I was carrying the novel I'd begun on the plane. I was about to retrieve it, when the man began speaking again.

'So your father's alive then?'

'Yes, he is. Old, but in good health, fortunately.' I felt bad as I said it.

'Perhaps he'll remember my father, then.'

'I could ask him. What was his name?'

'Antonio Palomino, like myself. Ask him when you get the chance.'

At this point, his phone rang. He put a single headphone bud into his ear. I looked out the window and saw we were close to Ciudad Lineal. Unusually, all four lanes of the highway were nose-to-tail.

'They're telling me from the base that there's a big delay. A truck turned over and caused a pile-up, and the police still haven't set up a diversion. We're going to take longer than expected, maestro.'

'Don't you worry on my account, Antonio. I'm not in any kind of a hurry.'

11

In Lima I worked with a well-regarded communications consultancy. I was part of a team of staff who advised large and medium-sized companies, as well as individual clients, when they needed to launch corporate or other kinds of campaigns. I spent my first year there developing promotional strategies that didn't exactly stand out for their originality. Then my journalism experience led me to focus on political and social content. Almost accidentally I ended up specialising in situation analysis, media training, electoral campaigns and crisis management. At the same time, I was teaching a course for the Diploma in Political Communication at the Catholic University. On top of that, I contributed to the country's most popular radio channel with a slot on current affairs that went out three mornings a week, and which confounded my predictions by becoming a real hit. An influential colleague I'd known from the days when we worked at a newspaper together offered me the spot, and despite the fact that I'd never sat in front of a microphone before, it suited me. The owner of the radio station had no fondness for me, or at least didn't share the ideas I expounded on air, but seeing that the slot had resonated so well with audiences he was obliged to smile at me when we crossed paths on my way to the recording booth. That radio presence garnered me a certain popularity in the circles I frequented. Producers of TV programmes began to invite me onto talk shows and discussion panels to dissect the news of the day. They liked the fact I was less starchy or serious than their regular pundits, and they used a phrase that had something paranormal about it: 'you go beyond the screen'. Appearing on television meant that people began to recognise me in public. Wherever I went, there'd be a couple of random strangers who would approach me in a friendly manner to say hello or even ask for a picture or an autograph. In no sense was I a celebrity, but my name and my face becoming recognised not only boosted my ego but fuelled that treacherous sense of complacency that I later – happily – managed to overcome.

Before leaving Peru I spoke to each of my bosses in turn, wondering if I could carry on doing some of this work in which I saw myself as irreplaceable. The director of the consultancy firm said he would happily keep me on, but did nothing about it, and between his intransigence and the urgent need to prepare the budget for the next year, the head of resources had no other choice but to cancel my contract. I received a decent severance, but I lost the regular monthly income that allowed me to sleep easily. The radio station owner, meanwhile, said right up to the last moment that he was 'very interested' in the 'material' I might be able to 'generate from Spain', yet once I was in Madrid, his responses to my emails landed less and less frequently in my inbox until they dried up altogether. Evidently, my departure had been the perfect excuse to get rid of me. Finally, the dean of the faculty was the only one to throw me a lifeline: she agreed to let me continue to deliver my seminar online, although with a reduced number of hours.

As soon as I set up in Madrid I threw myself into the creative writing course with total commitment. However, the level of students on the master's course, combined with the expectations of the faculty, left much to be desired. To earn my diploma I presented a series of stories linked by the theme of claustrophobia, set in both open and closed spaces that were asphyxiating in their own way. The jury described them as 'original and intriguing' when the fact is they were awful. I wouldn't like to say it was a waste of two years – I must have learned something from it – but once it was over I realised that I was at the same point as when I started: without a project in hand, nor even a clear idea about what kind of writer I wanted to be, or indeed if I really wanted to be a writer. In Madrid, I attended every book presentation going to see if they provided the necessary inspiration, but I almost always emerged disappointed from these soirées dominated by posturing, over-egged praise, and gossip. At this stage my savings, though in decline, still supported the rhythm of the life I was leading. This was not the fast-paced life of a bachelor in Europe, however, but more serene and easy, even if there was a smattering of music, alcohol, and flirting – or, to be more precise, attempts at flirting. I went to bars and forced myself to write about them, but all I got out of it were wasted nights, insipid anecdotes, and disappointing one-night stands. I decided to forget all about creative writing, or simply concluded that it was not my thing and focused on giving virtual workshops on communications and offering poorly paid consultancies to novice Spanish politicians. I never went back to radio or television and strangers never approached me on the streets again. It wasn't that I was a pariah, but I was clearly on another rung of the social ladder.

One night at the after-party of a concert by a band in which my Peruvian friend Hugo played, I met Erika. She was introduced to me by Teresa, the backing singer. I liked her right away, from her layered blond fringe to her little leather boots, by way of the tiny piercing in the side of her nose that I associated, perhaps mistakenly, with a laid-back lifestyle. She was German by birth but spoke Spanish perfectly. She told me that her mother had moved from Argentina to Berlin as a child, where she met her future husband. She also told me that she spent several summers of her own childhood moving back and forth between her grandparents' home in Buenos Aires and a holiday home the family rented in Mar del Plata. It was funny to listen to her speaking Spanish with a dry German accent but peppered with Buenos Aires slang. We laughed a lot that night, me at her and her at me, we laughed about the gloomy basement where we had met, and about the Last Maniacs, the terrible rock group we'd just heard, even if we agreed that the performances by our friends Hugo and Teresa were the best bit. At one point I dared to describe our meeting as 'improbable chance'. 'It's not chance, it's synchronicity,' she said. 'It's chance,' I pleaded. 'There is no such thing as chance,' she said. 'It's an accident,' I countered. 'There are no accidents, there are achievements and oversights,' she said. 'It's fate,' I insisted, exhausting my cards. 'Destiny doesn't materialise by itself, it happens,' she said. 'I can tell you're a Virgo,' I speculated. 'I'm a Gemini, but I don't trust the western zodiac,' she said. With no more tricks up my sleeve, I suggested we remedy our existential disagreements with a round of piscos, to which we would add another of tequilas, and a final one of absinthes, and five minutes later we were dancing and kissing, and were all over each other in a manner that I now remember as impetuous and premature. Now that a whole year has passed since the separation, I can see everything with a better perspective, or with some perspective at least, and I admit that what happened between us, more than an idyll at first sight, was something like a mutual salvation pact. She'd been in Madrid for a year, me for two, neither of us had settled in or adapted: for both of us there was much more lacking in our lives than the little we had gained. We fancied each other, sure, but perhaps we threw ourselves into each other's arms searching not so much for romance or excitement as for some warmth or protection or simply for a convenient remedy to the intimidating solitude of exile that, on a bad day, can lead you to renege on your intentions, abort your plans, pack your bags and retrace your steps with a defeated look on your face. In another context, furnished with other attitudes and words, we might not even have noticed each other. However it happened, the cycle of events that followed that night confirmed the initial impulse: we hooked up and eight months later we were living together in the flat on Calle de Ferraz. With certain reservations, I proposed that she move in with me, fearing our domestic routines might wreck the relationship, but from day one cohabitation proved not only bearable but surprisingly harmonious. Just as her blouses, books, handbags, candles and other personal objects gradually found their place until they became a part of our daily surroundings with striking ease, she too, with the songs she sang in the shower, the aromas she left impregnated in pillows, scarves and cushions, the jars of herbs and condiments she would habitually leave open in the kitchen, and even the good taste with which she arranged the furniture and the lightness with which she would throw herself into them, meant that the house little by little became imbued with her personality to the extent that it almost seemed insipid and meaningless without her presence. After nine months of this experiment, I proposed another, even less prudent one: to get married. Her affirmative reply only demonstrated a higher degree of madness to my own. Were we betrayed by emotion? Naturally. But at that moment we felt, or at least I felt, that marriage was the logical next step for a couple who, when it came to their everyday functioning, felt invincible.

12

If it weren't for the conversation with Antonio, I wouldn't have been able to put up with the traffic jam. When cars come to a standstill, all backed up, and there's no end in sight, I tend to suffer from severe claustrophobia. In Lima it happened twice on the Panamericana Sur and once on Avenida Grau. All three times in summer, when I felt not only trapped in the tangle of cars that constantly sounded their horns, but knocked out by the heat. Winding down the window or putting on the air conditioning did nothing to alleviate the symptoms: palpitations, anxiety, sweating temples and palms. It doesn't only happen in traffic jams. For years I've been unable to climb into the rear seats of a two-door car for fear that the reduced space would set off an attack. For the same reason I avoid caves, grottoes, crypts and catacombs on tourist trips. And I even skip narrow streets, maze-like markets, and busy alleyways, picturesque though they may be. In long underground tunnels of any kind, I have to concentrate hard to calm the anxiety at not seeing the light at the end. It's the same with getting an MRI scan: the four times I've had to undergo the procedure I drove the staff crazy, as I couldn't bear to be inside for more than a minute. I won't go the cinema or theatre if I haven't procured a ticket close to an emergency exit, or at least an aisle. Erika was once given tickets for the premiere of a highly praised production at the Alcalá Theatre, but the seats were right in the middle of the ninth row. And the rows were so very long, and the theatre so very full. Two minutes after the lights went down and the curtain went up, I looked left and right, calculated how many seconds it would take me to reach the corridors if I had to, and turned to Erika to say I couldn't stay. I pushed my way out. Aeroplanes were the worst. It was enough for me to think that I was trapped with two hundred other people in a metal tube thousands of metres above the sea, absurdly transgressing the law of gravity, for me to spend the flight in terror. I cured that one by drinking three or four glasses of wine before boarding, enabling me to fall asleep as soon as we took off. But wine has its limits. It does nothing for claustrophobic dreams. Sometimes I dream I'm in an enclosed venue, thronged with people, where a fire or explosion has occurred and I am fighting to get out, struggling in vain against the smoke and the weight of the crowd. Other recurring dreams leave me pale-faced in the morning: victim of a kidnapping, the criminals take me from one place to another in the trunk of a car, from where I scream curses and kick feebly, certain I am going to die of suffocation or a heart attack. But the nightmares that really make me sweat, that make my hair stand on end, are the ones in which I'm taking a decrepit elevator that grinds to a halt in a power cut and all I can do is slam the alarm button, which no one can hear, just as there is no doorman or neighbour to hear my cries for help, and pounding the metal walls I scream on the edge of a madness that feels so real that even after I wake up with a start the sense of jeopardy lasts for minutes more.

'This isn't moving,' I remarked, moving around on the back seat, rolling down the window, sticking my neck out the window in a vain attempt to see if there was any sign of the cars ahead starting up again.

'So, you are in a hurry?' said Antonio.

'No, but these traffic jams make me nervous. And I have a migraine, it must be the time difference.'

'Take it easy, it'll sort itself out,' he said, as if making a prediction. 'Is someone waiting for you at home?'

'Yes,' I lied.

'Better tell your folks you'll be late, then.'

'My battery's dead,' I countered. This much was true.

'You can use mine, if you like,' he said, holding out his own mobile.

I gave in.

'No one is waiting for me, Antonio. I've neither wife nor children.'

'I was just about to ask you if you were married.'

'Divorced, two months ago.'

'Oh, heck,' he said. He sounded like he really regretted it.

'Nah,' I responded, clucking my tongue. 'It was always going to happen.'

'You left her, then?'

I felt obliged to answer; I had been just as indiscreet speaking about the death of his father.

'Me? No. Well, I don't know. You never really know who ends things.'

'You always know, maestro. When someone says they don't know, it means the other person ended it.'

What I didn't acknowledge to Antonio was how easy I found it to fold my arms after the break up. When it happened I couldn't see it, but that's the way it was. I didn't fight. I gave in. I acted with indifference, as if I couldn't care less. I could have taken the initiative, I don't know, gone to Berlin, knocked on the door of her parents' house, tried to persuade her to return, written a deeply felt letter, sent her flowers or some other signal to smooth things over and pick ourselves back up. Was I so confused I was unable to react? Wasn't I supposed to love Erika so much that this love would reverse any setback? What I did, instead, was to resign myself, play the role of victim, flee to Lima, run back to my parents, and curl up among the blankets of my teenage bed. I reacted like an adolescent. I justified myself saying that she was the one who had broken it off, not me, a childish response whichever way we look at it. Perhaps a part of me did feel suffocated and wanted our relationship to collapse, except that, unlike Erika, I didn't articulate it, preferring to believe that we were going through a crisis that would sort itself out.

'No marriage is easy, but where there's a will, you overcome your problems,' he said.

'For me it's too late.'

'Didn't you say the divorce was two months ago? You could still…'

'Have you ever been divorced?' I interrupted.

'No, thank goodness, but we've been close. Things were pretty dicey for a while…'

'Just how dicey?'

'If I had to tell you I had to swallow my pride and forgive the thing that men find most difficult. My wife had an…'

'You don't have to tell me.'

'I don't mind telling you. I can talk about it now, in the past it might have been more difficult. My wife got involved with some guy from her university. He was a red, a commie. He was one of the ones imprisoned by the military. My old lady says they made a mistake in picking him up, that he wasn't part of Sendero, they called him comrade as a "term of endearment",' – his hands left the wheel to make air quotes at this point – 'but this asshole seduced her with his whole socialist spiel. Out of nowhere she started talking about Marxism, the proletariat, the people, the bourgeoisie, nonsense she'd never mentioned before. Like a mate of mine says, the right may launder money, but the left washes brains.'

'But at least she confessed it to you.'

'At the time we were already living together, and even though I forgave her, she went back to her parents. She said she felt bad for lying to me, and told me she wasn't sure about anything any more.'

'Look at it this way, she was honest,' I added, but it was as if I'd said nothing at all, as Antonio had been ignoring my remarks for a while now.

'What I did do was get the guy's name out of her. She made me promise not to do anything to him, but one day I blew a fuse, worked out where he lived and headed over. I banged on his door and told him what I knew straight to his face. You wanna know what the coward said? He denied it! That really riled me up, that he refused to face it like a man. His brother showed up just when I was about ready to punch him, so I took off, swearing that I'd get him on his own one day.'

Antonio smacked the steering wheel with the palm of his left hand.

'And did you... get him?' I wondered.

'Nope. The military came and took him away. After a few months I tried to find out what happened to him. A cousin of mine who's a cop told me that they'd done him in.' He was emotionless. 'My wife was in tears for days. She'd shut herself up in the bathroom. I just listened to her.'

'You did the right thing forgiving her, Antonio.'
'You reckon?'
'I don't reckon, I'm sure of it.'

I wasn't entirely sure that Antonio had got over his anger, but beyond satisfying my curiosity, asking him gained me nothing.

'Did she take a long time to come back to you?' I continued.

'After five or six months she returned. That separation hurt me more than the deceit. The anger lasted until we came to Spain. Here, with the kids and all, we were able to move on.'

'Getting out of those surroundings must have helped.'

'It was the distance, but it was also the kids. I didn't say before, but my daughter, the eldest, was born with hydrocephalia. We've adapted now, but when we found out, jeez, maestro, we were knocked for six, we had no idea what to do. We cried, we blamed each other, we turned everything over. In the end it brought us closer to God, and that in turn brought us closer to each other. We decided not to have any more kids, but you know how the Lord works: a year and a half later my wife was pregnant again.'

Antonio crossed himself as he said this.

'And weren't you frightened that...'

'...that the second one would have hydrocephalia too? Yes, of course we were. So when the baby turned out to be fine, you can't imagine what a relief it was.'

Antonio left the engine switched off, only turning it on to advance the three or four metres at a time the traffic jam allowed. People in other cars turned to look at each other, making gestures of despair or encouragement. The blinking warning lights on all sides had me hypnotised, to the point where I started to feel our conversation was marked by their flashing rhythm.

'You never wanted a family?' he asked bluntly.

'Sure, we tried, and we underwent tests, which suggested she was the one unable to conceive. The doctor encouraged us to try alternative methods, and I was up for it, but my wife said that would be forcing something that should be biologically pure. When we stopped trying I mistakenly thought she had accepted the limitations and that her desire to be a mother would gradually fade. I couldn't have been more wrong. Once that desire is there, nothing extinguishes it.'

'Did you think of adopting?'

'We never talked about it. She had a crisis that went on for a long time until one fine day we decided to go our own separate ways. I accepted that I should leave the flat, which is why I went to Lima. Do you know what it's like to have to abandon a house you don't want to leave?'

'I know what it's like to watch someone leave who you don't want to go.'

'It's the same thing. It feels like shit. I felt that I didn't deserve it,' I said.

Antonio took a second to look at me in the rear-view mirror before he said:

'Don't take this the wrong way, but don't you think we all deserve a little bit what comes to us?'

13

A few years ago, in Lima, a doctor recommended I take up swimming as therapy for my claustrophobia. 'It's best to swim in a pool,' he told me. 'The sea can bring its own anxieties.' Ever since, I've swum with a certain regularity. It does me good, it relaxes me, especially when I manage to disassociate the physical exercise from the mental, and it feels like one half of the brain is occupied in coordinating the succession of arm strokes, leg strokes and breaths, while the other sets about producing images that find in the water an essential element that allows them to form and stick in the memory. In the two months I was back in Lima I swam almost every day, trying to forget about my divorce, the same way that Kafka distracted himself from the war (there is a celebrated note in his diaries from August 2, 1941 that reads: 'Germany has declared war on Russia. Went swimming in the afternoon.') Just like in the past, I went to a club pool: I'd leave my towel and sandals on a bench, put on the synthetic cap, goggles and earplugs, warm up stretching my arms and legs for three minutes, then adjust my trunks, dive in and, in the restorative glare of noon, swim lengths for 1,000 or 1,500 metres. Swimming not only helped me to forget Erika, but to think about the separation in a different way, no noise, no people, pushing off from one wall to the next, surrounded only by tiles, inhaling the aroma of chlorine, as difficult to scrub from the body as certain memories. I didn't always find answers as I swam, but the water was a kind of relaxed language that made my questions less pressing. Upon my return to Madrid I started going to a pool in a gym close to the Malasaña apartment. It was one day while I was swimming that it occurred to me I needed to get a pet. The last one I'd had was Pascal, Erika's dog, who bared his teeth whenever I tried to stroke him, though he'd eagerly wag his tail if he needed fed or taken for a walk. The very next day I decided to buy a fish. I went to an aquarium store called Vida Marina and acquired a beautiful oval-shaped *Acanthurus triostegus* originating in the clear reefs of Indonesia. It is known as the convict surgeonfish because of the black stripes that traverse its silvery body. I took it home and placed the fish tank on a shelf where it received natural light. From day one I followed the saleswoman's instructions to the letter, feeding it with plankton and seaweed-flavour granules. I also bought some decorative rocks for it to hide in. I named it Fritz. It was only after a few weeks that it occurred to me that this was a German name. In the mornings I'd observe the frilling of its tail and fins, trying to understand the logic of its movements, wondering what it could see from inside the tank, how it avoided bumping into the stones at night, whether we'd develop some form of telepathic communication, and if he also felt something like claustrophobia in that glass sphere. When I fed him I couldn't help sharing my confidences the way people do with cats and dogs, without thinking that for him I was probably nothing more than a blurred shape that grew larger when his food arrived. It might sound naïve, but as well as providing company,

Fritz conveyed a kind of peace. When I went swimming I'd think about his regular breathing through his gills, about how nice it must be to be able to dive without goggles, without a swim cap, without having to pull your head out of the water every three strokes, disconnected from the outside world. I don't know if I made a mistake with his food or with his exposure to the sun, but I did something wrong because, even though the species can live up to twelve years, Fritz only lasted seven months. One day, returning home at noon, I saw that he was lying at the bottom of the little fish tank. I took the whole thing back to the store and placed it on the counter so that they could see it exactly the way I'd found it. It was a different young woman to the one who had sold it to me. 'Why did you only get one of them?' she asked, putting on a glove. 'The convict surgeonfish is gregarious, didn't my colleague tell you?' 'She didn't say anything,' I muttered. She plunged her forearm into the tank and tried to reanimate Fritz with a fingertip, but there was nothing left to reanimate. Her last words resounded in my ears for minutes after I'd left the shop: 'That fish died of loneliness.'

14

'All I'm saying is that sometimes, for wrong or for right, things happen to you that you don't deserve,' I said, countering his previous argument.

'It's like anything else: if it suits you, you'll say you deserve it; if not, then it's unfair,' Antonio replied.

'Tell me, seriously, do you think you deserved what happened with your wife?'

'I don't know. I'm no angel either, I had my slip-ups.'

'You mean with women?'

'No, no. I'm talking about gambling. One-armed bandits.'

'You mean, like slot machines?'

'Yeah. We'd moved to Rímac and there was a casino near our place that opened at midday. I was driving taxis then. One day I parked outside a store to buy a soda. The casino was right there and I went in to see what was up. The place was empty. I was hooked from day one. I'd spend an hour there easy, though when I started winning and losing, two, three, four, even five hours could go by, keeping going in search of that lucky shot that was always about to arrive.'

'Did you win much?'

'One day I won almost 800 sols, but I just carried on, trying to double or triple it. It was an addiction, I forgot everything else, I'd forget to pick up my old lady from the university, and she'd have to get the minibus home, in a rage. She was even angrier when she saw I was falling behind on the bills. "What are you spending all your money on, eh?" she'd throw in my face, and my alibi was always the car in the garage. That poor car suffered every defect imaginable. She only half-believed me.'

'Are you trying to say that your gambling addiction justified her infidelity?'

'It doesn't justify it, but it explains it, in part. I wasn't paying her enough attention: I was obsessed with money. I started to fall into debt, and our fights became a daily affair. One day she came home early, and someone on the block said they'd seen me at the casino, and she blew her top. She said horrible things to me. We said horrible things to each other.'

I fell silent again. My mind went back to the Ferraz apartment and I saw Erika and me in heated argument, one of the many over money. Not because we were short of it, though we were, but because of how we spent it. Or rather, how I spent it. While she went without, I was reluctant to make the slightest sacrifice. Her scolding reminded me of how my mother had scolded my father for the same reason, with one difference: he actively squandered money, on expensive drinks, imported cigars, brand-name shirts and watches that he liked to show off, even though his salary at the bottling factory where he was employed as a supervisor was not high enough to afford such extravagance. Fortunately my mother kept tabs on the household budget, or we'd have been broke and I'd have been kicked out of the university. One night she asked him for money to pay a bill, and he, without the slightest tact, displaying his usual ineptitude in choosing the right words, pulled some notes from his pocket and threw them on the dresser, telling her, 'You think I shit money, don't you?' Enraged, my mother began to list the unnecessary expenses he had been incurring, and pulling at him, scratching him with her fake nails, yelled that she didn't want the crumbs from his table, took the notes and tore them into pieces and threw them at him like confetti. My sisters claim they don't remember this scene, but I saw it, and the physical struggle and the torn money fluttering in the air shook me deeply. That's why these quarrels affect me so much. I was not, by any stretch of the imagination, a banal or compulsive shopper like my father, but nor was I a miser: if I was running late, I'd flag down a cab instead of walking to the metro or bus stop; I never checked restaurant bills in detail; I went to the supermarket without paying attention to the signs advertising special offers or discounts; I visited clothing stores without waiting for sales season to come round; I rented cars according to the model, not according to the amount of fuel they consumed per kilometre; I didn't calculate or negotiate the price of anything, nor refrain, for example, from having a few beers if I felt the situation warranted it. For Erika, these habits were unacceptable for a couple whose monthly income was barely scraping three thousand euros. I earned almost fifteen hundred with my classes, collaborations and consultancies, and she earned a little less working as an assistant at a construction company, a job I encouraged her to accept, from which she used to return disappointed, not understanding how a bachelor in industrial design graduated with honours like her could be unable to find a position where she could apply her skills or receive a salary that matched her expectations. 'We can't afford to throw money away,' she would chide me during those hateful fights. When summer approached, I was the one who pushed her to ask for a holiday so that we could – flying on low-cost airlines – visit London, Paris, Rome or Lisbon; at first she hesitated, but once there she let her guard down, she enjoyed it more than I did, we even indulged ourselves a little, although the next morning I saw her lying face down on the mattress checking figures, doing sums in a notebook, regretful at 'having overdone it'. Though in every other sphere of life she was happy to give in to superstition and a cabbalistic interpretation of reality, in financial matters she was resolutely rational. I didn't reject her methods, which were as effective as they were stingy; it was just that I was incapable of adopting them: I hated having to skimp and rein myself in, while she exaggerated her criticism, making it sound as though we were on the verge of ruin.

15

Regarding Erika's paternal grandfather, I am afraid I have not yet related the most important details, or what I found most important after I met him. And I'm not talking about his missing left arm, but rather the consequences of having lost it. His name was Ernst Hartmann. As I mentioned, he was a member of the Hitler Youth; but this is to say little. In reality he was one of the organisation's most committed militants, the most outstanding of his cohort, having joined at just thirteen years of age. In the *Hitlerjugend* camps the activities were not unlike the Boy Scouts: excursions, hikes, gymnastics, survival tactics. But as the weeks and months passed the indoctrination became more and more intense until they were undergoing quasi-military training in camps belonging to the army. There, the youngsters marched in perfect synch, sang the National Socialist anthem, the *Horst Wessel Lied*, performed the obligatory *Sieg Heil* fifty times a day, and were imbued with exaltation of the Aryan race, loyalty to the party, and blind adoration of Hitler. Following this training period they were supposed to be eighteen years old before they could sign up for the Waffen-SS and see active service. Erika's grandfather didn't have to wait that long. One morning in 1943, two Luftwaffe officers turned up at his high school, gathered all the pupils in the central yard, and following random criteria instructed twenty students to step forward. Ernst Hartmann was one of those selected. In a classroom where the blackboard displayed the slogan *Ein Volk, Ein Reich, Ein Führer*, after a lengthy speech on the inescapable duties they owed to the nation, it was explained to them that in two days' time they were expected to present themselves at a military base to join the air defence corps. Young Ernst was about to turn fifteen. That day, returning home glowing with excitement, he shared the news with his parents and siblings and went to bed before nine without dinner, without practising piano, without saying his prayers. Erika told me that the night before her grandfather joined the Luftwaffe, while the boy slept, dreaming of waking up as a soldier ready to defend the fatherland with his life, Erika's great-grandmother was up early with her sewing machine, altering his camouflage uniform to fit. Ernst was assigned an unexpectedly urgent task: manoeuvring, alongside five somewhat older soldiers, one of the powerful Flak 88 artillery guns in the anti-aircraft batteries. The kids learned on the job how to move around the gun carriage and how to operate the loading system to achieve the target rate of fifteen or even twenty rounds per minute, aiming at the Allied bombers flying at altitudes of as much as 8,000 metres. After several days of shredding dozens of British and American planes, sometimes shooting them down, sometimes only damaging them but forcing the crews to parachute into German territory, it became clear to the Nazi officers that cadet Hartmann was a budding prospect, and he was given greater and greater responsibilities. However, as would be the case on both fronts throughout the war, adversity took charge of scuppering the most promising careers. One night the battery of six was withstanding a heavy bombardment by the Royal Air Force. Lighting up the sky with electric search lights, they fired the artillery gun into the heavens, seeking out the Lancasters and the four-engine Stirlings that came and went, releasing their bombs over Berlin. One of them exploded just metres from the Germans' trench and the shockwave sent them flying. Two of them died immediately, their bodies shattered. The smoke took time to clear before the scene could be observed. Cries and groans came from all directions. Ernst raised his head with difficulty and, in a daze, understood that he was still alive. He saw the apparently lifeless body of a comrade and wanted to check if the man was still breathing, but when he stretched out his left arm he found it was no longer in its place. It was only when he saw shreds of bloody skin hanging from his disjointed shoulder and a jumble of blood-soaked nerves and tissue, among which he thought he could make out fragments of bone, that he cried out in pain and collapsed.

It goes without saying that he never fired an artillery gun again, nor even a rifle. He spent a month in hospital, awaiting a skin graft that never came. It was the officers who had noticed his potential and had put his name forward for one of the elite regiments who were most upset by what had happened. Ernst tried vehemently to convince them that, even without his left arm, he could still serve the army and he asked to be considered for other defence actions. To no avail. He was relegated to a desk flanked by archivists in an administrative office. As the years passed, and even after the war, he never gave way in his eagerness to prove his independence to others. I remember seeing him at a dinner viciously insulting a waiter who had come to help him uncork a bottle of wine. I couldn't repeat his exact words, as they were in German, but the authoritative tone spoke for itself. He sat back in his chair, took the bottle in his right hand, clutched it between his legs, painstakingly removed the lead foil, embedded the corkscrew in the top of the cork, twisted it right to the hilt, began to pull, his face reddened by the effort of compressing his thighs, while no one at the table moved, praying that the veins in his temple and neck weren't going to burst from the effort, as we fixated on the slow emergence of the cork and the constellation of drops of sweat scattering from his forehead to the tablecloth. The left arm of his shirt swung flaccidly, as if the missing arm was trying to come to the assistance of its pair. Erika made as if to get up to help him, but her father, with a firm gesture, held her in her seat. '*Opa* doesn't have to put on these displays!' Erika was saying, just as the cork emerged with a plop. We all clapped in relief. All those who had been holding in coughs began to cough. At the far end of the table, a frail old lady crossed herself. Ernst raised the bottle with theatrical flair, presenting it to the audience as if it were a trout he had just plucked from the river, wiped his face with a napkin and served the first glass. Just as we thought this exhibition was over, he picked up the corkscrew and began to untwist the cork from it with his teeth, earning another round of applause. While he drank the first sip of wine with calculated docility, he fixed the waiter with a murderous stare that said something like: *Don't ever doubt the ability and determination of a one-armed soldier again.*

It was during the war, soon after his encounter with a falling bomb, that these attributes were put to the test. As I've already recounted, due to his injury Ernst had been relocated to a distant building where he was assigned sedentary tasks circulating the regime's propaganda. He became a pliable yet insignificant pawn in the Nazi machine, and although he rose through the ranks and sat in on many a coordination meeting with some of the Wehrmacht's top cadres, he never achieved sufficient rank, status or prestige to be included in the circle of the chosen ones. Hurt by the bias against him, by his demotion from promising military cadet to nondescript bureaucrat, Ernst moved further and further away from the heart of power. Yet it was thanks to this estrangement that he was saved from involvement with the Nazi leadership and, who knows, from direct or indirect participation in the monstrosities it unleashed. A little discretion enabled him to reestablish his social life without prejudice to his family. I was able to find out all of this through my own research, behind Erika's back. The only time I asked her about her grandfather's past she assured me that her *Opa* was a 'hero' who hadn't been corrupted by Nazism and therefore had nothing to apologise for. Her reticence only deepened my desire to find out the details of this man's personal history. The two or three times we visited them at their home in Berlin, I took advantage of the fact my presence passed largely unnoticed to wander about, poke around the rooms, the library, the garden, ask prying questions of the less astute relatives: in short, to play detective. I didn't find very much, but I let the house speak to me. Houses always say something, they betray their occupants, they are a museum of their vanities. All I had to do was open my eyes wide: there were the uniformed figures in black and white, the volumes on the war with questionable titles, the vinyl records, the paintings, the portraits, the eagles, the swastikas, the mythologised symbols, in short, a whole series of scattered clues that led me to think that this jowly old man, who greeted and bade farewell to visitors with his single hand, white and cold as marble, had played or could have played a significant or sinister role in the years of the Second World War. The rest of the information I took from Internet pages where Ernst

Hartmann's name appeared in relation to anti-aircraft batteries. The first few times I heard Erika talk about the suffering of her paternal grandparents during the bombing of Berlin, I had been sincerely moved, but with what I learned later, her account came to strike me as a pitiful attempt to apologise for a sordid henchman of genocide.

TWO

The second encounter takes place on December 2, 1941, at twenty-five minutes past four in the afternoon.

Matías turns up unannounced on the porch of Gordon Clifford's house in Washingtonville. Hearing the bell, the banker goes to answer the door, wondering if his neighbour Mr Bennet, who that very morning had dropped by to ask for a loan of his lawnmower, needs something else. Through the peephole it takes him between four and six seconds to recognise the young man with the scrappy beard standing at the door with a rucksack on his shoulders. 'Matías!' he finally exclaims, as he opens up. The embrace he offers is both warm and gruff, as he takes the backpack and invites him in. 'How've you been, my boy?' he asks. 'Very well, it's a pleasure to see you, sir!' replies the other. Clifford is amused that Matías continues to treat him so formally. They embrace again, laugh, step back and look at each other before repeating the gesture with reciprocal effusiveness, as if it has been just twenty-four hours and not more than two years since they disembarked from the *Santa Bárbara*. The young Giurato advances from the lobby into the house, taking stock of the interior decoration: elegant yet dated lamps, fine but threadbare carpets, faded plants in chipped pots, and sagging armchairs arranged with no clear logic, or rather with the logic of a withdrawn banker who – nearing retirement, satisfied with his earnings and tired of dealing with partners, speculators, litigants, executors and lenders – spends too much time alone, immobile and abandoned. On a shelf, beneath a thick layer of dust, stand mismatched cut-glass goblets that must have been party to memorable toasts in the previous century. Matías pauses before a low, three-part credenza, where he sees the family photograph, now framed, that he discovered in the leather portfolio that day, back in Salaverry, before boarding the boat: the photo of Gordon, Manuela Altamirano and Samuel. 'She's still in hospital,' Clifford says, looking at the smiling image of his wife and wiping dust from the picture frame. 'The medical prognosis is not encouraging,' he adds. Then he touches the glass by Samuel's face. 'Yesterday was his birthday, he'd have turned eleven,' he says, with a jaunty rather than a solemn tone, the celebratory voice of someone who refuses to be downcast by the weight of accumulated sadness. 'I even ordered a cake. Would you like a slice?' Matías accepts readily, takes off his jacket and sits down on the sofa, delicately crossing his legs. From the kitchen, Clifford can get a different view of the lad: he notes his young friend's robustness, his adult size, the physical confidence of his twenty-one years. It is good to see him. They have exchanged two or three letters since they went their separate ways at the dock in New York, but seeing each other again in person is different: it is real. Clifford returns to the lounge with two plates of cake and two bottles of beer. 'Have you written to your parents?' he asks. Matías nods. He sent identical letters to Trujillo and to Hamburg, addressed to his mother and his grandfather respectively, recounting his days in New

York. He's been a waiter, a dishwasher, a bartender, he's worked at a dry cleaner's and in a jewellery store, and he's been an office boy in a factory. He's also spent months scrubbing tiles in the Harlem public library, pumping water for the horses at the Belmont Park racecourse, and even handing out flyers and sticking up posters with the face of Wendell Willkie for the electoral campaign that saw Roosevelt elected for the third time. For the last three months, he tells Clifford, he has been on probation at a second-hand car dealership in Brooklyn, where for forty cents an hour he shows customers the folding seats of the Plymouths, the semi-automatic gearbox of the De Sotos, the eight-cylinder engine performance of the Packards, and the bonnet ornamentation of the Studebakers.

Together with a couple of workmates, he is renting a room in a boarding house on the Lower East Side, at Madison and Montgomery. No quiet neighbourhood, a horde of vagabonds, hoodlums and drug addicts throngs these city blocks with their barred stores, greasy pavements, washing hanging to dry on improvised clothes lines, and squalid alleyways where the impact of the Depression is still felt. The only good thing about it is probably the view of the Manhattan Bridge from the window of his room, big enough to forget the discomforts of the lodgings and their surroundings. In any case the three youngsters do little more than sleep there, spending much of their time wandering the streets, eager to explore the Big Apple, losing themselves in its endless grid, visiting its corners redolent with symbolism, plunging into its abundant customs, distinguishing the languages that blend in the air creating the impression of a single intricate, hypnotic tongue, and vanishing among the vast blocks of red-brick buildings in Little Italy or Greenwich Village, with their exterior metal fire escapes, towering above bakeries, barbers and fishmongers, and their residents sitting out on the front stoops, on the broad steps leading up to the main doors, and on the kerb, gossiping or reading the daily news at leisure, or passing the time observing the beat-up cars and equally beat-up people go by. Even for his roommates Steve Dávila and Billy Garnier - New York natives who grew up in Chinatown and the Civic Center respectively, the first the son of Latinos, the second of French and Spanish descent - the city was a cornucopia that adapted itself to their meagre finances. Leaving their work in the evenings, as often as not they'd head to Times Square to watch dilettante actors perform in cheap theatres, decadent, clandestine cabaret shows, or seek out the hidden clubs where jazz bands played with musicians whose names were not yet as famous as they would one day become: Billy Taylor, Dizzy Gillespie, Thelonious Monk. Other nights, they'd play darts in the Bowery pubs or go bowling in a Union Square salon. In both, the precise aim of Matías, hitting the bullseye or knocking down all the pins in one go, helped pay for bottles of beer. Or failing that, they'd head to the cinema when movies like *His Girl Friday*, *Santa Fe Trail*, *The Letter* or *The Philadelphia Story* were being premiered and would crowd round the exit trying to catch a glimpse of their stars Olivia de Havilland, Bette Davis, or Jimmy Stewart. On Saturdays, if it was warm, they'd take the subway at noon and travel for over an hour the twenty stops to Coney Island. There, they'd set up on the crammed beaches, spend hours beneath a faded umbrella, play at interpreting the indecisive actions of the crowd, take a dip in the sea, eat hot dogs for lunch, wander around the amusement park, ride the Cyclone or the Parachute Jump, pay a few dimes to ogle the best legs contest at Billy's urging, or gawk at the freak shows (Steve's favourites were the Elephant Girl and Marian the Headless Woman), and finally watch Matías lay bets at a target shooting booth before gleefully aiming at the clown heads and spinning pipes and hitting the jackpot. At dusk they walked up and down the boardwalk looking for girls from Tudor City or Park Slope who they duped into believing they were college kids from the suburbs of Queens, and the girls would let them kiss them and fondle their breasts over their blouses on the warm sand until it began to grow dark. The most gullible among them even fell for the story that they were in training with the Yankees and allowed more intrepid dalliances in the crummy hotels on the final blocks of Henderson Walk. Their sex lives wouldn't be the same without the Yankees, they joked among themselves. As a sign of their loyalty to the Bronx Bombers, when the crucial games of the season were played, they suspended their street forays to flirt with Mrs Morris, the spinsterish owner of the boarding house, beg her to change the radio station where she listened to the adventures of *The Lone Ranger* or lachrymose episodes of *The Right to Happiness* at full volume, and to allow them to follow the broadcast from Yankee Stadium, where DiMaggio's bat was always about to set a record or knock a statistic into oblivion.

Inspired by the account of these wild exploits that he wishes he had experienced in his own youth, Gordon Clifford puts out the pipe he has just lit and asks Matías to put on his jacket and accompany him out of the house. As he closes the door, he hands Matías the keys to the Pontiac and, once in the car, tells him that they will go to Flushing Meadows to visit the exhibition that all of New York has seen or wants to see: *The World of Tomorrow*. The fact that Matías doesn't yet hold a driver's license is neither here nor there for Clifford, who leans back in the passenger seat, trusting in the boy's skills and his own instincts to get the machine moving. Matías orchestrates his movements with the pedals, the steering wheel, the gearshift, and the Pontiac's white-banded tyres glide down those roads as wide as rivers, into the suburbs where the streets are lined with two-storey homes and children are forbidden to trespass beyond the front gates, and where every ten blocks well-kept police stations are guarded by drowsy officers.

The fair is astonishing. Across a dozen aerodynamic metal pavilions, with futuristic architecture and fluorescent lighting, three-dimensional artefacts, mechanical calculators and technological advances are displayed, such as an android that talks, takes orders and lights cigars. But the main course, the one that captures the attention of young and old, is the vast diorama of a metropolis with 100-storey skyscrapers, criss-crossed by highways, interspersed with woods and rivers, set against mountains made of folded cardboard. Matías is amazed by this miniature world and for minutes on end he observes the tiny cars that go back and forth, the beautiful inanimate trees whose tops seem to sway in an illusory wind, and sees the diminutive inhabitants of these buildings move between living rooms and kitchens, go up and down stairs, watch television, sit behind desks, leading an artificial life that for brief moments seems overwhelmingly real. The final piece is the famed time capsule, an indestructible, two-metre, torpedo-shaped container buried in an underground crypt, inside which objects representative of the twentieth century are stored in the hope that they will be a message to eternity: a telephone, an incandescent light bulb, an electric razor, microfilmed magazines, musical scores, works of art, a roll of film with newsreels, and even messages from Albert Einstein and Thomas Mann that some living being will read in five thousand years' time, surely to find them antiquated, bizarre or fascinating.

On the way out, Matías suggests they go into town for a drink. Gordon Clifford counters that it is late, but he doesn't take much persuasion. They come to a bar on Baxter Street. A bar that could be mistaken for a gloomy basement where, apart from a few distant bulbs emitting a coppery light, everything else is in darkness. A heavy miasma envelops the patrons. Like everywhere, there are happy drinkers and there are sad drinkers. From the kitchen comes the smell of fried food. Accustomed to the opulence of English-style pubs and the exclusivity of smoking lounges, the banker regards the premises with suspicion, but the first sip of martini and the background music, tunes by Tommy Dorsey and Freddy Martin, swiftly quell his misgivings.

'I have to tell you something,' Matías says, timidly, anxiously folding a napkin.

Clifford notes that he used the expression 'have to', and observes in it something verging on debt or loyalty.

'Should I be concerned?' he asks.

'Not at all. Do you remember on the boat you asked me how many girlfriends I'd had?'

'I asked you how many girls you'd fallen in love with, which isn't the same thing at all.'

'And I replied that I hadn't ever fallen in love, do you recall? The thing is, now there is someone.'

'And what do you mean by "someone"?'

'A woman, of course.'

'Right, but tell me more. What's her name?'

'Charlotte. Charlotte Harris.'

'Harris. Where is she from?'

'Her father is English, her mother Hungarian, but she was born in Georgia.'

'And where did you meet this Miss Harris?'

'At the lot. She's the sales supervisor, she's one year older than me.'

'And do you like her very much?'

'I think about her every moment of the day.'

'Is she pretty?'

'Pretty, no – she's beautiful, the most beautiful woman on the planet.'

Clifford smiles as he notes that his friend hasn't lost his tendency to hyperbole, just as he retains the habit of scratching both elbows at once.

'Given your excitement I'm guessing this sentiment is reciprocal?'

'Very much so.'

'Are you together, then?'

'Not yet.'

'So what's the issue?'

'Well, there's a… how should I put it? A barrier to overcome…'

'A barrier? What barrier?'

'Sorry, more than a barrier, it's an obstacle, that's it.'

'What kind of obstacle?'

Matías takes a sip from his glass, summoning courage.

'Come on, out with it!'

'The thing is… Charlotte has a fiancé.'

Gordon Clifford almost spits the olive into his martini glass.

'You can't be serious, Matías, that will bring nothing good for the three of you.'

'Allow me to finish: the fiancé has spent a year in bed after he was hit by an automobile, destroying his legs. It's unlikely he'll walk again, and the impact also left him with neurological issues: he cannot speak, Charlotte visits him at his parents' home when she can, feeds him, supports his recovery, sympathises with him, but for a year she has felt more like a nurse than a partner, and her feelings towards him are wholly undefined right now.'

'What does *wholly undefined* mean?'

'It means whatever it means, but she no longer loves him.'

'And do you believe her?'

'Should I have any reason to doubt?'

'I don't know. Had they been together long?'

'They had got engaged one month before the accident.'

'Goodness, that complicates matters further.'

'What can I do?'

'Nothing.'

'Nothing?'

'You must wait.'

'Wait for what? To see if the fiancé recovers?'

'No, kid, for her to take a decision. In the meantime you can be friends.'

'That's unthinkable! We like each other, we love each other, we can't go back to being merely friends! Do you understand what I'm saying?'

'Tell me this, Matías. Do you love her?'

'Yes, I love her.'

'Well, if she feels the same, she will find a way to do the right thing. The worst you could do is to pressure her, to demand an answer. Sometimes the most appropriate strategy is to remain quiet until things fall into place, or collapse under their own weight.'

Matías sighs in relief: he needed to hear these comforting words from his friend, to feel the input of his wisdom. They raise their glasses, look at each other and knock back the martinis in one.

'Shall we switch to gin?'

They laugh heartily.

'Only if you let me pay,' Clifford replies. He pulls a pack of Chesterfields from his inside pocket while, almost simultaneously, Matías retrieves his Wieden lighter from his left trouser pocket to light one for him.

'And your pipe?'

'I left it behind.'

'I hope you didn't leave your portfolio, too.'

They laugh again. Oblivious to the hour or to the changing occupants of the tables around them, midnight surprises them discussing the exhibition they'd both seen at Flushing Meadows, the progress of technology, tomorrow, the future – and in particular Matías' own future.

'Selling and renting cars is no bad thing, but you should consider studying,' Clifford proposes, trying to avoid sounding too paternalistic, though it is a rather ineffective or ill-advised precaution considering he is the lad's adoptive father. A distant adoptive father, he says to himself, as if wishing to make explicit (to whom? for what purpose?) that he is merely Matías' guarantor in the eyes of the law, and it is not his role to assume any other position of guardianship. Yet there he is, speaking as if he were the parent, asking him what career he would like to pursue.

Matías is reluctant to make a choice; he has a vague notion of travelling to Hamburg, meeting his mother's family, perhaps settling down there, but he knows he needs to earn more money, and above all to save it, he knows he needs to throttle the fast-paced life he has led to date. Clifford suggests various options, which Matías listens to without interest, or rather with suspicion. He mentions another possibility: taking correspondence courses, but Matías infers that he would have to postpone his trip indefinitely if he were to devote himself to formal study. Finally, over the third round of gin, smoking the fourth cigarette on his tab, Clifford tells him bluntly what he has always thought about that infamous trip to Germany.

'It's a crazy idea, Matías. Don't you read the newspapers? The Germans have occupied Holland,

Poland, Norway, France. Hitler has half of Europe in turmoil. Just imagine if he were to invade the Soviet Union! The Brits can't handle him alone, anyone with any sense is trying to get out of there, yet you want to step into the lion's mouth!'

Matías listens attentively to Clifford's disquisition, aware that he is right, just as his grandfather Karsten was right when, in his last letter of May 1939, which arrived a few weeks before he left Trujillo, having heard that he was boarding a boat for the United States intending to continue on to Hamburg, abandoned the balanced tone of his previous missives and begged Matías to desist:

The Nazis are steering this country to catastrophe, it's happening any day now. We good Germans are not inclined to fight, even those who support this abject dictator, and even those toadies who pay obeisance to him today question the utility of war. But I fear there will be no shortage of those who will decide to bow to it. There is nothing to be done. Geographically, Hamburg is vulnerable by sea, land and air. Don't come yet, beloved Matías. The painful memories of the hardships of the Great War are still fresh in our minds. At the thought that such a thing could happen again with you among us, your grandmother and I sink into absolute despair.

The personal struggle Matías waged against his father and his determination to leave his home and Trujillo in order to become another person, had led him to board that boat, ignoring the warnings of Karsten, who implored him not to mention that last letter. That June morning of 1939, Edith Roeder accompanied Matías to the port of Salaverry believing that her son would travel to New York to stay for just a few months, at most a year, with his uncle Enrico Giurato before returning to Peru to study law or economic science. His true intentions were different. And they are still different now, two years later, despite all that Gordon Clifford is telling him in

113

this bar on Baxter Street where the miasma has begun to disperse, revealing empty tables.

'Have you given any thought to what you'd like to do, to where you'd like to be in five years' time?' probes the banker.

'All I know is I want to fly, to travel the world.'

'Hadn't you promised your mother you'd return and study to become a lawyer?'

'It wasn't a promise, it was a *non-binding agreement*.'

'Oh come on, Matías, it was a promise.'

'If I hadn't promised, she'd have put up a thousand obstacles to my leaving Peru.'

'That is to say, you lied to her.'

'Let's say that I saw an opportunity and I didn't want to waste it.'

'If you're not planning to go back, don't you think your parents deserve to know?'

'I'm still not sure what I want to do. All I know is I'm twenty-one years old, I'm barely scraping a living in New York, I want to visit other countries and, at the right moment, that is, when the war in Germany is over, to travel to Hamburg, meet my mother's family, see if we get along. That's all I know.'

'You're obsessed with Hamburg! First you should find a career, work!'

'Why do you think I'm here asking for your advice?'

They drink in silence. The waiter leaves off polishing the bar with a cloth, approaches to serve a final gin and let them know they'll be closing in twenty minutes. Clifford asks where the washrooms are. 'Down the stairs, on the left,' he replies. As he stands before the sole urinal, the banker entertains himself with the inscriptions on the walls and the jumble of posters. 'Is that guy from the neighbourhood?' asks the waiter as he collects the ashtrays full of lead-coloured mountains. 'No,' replies

Matías, 'is there a problem with that?' 'None, kid, it's just that you can tell he's from the other side of the Hudson. I mean the way he dresses. Is he your father?' 'He's a friend.' The waiter smirks. Clifford comes out of the bathroom, hurries up the stairs and, without sitting down at the table, makes his way over to Matías:

'I've got the solution to your dilemma!'

'My dilemma?'

'That's right, I think it's a great idea.'

'What happened in the washroom. Did you have a revelation?'

'More or less.'

'Could you tell me what the devil you're talking about?'

'On the washroom wall there was a cover from an *Uncle Sam* comic.'

'I don't follow.'

'What does *Uncle Sam* do?'

'I hate playing charades.'

'Matías – military service!'

'What about military service?'

'You could sign up! I have contacts in the Air Force.'

'Sounds great, but since when is the United States at war?'

'Damnit, Matías, don't you get wind of anything that's going on? We've been at war ever since we've been sending soldiers and food to England, and ever since we provided China with weapons produced by General Motors; very soon we'll be in it up to our necks, mark my words. I've read countless articles in *The Times* predicting a conflict with Japan, you just have to interpret the scenario, look at the sequence of events: the Japanese enter into an alliance with Germany and Italy, Roosevelt blocks them economically, takes away their oil, bans exports to Tokyo, and – naively in my view – orders them to withdraw from Indochina, do you see? But if we go to war, listen carefully to what I am going to tell you, if we go to war, I take it for granted that the United States will pulverise the Japanese in two days flat – four at the most. You could sign up, become a pilot, complete a year and a half of service with all the benefits it provides, then get discharged and go into commercial aviation. The future is up there – isn't that what you want: to fly?'

Before Clifford has even finished talking, Matías has made up his mind. After all, he is a U.S. citizen, and in his short time in this country he has developed a sense of belonging he never felt in Peru. Now he feels that he is *on the inside*, in the whirlwind of history, inserted in the great narrative of humanity, not on the margins, no longer a humble footnote like when he lived at the Chiclín hacienda, thirsting to break those borders that oppressed him every day. What's more – and this is key – his two years in the United States are marked by firsts: earning his first wage and frittering it away, making friends, discovering love, losing his virginity, learning to drink and smoke without moderation, learning to drive, breaking the rules. For the first time he has been free and this freedom has allowed him to discover that certain places are the same as certain people: in just a few months they can become as beloved and indispensable as others never did in far more time. It is still too soon to see himself as a patriot, but he is excited or says he is excited or wants to be excited at the idea of paying back the United States for the chance to become a different person, not to see himself as a foreigner there. Of course, when he says *United States* he means *New York*, the only city he knows, and he's not even thinking about the city as a whole, but the individuals who embody it for him. In this sense the image he has of the country is one in which the faces of Gordon Clifford, Steve Dávila, Billy

Garnier, Charlotte Harris converge, one which includes the faces of each of the bosses who hired him for his temporary jobs, and even the face of the discreet Mrs Morris, the owner of the boarding house, who asks him each week if he is happy in that room and in that neighbourhood which – now he thinks about it – perhaps isn't so insalubrious after all.

'Say something, my lad, isn't it a good idea?' the banker pushes him, rubbing his hands in satisfaction.

Matías stands up and embraces him, slapping his back. Once again Gordon Clifford has saved him by marking out the path ahead.

Just five days later, at 7:48 in the morning of December 7, 1941, the grim portents described by Clifford are fulfilled to the letter. A formation of aircraft is streaking across the skies above Pearl Harbor. A red disc can be seen on its fuselage. More than 350 Imperial Japanese Navy planes are ready to shower the American harbour with their cargo of bombs and shrapnel. Under the waters of the Pacific, thirty Japanese submarines attack U.S. naval vessels, but their torpedoes only manage to sink one old armoured transport ship. It was the planes that hit the bay hard; it took them just ninety minutes to sink two battleships and to damage or destroy a further seventeen vessels, destroy more than a hundred aircraft, kill more than two thousand service men and wound another eleven hundred. The next day, newspapers in the U.S. bear a headline in huge type: JAPS BOMB HAWAII. By noon, President Roosevelt has declared war on the Japanese Empire. Thousands of Americans who a week earlier opposed their country getting involved in a foreign war, invoking the principle of neutrality to ensure a peaceful life, now demanded exemplary punishment of the aggressors. In the following months, a wave of racism and stigmatisation unleashed against Japanese immigrants and Japanese-Americans led the government to order the evacuation and relocation of more than 120,000 of them in camps, isolating them from the society to which they legally belonged.

The clamour for war had preceded the attack on Pearl Harbor, however. Once Roosevelt activated the Selective Service program – a recruitment lottery – young men were called up to serve. Actors like James Stewart or baseball stars like Hank Greenberg of the Detroit Tigers didn't hesitate to make themselves available to the armed forces, leading to contradictory feelings among their fans – some thrilled to see them defending the nation, others terrified they would come home in a coffin. On television, Abbot and Costello roused their compatriots to buy war savings stamps and war bonds to finance logistical operations. Advertisements multiplied in streets, supermarkets, train stations.

The enthusiasm is such that when Matías tells Steve Dávila and Billy Garnier that he is going to join the Air Force, he doesn't have to work hard to convince them to follow in his footsteps: they too want to enlist, shoot down the Japanese, seize their sabres, capture their flags, return as national heroes and become an inseparable part of the pompous military paraphernalia. One evening, following another piece of advice from Clifford, Matías sits down to write three letters: to his mother, his grand-father, and to Charlotte Harris. He asks his mother not to worry about him, he'll be fine, he'll come out on top, win medals; he doesn't add a single line for his father. To old Karsten he confesses that he wants to confront the Japanese in the Pacific, learn to pilot aeroplanes and one day, after the British and the Russians overthrow the Nazis, fly to Hamburg: 'you know the plan, *Opa*, I'm still going to visit'. He tells Charlotte to wait for him, that it will be two long years, that they will remain in touch: 'perhaps you can resolve the matters that trouble you today, and on my return we can begin a new life together'. Matías posts the first two letters, but decides to deliver the last one in person. One day before he resigns from his position at the Brooklyn car dealership, he approaches Charlotte's desk.

'I need to speak to you alone. Is tonight possible?'

'I'm sorry, I need to take care of Paul at his parents' house, they have a dinner.'

'I'll come there. It will only take a moment.'

'Tomorrow would be better, somewhere else.'

'It's important.'

She asks him to come at eight, as Paul's parents won't be back until eleven. Matías arrives on the dot, feeling strange in that house. He inspects the photographs hanging on the walls, of trips, Christmases, graduations, one in which Paul appears healthy, his arms around Charlotte. He was handsome, Matías thinks, using the past tense, as if the guy were dead or he wishes he was.

Charlotte emerges from one of the bedrooms, closes the door, and sits down in the lounge opposite Matías. 'He's asleep,' she says. 'What do you need to tell me?' Without beating around the bush, he informs her that in two weeks' time he will sign up at Mitchel Field Air Force Base to serve in the war. Charlotte doesn't know how to react. She drops her head, covers her face, weeps. Matías gently strokes her shoulders, dries her tears, whispers words of consolation in her ear, phrases he's written in the letter he is carrying in his jacket pocket and which in the end he won't hand over; the modulation of his words suddenly changes, the kisses on the cheek become more urgent and, without any deliberate intention, as if the sombre news of the war had triggered a vital outburst in both of them, they begin to kiss and touch each other, with a haste that comes from the most primitive reactions; now they find themselves on their feet, pressing closer and closer, until they mould to each other's forms and feel the turmoil in their bodies. They need no other language than a succession of impatient caresses and syncopated moans, Charlotte takes off her heeled shoes with the help of her feet, their tongues are still joined by instinct, Matías moves backwards, lets himself be led and soon notices, out of the corner of his eye, that they are heading for the second bedroom of the house, the parents' bedroom. He is captivated by Charlotte's audacity, offering her neck without reserve, as Matías advances across that territory between the chin and collarbones with the blind audacity of a stray animal that hasn't seen the street in weeks. 'Don't make a sound,' says Charlotte, mechanically stretching out a hand to turn the doorknob. As they cross the threshold they stumble without losing their balance, they fall onto the bed, he underneath at first, then on top, so it's easier to push the pillows aside, get rid of the jacket, tear off the belt, strip off the trousers, pull up Charlotte's flared skirt, imperiously remove her nylon stockings, toss them to the floor; even with the lights off, the girl doesn't dare open her eyes, instead choosing to imagine the ceremony, perhaps out of modesty, perhaps guilt, perhaps the conviction that her imprudence would not be the same under the yellow glow of the lamp, she undoes her bra but does not allow Matías to unbutton her blouse, he thinks that maybe she is hiding a skin blemish and resigns himself to not seeing her completely naked, to not kissing or nibbling her breasts, he is content to touch them from the outside only, even if far from gently. Then he moves down, his nose grazes her belly and embarks on a journey in a straight line, as if following the invisible trace of a long scar, he imprisons her hips and, without asking, nimbly removes Charlotte's underwear, rubs her thighs impetuously two, three times, spreads her legs apart at the knees, notices how they tremble, how they offer resistance, how they give way completely, then he plunges his head between her legs, savouring the bitter-sweet taste. He licks Charlotte's sex feverishly, while she writhes, and emits a hoarse grunt of a new kind, she bites her lower lip until it bleeds, she knows that her defences have been overwhelmed and she buries her nails in her man's head, she tangles his hair with her hands that beg him to continue. Matías moistens two of his fingers with saliva, and she pulls him up, whispering to him, *please, be gentle*. Matías kisses her ardently as if to tell her *I love you*, thinking that he's telling her, perhaps he does tell her. At that moment, a clatter of breaking glass shatters her concentration. 'Did you hear that?' whispers Charlotte, her eyes wide. 'No,' replies Matías muffled, still moving his fingers down there. 'Wait, I think it's Paul.' 'You thought,' he stammers, excitedly, without restraint, seeking her tongue again. 'I said wait!' Charlotte raises her voice, sitting up abruptly on the couch and drawing her legs up against her chest in an impulsive but coordinated movement. Suddenly there is a clear growl from the next room: the gruff noise of an animal caught in a trap. Her hair wild, Charlotte jumps to her feet, covers her body with the sheet, leaves the bedroom on tiptoe, takes three strides, opens the door with a trembling hand, and stops abruptly when she notices a pool of water on the floor and a shattered glass tumbler. From the bed, staring at her, Paul gives a furious shriek, frothing with rage or frustration. His legs are still stiff as iron masts. Inside his trousers, his right hand is jerking.

THREE

On Thursday January 8, the day before he is to enlist, Gordon Clifford phones Matías to provide him with detailed information on the rank, name and appearance of the person he should ask for when he presents himself at Mitchel Field. Clifford suddenly fears he might not see Matías again, that he has placed the young man's life in danger and can do nothing to prevent it. In anticipation of this, he has asked his friend from his youth, now Lieutenant Colonel Robert Ellsworth, one of the commanding officers at Mitchel Field, to keep the boy safe and, if possible, not to expose him to high-risk missions, a request that Ellsworth will soon fail to heed.

'One last thing,' Clifford says into the heavy black mouthpiece, giving his words the right emphasis so that Matías understands the importance of what he will say next. 'For the duration of your service, you must promise me you won't write to your grandfather.'

'Why not?' Matías objects.

'Our short-term battle is against the Japanese, but don't forget that the number one enemy in this war is Germany: Churchill said as much in Washington two nights ago. Therefore, any association with the Germans will arouse suspicion.'

For Matías this is a terrible argument, but he promises anyway.

'And for this reason…' Clifford adds, with a tone that suggests these will be his last words, and they will be uncomfortable ones, '…if on the ship I recommended you change your father's surname, now I believe you should do the same with your mother's.'

Matías shakes his head, as if Clifford could see him reject this suggestion that feels like a step to far.

'In the United States no one looks twice at your surname,' he says.

'From tomorrow, the Air Force will be interested in your past and your family, they could investigate you, label you as a spy, who knows, they could even haul you up before a tribunal,' Clifford replies.

Matías hangs up without feeling wholly persuaded.

The next day, having spent the night mulling options – while also knocking down bowling pins and knocking back beers with Billy and Steve at the bowling alley – when he faces the recruitment form, he seeks to distort his maternal surname as little as possible and registers as Matías Clifford Ryder. This will be his name from now on, his new identity as a U.S. airman ready to go to a war into which fortune or fate – it is still too early to tell – has thrown him headlong. His mother, Edith, who is only concerned that her son's letters continue to arrive, without delving into the how or when, overlooks this chicanery when Matías fills her in. Not so grandfather Karsten, who protests when he learns of the strategic suppression of his surname, but continues to write to his grandson. On his convoluted path to becoming someone, the young Trujillo boy's original signs of identity continue to fade like the words drawn by aircraft in the sky.

At Mitchel Field base, bus loads of young men are continually being disgorged. Conscripts and volunteers alike, all are eager to wear the uniform and to go into battle. There are thousands of them. None over twenty-five years of age, and even some as young as seventeen or eighteen whose spotty faces still betray the marks of puberty. They come from all over the country. They stare at each other, examining features, hearing the variety of accents, from the north, the south, the north-east, the Great Lakes. They come from modern metropolises, from rural towns, from remote farmsteads. Some are recent graduates or independent professionals, while others barely finished elementary school and spent the rest of their adolescence rising at four in the morning to grab their tools or drive tractors whose engines and carburettors they know inside out from taking them apart so many times.

Matías observes the group through the window of the waiting room outside Lieutenant Colonel Ellsworth's office. He asks himself who of them will become his friends, who will survive, what they'll look like the day all this is over and they see their families again. He asks himself if this will ever really be over. After receiving nothing more from Lieutenant Colonel Ellsworth than generic instructions, Matías passes the initial medical and psychological tests. Hundreds of applicants are rejected for physical or neurological limitations they were unaware they had: colour-blindness, inadequate hearing, lung conditions, venereal disease, asymmetrical foot bones, claustrophobia. When they are given to understand that they have an impairment ('not fit to serve'), the boys head out of the barracks begging for another chance. Few of them take the rejection well. Some fall into depression, others try to commit suicide, a few succeed.

Those accepted are gathered on the vast parade ground under the watchful eye of an officer who yells the roll call. This is where they hear for the first time the names and surnames they will become familiar with to a degree they cannot yet begin to imagine. They climb back into the buses to be transferred to different centres, where they are given buzz cuts, they collect their gear at the quartermaster's, are vaccinated against tetanus, measles and yellow fever, are assigned a barracks, and finally a service number of their own.

Matías, Billy and Steve all remain at Mitchel Field and at each successive interview they ask to be trained as pilots – specifically fighter pilots. The bad news is that most of the applicants ask for the same thing: they can only imagine themselves inside a monoplane, an Airacobra, a Douglas, a Curtiss, manoeuvring them at unprecedented speed, spraying ammunition at will, conquering the skies like the daredevil Eddie Rickenbacker, the Ohio ace of aces, who in 1918 achieved the feat of twenty-six shoot-downs aboard his versatile Nieuport 28; or like the unpredictable Billy Bishop, the Canadian fighter who would not back down from anything, a specialist in solitary but daring missions that no one else wanted to carry out; or even like the 'Red Baron', that risk-taking, bloodthirsty German of whom Karsten Roeder spoke to Matías in his letters, and who once brazenly confessed: 'When I have shot down an Englishman, my passion for killing subsides for a mere fifteen minutes.' The recruits want to emulate these indomitable legends, but it will be the rigorous basic training of the first few days, along with tests to measure nervous reactions, concentration, speed of decision-making and self-discipline, that will determine which sector of the air corps each will serve in.

Matías excels in the rifle shooting tests – the precision with which he hits the targets has the officers mesmerised – yet they decide to send him not to an artillery school, as might be expected, nor to a pilot school as he had hoped, but to a bomber school. There, the instructors unanimously agree, they will get more out of the boy's superlative talent for hitting targets, his mathematical skills – once applauded and encouraged by the Marist priests at the seminary school – and his mechanical skills, acquired at the Brooklyn dealership by examining the engines of all the old bangers that were neither rented nor sold. The officers' verdict is so firm that Lieutenant Colonel Robert Ellsworth unhesitatingly signs the papers to transfer Cadet Matías Clifford Ryder, registered C-2808, to one of the main bases: Westover, Massachusetts, almost three hours away.

He arrives at the camp on a Friday morning, by bus, in the company of other cadets, but leaving behind Steve Dávila and Billy Garnier, who will be attending a navigator's school in Louisiana and a radio operator's school in San Francisco, respectively. The day before, the friends wished each other luck by repeatedly bumping foreheads to vent their anger at the separation, hard to stomach for all three. Before the goodbyes and eloquent embraces, recalling the exultant New York nights spent without a penny in their pockets, they vowed to meet as soon as fortune allowed. Each retreated to his barracks and crawled under the blankets to wait for dawn. They would never see each other again.

In Westover, Matías meets the members of the squadron that would be his home for the next three months, together with his immediate superior, Sergeant Clayton Lakeman, thirty-two years of age, who sports a lush but well-trimmed moustache that he twirls in an intellectual manner when he delivers orders, and which matches his prematurely grey hair. Lakeman is also behind the peremptory slogans that can be read on the walls of the classrooms and the NCO mess: 'We don't want martyrs, but men who fight for glory', 'We don't want soldiers for war, but pilots for life', 'There is no time for softness or laziness here', slogans that he constantly utters during ground training and which, after so much repetition, boasting of having devised them himself, gradually penetrate the minds of the youngsters. On the morning of his presentation, walking among the rows of the one hundred and eighty subordinates under his command, scrutinising them one by one, trying to detect in them signs of mettle or of cowardice, Sergeant Lakeman reminds them that the best bomber crews in the squadron will see action in the Pacific and in Europe. To kindle their enthusiasm, he draws their attention to the aircraft lined up in front of the hangars that, in a few months' time, will become their habitat. The squadron of imposing B-17s, four-engined flying fortresses designed to drop vast numbers of bombs on the military infra-structure of Axis countries, leaves the cadets in awe, as if they were standing in front of a mighty herd of prehistoric beasts. Matías has heard of the Mitchells and Marauders, but these planes, he thinks, are on a different scale. He peers into the nose of the craft, the glass snout, that conical, transparent cubicle like a fishbowl or glasshouse from which the bombardier identifies targets through the viewfinder and drops the bombs to destroy it. He already wants to be in there, to occupy the tilting chair, to learn the knack of each device, to hear the roar of the engines as they ignite, to take off from the ground for the first time, to cross the skies, to watch cars, forests and buildings become indiscernible from above. He wants to drop the bombs, to complete the stipulated number of missions, or more if necessary, to become the most skilled bomber not only at Westover but all the American air bases, to make a name for himself; and to return – to return triumphant, in style, although he does not know where, or who might be waiting for him.

'I'm talking to you, airman! Are you deaf? How the hell did you pass the hearing test?'

Matías' daydreams are interrupted by the rough barking of Sergeant Lakeman.

'No, sir!' he replies, nervously.

'No, what?' Lakeman dresses him down, from inches away.

'No... I'm not deaf, sir,' Matías answers, triggering a chorus of stifled giggles.

'Silence!' the sergeant screams at the top of his lungs, glancing from left to right, blowing his whistle forcefully, and pulling at his moustache. 'Your full name!'

'Matías Clifford Ryder.'

'Louder, soldier!'

'Matías Clifford Ryder!'

'Not in that faggot's voice!'

'Matías Clifford Ryder, sir!'

'*Matías*?'

'Yes, sir!'

'What kind of name is that?'

'The name my parents gave me, sir!'

More laughter.

'I said silence!' yells Lakeman, drawing closer. 'I don't give a damn who chose it, it's a ridiculous name and unsuitable for a bombardier in the United States Air Force, am I right?'

Matías stammers.

'Right, soldier?'

'Yessir!' he gabbles.

'What's that?'

'Yes, sir!'

'How about *Matthew*, that has a better ring to it, does it not?'

'Yes, sir!' Matías repeats, still uncertain whether he is the victim of a joke.

'From now on you shall report to this squadron as Matthew Clifford Ryder, understood?'

'Understood.'

'I didn't hear you, soldier!'

'Understood!'

'Understood, what?'

'Understood, sir!'

'Stop calling me *sir*, look at my badge, you son of a bitch!'

'Understood, sergeant!'

'Sergeant what? Don't you know how to read?'

The officer stabs the patch on his uniform bearing his surname with his finger.

'Understood, Sergeant Lakeman!'

On the parade ground no one blinks. There is no sound beyond the squeaking of the sergeant's polished boots. Matías waits for the head of the battalion to move away and only then does he exhale all the air he had been retaining. The colour of his face returns to normal, that is, pale. At the sound of Lakeman's whistle, the group breaks ranks, and he is lost in the din. On the way to the mess hall, Matthew reflects that it was not the smartest way to make himself stand out, but he takes it for granted that the sergeant will not forget his name, that is, his new name, the name that has been imposed on him, Matthew Clifford Ryder, a double, an impersonator of his former self, Matías Giurato Roeder, who, for all practical purposes, at least until the end of the war, has ceased to be, ceased to be worth anything, ceased to exist.

At the end of four weeks of intense training, with days that start at five in the morning and leave the cadets shattered, Matías completes his preliminary preparation. He has received detailed instruction in the operation of the Norden bombsight: now he can adjust the dials from memory to produce the right target angle, and correctly decode every digit that appears in the scope quadrants. He has read whole books on the free fall of bodies to understand the adverse variables and meteorological phenomena that can affect the trajectory of a bomb, and he can accurately specify the values of the altimeter, compass and exterior thermometer. Likewise he confidently handles the aerial cameras, swiftly operates the oxygen equipment, and can assemble and disassemble a parachute blindfolded. He knows how to distinguish fog from haze, clouds from thunderclouds, normal storms from thunderstorms, and accurately identify the emblems, strengths and weaknesses of the other side's most prestigious fighter planes, such as the Japanese Mitsubishi A6M Zero or the German Messerschmitt BF-109.

For an hour a day, together with an instructor, he sits on a very tall, rolling tripod, a simulator from which he practises the routine to be carried out in the aircraft. This particular craft is an AT-11, considerably smaller than the B-17 but ideal for low-altitude training. The night before his first real flight Matías doesn't sleep a wink, but sits at the door of the barracks scanning the star-filled sky. By four a.m. he is on his feet, dressed in his grey jumpsuit and cap, ready for breakfast despite the tingling feeling in his stomach and legs. At six he climbs into the plane's nose, accompanied by the instructor and a pilot. He passes his fingers delicately over the surface of his instruments. 'Talk to the sight,' the instructor tells him. 'Excuse me?' Matías replies, thinking he's misheard. 'Talk to her, like she's a pet. Officers talk to their planes, you've gotta establish a relationship with them, you'll see.' Matías forces a smile and puts on an expectant face as he hears the engines start up and the three solid metal blades of the propellers begin to spin until they blur. As soon as they take off, with the plane suspended in the air and the vertigo pressing against his belly, he pretends to hear the instructions, but all of his attention is fixed on the vast expanse on the other side of the plexiglass window. The AT-11 glides over the base, leaves it behind as it crosses vast fields to the south in the direction of Springfield, following the straight black vein that is the Connecticut River, a strangely tranquil torrent from 7,000 feet up. The vertical views from the nose remind Matías of the futuristic diorama that had made such an impression on him at the New York expo: a real-world scale replica so faithful that he asked himself that day whether this was how God orchestrates or directs his creation, and whether human beings were nothing more than insignificant decorative figures in a greater model, more complex, whose subtle meshings grant cohesion to our existence, yet fail to hide its triviality. The vision of all those miles of fields and parks brought back a memory of childhood, and he saw himself at the age of ten or eleven, wishing he could fly over the rough plantations of the Trujillo hacienda: he flaps his arms, slowly at first, then faster and faster until his feet leave the ground and he levitates like the saints from the Bible, like Icarus before the sun melted the wax from his wings. He flies at a medium height, the ideal height not to be seen but from where he could spy on his friends in the school yard, and survey the meanderings of his father along Jirón Sosiego or the bars of the centre. At that age Matías believed that, with just the right amount of concentration, he could imitate the birds and fly with the planes, a dream or miracle that suddenly appears fulfilled aboard the AT-11, where the pilot is now asking them to prepare for landing.

Over the following seven weeks the squadron is wholly dedicated to aerial exercises, with ever-longer flights, flying in formation, morning sweeps, low-level patrols of the area around the base. Nevertheless, every night he goes to sleep or rather dozes feeling a lack of readiness. There's not an instructor on the base who hasn't heard him complain about how far behind the bombardiers are compared to the pilots, gunners, navigators, engineers and radio operators. 'How can they call us bombardiers when so far we haven't released a single bomb? How do we know if our trigger fingers are firm and our judgement accurate if we are only given reconnaissance flights?' Matías protested.

The long-awaited simulacrums took place during the last four weeks of training. Finally, Matías learned to drop bombs of different weights, by day and by night, at every possible temperature and altitude, with flares for guidance in the darkness, with tail or head winds. Every time he takes control of the aircraft once the navigator positions it over the target, and every time he aims with the finder grid, opens the bomb bay doors, fires the trigger, shouts 'bombs away!' into the microphone of his headpiece, and every time he sees the cylindrical projectiles leave the aircraft's belly and rain down in clusters, and every time that he sinks abandoned ships off the coast, Matías feels radiant, singular, fulfilled. He is astonished by his effectiveness, as if his aptitude for absorbing this specific technical knowledge had always been lying inside him, dormant, waiting for the precise stimulus to reveal itself. His rectitude prevents him from saying so, but deep down, even though he knows that the fate of every mission depends on teamwork and that all crew members are equally important, he believes that when they are up in the skies, he is the real architect of their fates. Sergeant Clayton Lakeman, impressed with his progress, proposes that he receive honours on graduation day. More than one officer predicts that the leadership and marksmanship of Matthew Ryder – by now everyone calls him that – will be key in the missions to come, the real missions, where they will have to endure inclement weather and the fury of the enemy, missions from which they will return either as heroes or corpses.

By the end of April 1942, Japan has invaded Hong Kong, Thailand, Guam, Singapore. It has savagely bombarded Port Darwin in Australia (where more bombs were dropped than at Pearl Harbor), and it has taken control of New Guinea after subduing it by air and by land. It has expelled the British from Burma and defeated General Douglas MacArthur in the Philippines. The United States counterattacks, bombing Tokyo and five other Japanese cities, a psychological reversal for the Empire that believed itself untouchable.

On every U.S. base this news is heard over the radio, read in the newspapers and magazines that do the rounds of the messes, or conveyed by the squadron instructors and chiefs, who take care to soften its impact on the airmen so as not to distract them from the task ahead.

FOUR

The day of their graduation as bombardier officers, following a brief ceremony to which neither friends nor family are invited due to the urgency of the war, Matías and his companions celebrate in a Westfield club. They enter bearing the golden wings of their new badges that, placed just above the upper hem of the left-hand pocket of their mustard-coloured shirts, have a magnetic effect on those present, who mechanically swing round to look. The officers rest their elbows on the bar, knock back whiskies with the ease that comes from not having to report back to base for another week, hug the girls who come up to them, attracted by the uniforms, sing *Yankee Doodle* and *Blood on the Risers* ad nauseam, and bend their heads together to speculate where they will be sent after the break. Sergeant Lakeman has assured Matías that he will crew one of the B-17s at the Allied base in Australia, where General MacArthur has been tasked with repelling the Japanese advance in the southwest Pacific. Yet, seven days later, it is Lakeman himself who informs him – emphasising his 'outstanding performance over the past four months' – that by decision of the General Command, he is to join the 97th Bomb Group of the Eighth Air

Force, which has left its base in Florida to station itself at Polebrook, in the United Kingdom. This is not welcome news to him, or at least he doesn't know whether it is. It is a promotion, without doubt: the U.S. has been positioning heavy materiel in England and now it is to send some of its best troops to the south-east of the British Isles with the goal of invigorating the European northern front, where the Royal Air Force, despite the shiploads of bombs it has dropped on Lübeck, Cologne, Essen, Dortmund, Genoa, Turin and Saint-Nazaire, and the significant victories it has won, has still failed to neutralise the power of the Luftwaffe.

Three days later, on a Beechcraft C-45, Matías is transferred to Polebrook alongside a large contingent of U.S. soldiers. Finally I will see Europe, he thinks, resting his head on the window, seeking solid forms among the shifting shadows of the clouds gathered outside. He thinks of his grandfather Karsten, his Roeder family, and he imagines his friends Steve and Billy, wondering whether they'll get back to the lives they were leading in America when the war is over. When will I return? Will I return? He writes to his mother and to Gordon Clifford to pass on his news, but without going into too much detail in order to evade the censors, who meticulously scrutinise letters from personnel for coded leaks that might compromise the government and the nation. He also prepares a blank sheet of paper to write to Charlotte Harris: he adds the date and composes and rereads two paragraphs before deciding they are redundant, inconsequential. He had wanted to try again, but is brought to a halt by the bitter aftertaste left by the last time he saw her: the sexual vignette interrupted by Paul's roars from the other room, the image of Charlotte running down the corridor terrified by her fiancé's reaction, and then her cries begging him to get dressed and disappear. He gives up writing to her because of that memory, as if to punish her for that night of failure.

He presents himself at Polebrook and within a couple of days all the confidence gained during his training at Westover vanishes like sand between his fingers. The schedule is exhausting, the climate is hostile, the officers are wilier and more competitive. Another source of discouragement is the intransigent Colonel Cornelius Cousland, group leader, who enters the barracks at four o'clock in the morning with a saucepan and soup ladle to wake up the three squadrons under his command, and is stern in the extreme when going through the dress review. Twice now he has made subordinates march for three hours, barefoot and with their parachutes on, when he has caught them with their belts incorrectly fastened or their shirts not neatly ironed. In contrast with Sergeant Lakeman, Cousland rarely raises his voice, but his silence, his imperturbable gestures, the impossibility of knowing what he is thinking are all the more intimidating. For Matías these details fade into the background when he finally takes possession of the B-17 nose assigned to his crew, calibrates the lens of the bombsight and presses the button that deploys the bombs from their racks. Although it is far from the perfect aim he boasted of, his average hit rate rises with each sortie. And like him, each member of the crew improves their skills until together they are working like a well-oiled machine. So far, their missions haven't involved facing anti-air guns or enemy fighter planes. With the exception of a bumpy take-off that complicated the aircraft formation and caused their B-17 to almost collide with another, they haven't felt at risk of death. If there has been a difficult obstacle to overcome, it is the cold, not on the ground, where coal-fired stoves remain lit throughout the day, but in the air, where there is no heating and where at over 23,000 feet, even on hot days, it can reach twenty degrees below. Thermal underwear, full-length explosion-proof suits, woollen gloves, sheepskin-lined jackets and boots help to ward off those bone-chilling drafts to some extent, as do the thermoses of boiling coffee, but none of that takes away from the fact that the low temperatures leave the men feeling cold. In the first week, the flight engineer's oxygen mask became blocked up due to his own breath freezing, and he fell unconscious. The rear gunner took off his gloves to unblock his machine gun and in less than a minute his fingers were like blocks of ice, and he was out of service for a week. Other crews have had it worse; a co-pilot had to amputate two fingers with a saw to free his frozen hand that was stuck to the cockpit window.

'I'd rather the cold than the damned Pacific heat, I can tell you,' says Dave Hillard, pilot and captain, before sleeping, as he leafs through a copy of *Esquire*, 'and you don't have to whack scorpions and ticks and the rest of them.' Hillard grew up in the snowy Huron of South Dakota and is the kind of man who never distrusts his instinct and, despite his lesser weaknesses, such as his aversion to insects, emanates authority. Charlie Dufresne, the navigator from Wyoming, adds as he takes off his boots: 'Cousland reckons the only antidote to the cold is the hunt: as soon as you get out there your body warms up.' 'The only thing you need to know about fighter planes is that they are first, a spot in the sky, second, a lightning bolt, and third, 2,300 bullets per minute. I read that in *Stars and Stripes*,' Hillard comments, scratching the hair on his chest under his jersey. One of the amber lights of the barracks reflects off the dog tags hanging round his neck. 'Hey guys, if we fly with escorts then we only need to worry about getting there and bang, bang, bang, hitting the target,' pipes up Brandon Connolly, the co-pilot, crossing his legs on his camp bed, a Pall Mall between his cracked lips, while he shuffles a pack of cards for a new round of solitaire. 'Ha, if you had to be down below like Morty you wouldn't be saying that,' laughs Dufresne, referring to skinny Morton Tooms, the gunner in the ball turret, the transparent rotating sphere affixed to the belly of the B-17s. 'No way, the fighter planes don't bother me,' Morty remarks from his top bunk, chewing on a toothpick. 'What really shrivels my balls is the landing gear failing on the way home; in the mess I heard about a plane from another base that got its gear stuck, and as soon as the plane touched the ground the ball turret was crushed.' Eugene Moore, the blond radio operator, returning from the showers with his wash bag under his arm and towel round his shoulders, puts on a gruesome voice to add: 'I heard the same story, Morty, did you know the gunner's guts were left smeared across the landing strip and it took three days to clean them up? They had to hose out the turret to get the last bits of flesh out of the cracks.' 'Get out of here, I don't believe a word!' Morty Tooms erupts, turning around to discreetly make the sign of the cross. He's happy to say he disavows his religious upbringing at Prattville High School in Alabama, claiming to be agnostic and only to have faith in the horoscope, but sometimes, when his certainties are shaken, he resorts to crossing himself, not without embarrassment. The other members of the crew, four gunners and the flight engineer, have been dozing for several minutes now. 'Connolly wouldn't be allowed in the turret anyhow, he doesn't know how to shoot,' guffaws Hillard, peering over his magazine. Connolly removes the cigarette from his mouth to defend himself: 'In Kentucky, we start shooting buffalo and deer from the age of eight.' 'Sure, sure, with rubber arrows no doubt,' Dufresne snorts. 'With rifles, dumb-ass,' hits back Connolly, gritting his teeth. 'A standing buffalo is hardly a Zero or a Stuka at 10,000 feet,' objects Hillard. 'Well we also shot at the Apache and the Sioux, and they sure knew how to run,' jested Connolly. On the floor, doing push-ups in an effort to lose the eight pounds he's gained

139

since he arrived in Polebrook, Matías intervenes: 'Brandon, how about you fire up that harmonica instead of sniping at each other?'

Still pissed off at the argument, Connolly tucks his deck of cards under his pillow and pulls the silver instrument from the trunk where, in a disordered heap, he keeps socks, chocolates, photos of his sweetheart, condoms, men's magazines, razor blades, medals, a horseshoe, rabbits' feet and other knickknacks. Every airman has a similar chest at the foot of their bed. Matías has engraved the initials MCR on his with a knife, and uses it to store his mother's letters, a photo of him with Steve Dávila and Billy Garnier on the boardwalk at Coney Island, a bracelet from Charlotte Harris, the Wieden lighter from his grandfather, and a stack of dog-eared romance and science fiction novels that Mrs Morris lent him when he signed up and that he now reads religiously every night before bed. 'Sweet dreams, boys,' Dufresne mutters. The melody from Connolly's harmonica transports them to the empty plains of the west; he learned it from his father, the final link in a long line of Montana cowboys. Within minutes a languid cornet is heard from the yard. The four bare lightbulbs hanging from the ceiling are extinguished. Lit only by a slice of moon that sneaks in through the side windows like a lighthouse against a cliff, the men lie there, unaware of the misfortunes that await them. Tomorrow the skies will be clear. A fabulous day to go bombing.

When not out on missions, the crews play baseball at camp, play billiards in the officers' mess, write letters home, or simply discuss the latest news from the war. In the mess, Dave Hillard distributes copies of *Yank, the Army Weekly* that describe the damage caused by the Japanese navy to the U.S. aircraft carriers in the Battle of the Coral Sea, and the U.S. victory at Midway atoll, or the triumph of the Axis forces' attack on the Allied port of Tobruk, commanded by

Erwin Rommel. The young men pore over the account of the Battle of Malta, above all for the prowess of George Buerling, the loose cannon Canadian pilot just twenty years old, who shot down five Italian bombers in a single day, peppering them in the fuel tank, rear engine, and the starboard wing. Buerling marked thirty-one crosses on the flank of his Spitfire, as if it were a piece of cake, silencing those who called him undisciplined for frequently breaking squadron formation and zigzagging after German fighters on his own. His reputation as an executioner fully justified the nickname that was to outlast him – The Maltese Falcon – but what shocked them most was the Canadian's remarks on his off-colour practice routine in his spare time: 'I train by firing my revolver between the brows of stray dogs and any living thing that presents a challenge, from rabbits to beetles.'

'I vote for *Return to Glory* or *Homesick Thunder*,' ventures Charlie Dufresne.

'Are you crazy? It's supposed to be a girl's name, something like *Little Eva*, *Mary Ruth* or *Pink Lady*, and a drawing of one of the *Esquire* models,' counters Dave Hillard.

They are gathered in the yard to name their aircraft, on the orders of Cousland. On top of their service number, they each need a distinctive nickname to simplify identification of each unit. Cousland doesn't say so, but he knows there will be heavy casualties on the next mission and it is better to avoid the sad task of counting the aircraft that won't return.

'How about *Lucy Bell*?' asks Phillip De Stefano, the top turret gunner.

'And why Lucy, who the hell is Lucy?' inquires Brandon Connolly.

'My girlfriend,' confesses De Stefano.

Disapproving whistles and a rain of chewing gum and cigarette butts put an end to his initiative.

'In that case we might as well call it Peggy after my girlfriend – I'm not the captain for nothing,' says Hillard.

'And how about we call it after your sister instead?' Dufresne needles him.

Hillard makes a gesture as if to punch him.

'So what do you say to *Lorelei*?' Morton Tooms proposes.

'Don't tell me that's your girl's name?' exclaims Dufresne.

'Of course not!' Tooms retorts. 'She's a mythological woman who attracted men with her legendary beauty and singing.'

'I like the sound of that!' mused Hillard.

'Not so fast,' interrupted Eugene Moore. 'Morty's only told you one part of the myth. *Lorelei* is a pitiless woman who takes revenge on men causing disasters and shipwrecks, is that what we want?'

Everyone turns to look at Tooms, who tries a different tack.

'So… what about *Dame Satan* or *Hell's Angels*?'

'You're nuts, Morty,' Hillard shakes his head.

'Don't you like *All Americans*?' inquires Eugene Moore.

'Sounds great, except that, as far as I can see, not all of us are Americans by birth,' says Connolly, looking around him with an insidious gaze, poisoned by his prejudices as a middle-class boy brought up in a thriving neighbourhood of Erlanger, Kentucky.

Matías feels an urgent need to clarify his background, but the flight engineer Agustín Ferreiro gets there first.

'Hang on, Brandon, I was born in Portugal, but from the age of six I've been as American as you or any of us.'

The bucktoothed Ludwik Sosnowski, left waist gunner, takes the floor.

'My whole family is Polish, but I'm a Yank like the

rest of you, from the first block of Walton Street, Noble Square, Chicago, Illinois.'

'Over here, an Irish-American, born in Orleans, Vermont,' comes the conscientious report from Kenny Doods, right waist gunner.

'And don't look at me like I'm a louse, I'm Mexican-American, from Sugar Land, Texas, to be precise,' says Harold Median, tail gunner.

Before the silence grows too long, Matías speaks.

'I'm American by adoption, I was born in Trujillo, Peru.'

The group spirit takes its effect.

'All right, all right, we'll call her *All Americans*,' Hillard concedes, reluctantly. 'But I'm doing the drawing! That ain't negotiable!'

Three hours later, by the plane's nose stretches a smiling blonde in a bikini, half woman, half bomb, in profile, as if she were another crew member of this B-17, part captain, mother, friend, lover and saint protecting each of the boys.

The following day, Monday August 17, the three squadrons meet early in the briefing room. At breakfast, Matías noted that the usual fried eggs had been replaced by boiled eggs (after a few months he would reach the conclusion that whenever boiled eggs were served it indicated a tough mission ahead; and if they came with a couple of sausages and rashers of bacon, then the breakfast could well be your last). Cousland enters abruptly and climbs onto the dais. The airmen stand to attention and quickly take their seats again. On the wall, a black curtain hides the blackboard with the day's mission. The command has chosen to unveil the missions at the last minute to avoid, as has already happened at other bases, snitches or desertions. Cousland pulls back the curtain, revealing a map, and with a pointer informs them: 'Our target today is the railway station at Rouen, northwest France; twelve of our B-17s will fly over the English Channel in closed formation. The lead bomber will be commanded by Major Paul Tibbets and Colonel Frank Armstrong. Any questions?' An airman's voice breaks through the rarefied air: 'Will we have an escort?' Cousland replies in an even-handed tone: 'Yes, officer, four squadrons of British Spitfires, but they won't accompany you for the whole trip, because of their range. A ripple of murmurs spreads from the front to the back of the auditorium. Another voice is heard: 'Are you expecting anti-aircraft fire, Colonel?' Cousland, unperturbed, with his marble coolness, absolves the doubt: 'Affirmative, gentlemen, a number of flak batteries will be awaiting us.' The men know what that entails. They have heard of their devastating effectiveness. They have heard that the 88-millimetre guns are capable of firing fifteen shells per minute, and that just one of these shells is enough to blow an aircraft to pieces. They have heard that these guns reduce the chances of survival by twenty-five per cent. So the men remain silent as they synchronise their watches, take note of the weather forecasts and review the notes written on the map hanging on the wall. That's why they ask the chaplain to bless them, to give them communion, to tell them briefly what to expect. That's why some of them sneak a swig of whisky, light and extinguish cigars as they engage in soliloquies, or devour chocolate bars and chew gum as they walk around the tanker trucks, waiting for the airfield workers to finish refuelling the planes and the armourers to reinforce the machine guns and assemble the bombs on the racks. Or perhaps wishing they'd never finish. That is why some vomit as soon as they board and take their positions, holding back the tears, sure they are on their way to certain death.

'If the Grim Reaper gets me, boys, then bury me with one of the propellers,' Agustín Ferreiro says over the radio.

'We're all going to come back unbowed, dammit!' decrees Dave Hillard. 'We'll bust their asses and head home, all right?' 'Agreed, Captain!' they nod in unison, emboldening each other with a reckless but genuine fervour. As soon as they are clear of the English coast, the gunners test their weapons with a volley of shots into the void. At Hillard's request, Charlie Dufresne reports their altitude and the distance to Rouen: 'We'll be over the station in one hour and ten minutes.' Eugene Moore asks permission to put some music on the radio. Glenn Miller's 'I Know Why' is playing as the weightless Spitfires make their appearance, joining the choreography from the rear. 'Our little friends have arrived,' celebrates Phillip De Stefano from the top turret. 'Watch out for the fighters, Phillip, you're our eyes up there,' Brandon Connolly chimes in. The minutes pass with exasperating slowness, the sky is a grey wasteland that at times reveals the blue gleams of the Channel below. 'If it weren't for the war, I'd be in Newport right now, in the church in the suburb, playing the piano with the band,' Kenny Doods suddenly says, from behind his Browning 50-calibre. 'If it weren't for the war, I'd be with Elsie and Lucas in Walton's supermarket buying almonds to make Mazurkas,' continues Ludwik Sosnowski, holding the microphone close to his oxygen mask. 'If it weren't for the war, I'd be doing it with Peggy in the shower in her parents' bathroom,' laughs Hillard. 'I envy you, Cap; if it weren't for the war, I'd be narrating the Galveston rodeo trials, rotting like a sweet potato in the heat,' adds Harold Medina, seated in the tail, both index fingers stroking the triggers of the machine guns. The game continues for a while. 'If it weren't for the war,' says Matías, 'I'd be visiting my grandfather for the first time.' No one else continues. A thick shroud of silence hangs over the craft's different spaces. Then De Stefano's voice, breathless, shakes the crew into readiness: 'Red alert, bandit squadron at twelve o'clock, north-west!'

The German fighters, four Focke-Wulf FW 190s, the infamous Würgers, burst into view and whiz past. A jolt of electricity shocks the cockpit from one end to the other. 'Shit, Cousland was right, I forgot about the cold soon as I saw them,' says Sosnowski. The Spitfires chase after them. Bursts of fire ricochet back and forth. The hunt is relentless. From their flanks, the gunners keep their eyes peeled, hoping for a chance to take aim at the enemy aircraft. Shrapnel from the Würgers hits the B-17's fuselage constantly, a metallic clatter that unnerves. 'How're we doing, Dufresne?' asks Hillard. 'Ten minutes to target!' the navigator reports, marking lines on the map with a compass. 'The dance is about to begin, boys,' Connolly announces. The twelve B-17s advance in formation, keeping their distance. In the nose turret, Matías ignores the machine guns, removes the cover of the sight and pulls a white cloth from his right-hand trouser pocket to clean the lens. At that moment the German anti-aircraft guns are heard for the first time, *boom! boom! boom!*, an inconceivable, thunderous sound that instantly has his pulse racing. Each shell produces dense billows of black smoke, smudges that dirty the sky as if someone had clumsily scattered droplets of ink over an immaculate page. The incoming flak can't be seen, and the men have no idea if the next hammer blow will finish them. More explosions, and the black clouds multiply above, below, on all sides; Matías has the sudden impression of navigating a bat-filled cemetery. In the middle of this frenzy, a fat shell takes them by surprise from underneath, causing the plane to rattle violently, and flames flare out of engine number three. 'Oh God, we're all going to die!' howls Kenny Doods over the radio, continuing to fire at the fiendish German fighters as they chase the Spitfires. 'Shut up, Kenny! If I hear you whining again, I'll shoot you myself!' Hillard briskly orders. 'Ferreiro, how's that damn engine? Can you manage it?' 'I've got it under control, Dave, but we've lost some fuel,' the flight engineer reports, his mittens smeared with oil, after shutting down the conflagration and ensuring the other engines are still operational, though already overheating. 'One minute out,' advises Dufresne. 'Just sixty seconds, sixty seconds,' Medina says, commencing a countdown in his head. 'All ready down there, Matthew?' asks Connolly. The din of the anti-aircraft guns is relentless, with each round of shells shaking the security of the operation a little further. Matías glues his face to the viewfinder and the Rouen railway station soon appears clearly under the lines of the crosshairs. 'Almost there,' he says. 'Bombardier, autopilot engaged, the plane is all yours,' Hillard tells him, glancing at the altimeter needle and the fuel levels, adjusting his cap and leaning back in his chair for the first time since take-off. Following protocol, Matías briefly takes over control of the aircraft, which continues to shake. The fighters orbit like wasps at such a speed they blur into invisibility, appearing and disappearing as they execute evasive manoeuvres. No training, no patrols, none of the missions conducted so far have prepared him for a situation like this. Matías knows he cannot fail, that the calm of his comrades depends on his steady hand, that back at headquarters Colonel Cousland is hanging on his every move. Then, overcoming the hesitancy between jumping the gun or waiting too long, he flicks the switch that opens the bomb bay doors and shifts the lever: the bombs begin to fall one after another with a mournful whistling sound. 'Bombs away!' he reports, and within seconds a chain of explosions can be seen, as the other B-17s in the formation also release their loads. The rough voice of Major Tibbets, pilot of the lead plane, is heard in all twelve craft at once over the group channel: 'Well done boys, time to head back.' The craft regain altitude, dodge a final wall of anti-aircraft fire, take their place in the open blue sky and are soon out of range of German radar. Only then, still breathing heavily, their hearts still racing, do the men check themselves over for bruises or fractures. They've saved their skins.

Upon landing back at Polebrook they exit the aircraft by the front hatch. Some sing, pray, kiss the ground. The ground crew race to check over the craft, and the commanders come to congratulate them, as all personnel have returned unharmed, and of the twelve bombers sent out only three suffered minor damage. Having passed through the operation debrief room, the crew can visit the showers and get changed: they are counting on Cousland's blessing to be given a pass to go to London to celebrate the success of the raid on France.

'It's less than two hours in the jeeps,' estimates Hillard, sitting on his bunk and checking that the elastic of his socks matches the curve of his shinbones.

'Cousland's gonna lend vehicles for everyone?' asks Eugene Moore, tucking in his khaki trousers.

'Today, he'd probably lend us the planes,' jokes Morty Tooms, as he trims his moustache in a pocket mirror perched on a shelf.

'Does anyone know any places in London?' wonders Kenny Doods, doing up the top button of his shirt.

'What do you mean by *places*, Doods? The plan is to find a bar, get drunk, meet some girls. Or is good Kenny here after whores?' jokes Connolly, pretending to be scandalised. The rest laugh.

'What would the kids back at the church in Vermont think if they knew their band's pure pianist is a pervert who can't stop jerking off thinking about the whores he can't afford?' Dufresne puts his oar in, making lascivious faces and rubbing his crotch.

'Don't act like idiots, you know what I'm talking about,' protests Doods, blushing.

'I've heard of a place called the Star and Bottle,' suggests Medina, brushing his curly hair with one hand.

'That hole is a dump,' proclaims Hillard, knotting his tie. 'It doesn't compare with The Grapes in Limehouse, the Black Raven in Chelsea, the French House in Soho, or the Rainbow Corner in Piccadilly Circus.'

The others stare at each other, stunned at the captain's encyclopedic knowledge of the night-life.

The convoy of jeeps stampedes out of the base in a cloud of brick-red dust, leaving behind the barracks, the central tower and the prefab modules that house the mess, the hospital and the administrative offices in a rare calm. In the hangars, behind the sandbags that form a containment wall, the planes slumber amid the vaporous summer shadows; while on their fuselage, as if it were a billboard, embellished with those glitzy new names – *Piccadilly Lily*, *Sho Sho Baby*, *Pete-Repeat*, *Double Trouble*, *Reluctant Dragon* – the girls stand watch with their overloaded eyelashes, tiny waists and suggestive smiles.

The men occupy three adjacent tables at the Rainbow Corner. They feel exposed before the gaze of so many civilians: specimens from the same genus, but belonging to different families, such as geese with crows, or turtles with alligators. Some squadron commanders, plus a handful of colonels and generals, are already there, including Cornelius Cousland. With his small-town manners, Cousland orders a waiter to pour a round of brandy. General Carl Spaatz ceremoniously clears his throat as he takes the floor and addresses the men with a bombast that is out of place here: '…as far as today's mission is concerned, I can only applaud the fact that, despite the complexities of warfare and the challenging situation we faced, you gentlemen have honoured the uniform by acting before the adversary as true patriots, in the interest of a…' Noting the soporific character of the speech and fearing that it might go on for considerably longer, Colonel Armstrong interjects effusively, 'We destroyed Rouen!', provoking a series of cheers, acclamations and clinking of glasses, with which General Spaatz resignedly joins in. The music blasting from the loudspeakers at Rainbow Corner encourages couples to dance, the group breaks up, swaying through the crowd, each in search of his share of fun. The hours go by faster here than up there, Matías thinks. From his seat he sees Ferreiro making acrobatic moves on the dancefloor with a red-head, while Sosnowski mimics him with the style and coordination of a puppet. A Pole is never going to have better rhythm or dance with more grace than a Portuguese, he thinks. A few steps to the right, stationed at the bar, De Stefano and Dufresne drink one beer after another, escorted by four girls who, in the establishment's dim lighting, look as if they might have turned twenty. Looking around, he sees the co-pilot, Connolly, transfigured into a lecturer, preacher or windbag, at the centre of a circle of civilians who listen to him with fawning intrigue.

'Isn't this all a bit much?' Eugene Moore asks him sourly as he comes to sit on his left.

'You mean the celebration?' asks Matías, drumming his fingers on the table.

'Yeah, I mean, we were only doing our job.'

'Sure, Eugene, but it's normal to take a break, be glad we're still alive, don't you reckon that's something?'

'But would you say we were really risking it up there?' Matías stares at him.

'Is that a serious question? Didn't you feel the flak? Didn't you see the fighter planes?'

'Sure, Matthew, I saw them, I felt them, but we had escorts, they barely shook the plane a couple of times.'

'I don't get what you're trying to prove with that attitude,' Matías shakes his head.

Moore drags his chair closer.

'Listen, I heard Cousland in the washrooms saying

to a colonel that today's mission was more of a political victory than a military one.'

'In what way?' Matías asks warily.

'It's plain to see, Matthew. They needed the first shared mission with the Brits to be an "overwhelming victory". With Rouen the command showed Churchill and Roosevelt that we can take care of the daytime attacks, leaving the nights for them.'

'And what difference does that make?'

'It doesn't suit us to fly by day, does it? The planes are visible, the chances of dying are much higher – they're treating us like guinea pigs!'

'You just talk shit cos you've got a mouth,' Matías erupts, jabbing his index finger into the table. 'We take care of the daytime missions because we're more accurate than the Brits, because we've got better technology, and because they don't care where the bombs fall or if they hit civilians – but we do!'

'Wait 'til we go out on first-class missions, Matthew! Wait 'til we're not twelve but fifty, one hundred, five hundred planes!'

'What are you talking about, Eugene? We're never going to fly so many B-17s at once.'

'Don't you know how many bombers the RAF sent to Cologne two months ago? More than a thousand, Matthew! A thousand planes in a single night! Do you have any damn idea how many anti-aircraft guns will be waiting for us when we head out on more difficult daytime missions? How many fighters do you think they'll send to shoot us down and how many Spitfires will escort us? Can you even aim a damn bomb in the middle of that kind of hell? Nothing is in our favour! Am I the only one who can see this?'

'Look, Eugene, all I'm going to say is this: try and enjoy this night and stop being an ass.'

Matías drains his glass of brandy, slams it down on the table, stands up and takes a long tour around the venue. Moore's rebellious words resound in his ears for a good while before fading, but by two in the morning, at the apogee of the party, when he sees the rest of the *All Americans* around the piano, holding young ladies with tight skirts and rosy cheeks round the waist, singing along euphorically if out-of-tune to the ballads gunner Kenny Dodds is playing – Gene Autry's 'Don't Fence Me In', Perry Como's 'Deep in the Heart of Texas' – boasting a self-possession that stands in striking contrast to the uneasiness with which earlier, in the air, they were counting down the minutes and seconds to return to the earth; when Matías sees all this, he thinks that maybe what the radio operator said was true: maybe so much revelry is a mistake.

The scene in the barracks the next morning is deplorable: Hillard, Medina and Doods, still in their pyjamas, are inhaling oxygen from a balloon to cure their hangovers. 'I shouldn't have left the base, I don't know why I went,' moans Doods, ravaged. 'Cut the crap, Kenny!' grumbles Sosnowski the Pole, drowsily. 'We saw you enjoying yourself like a pig, don't come over all innocent now.' Morty Tooms, still tipsy, stiff-haired, swears he proposed to a girl whose name he can't remember: 'Was it Janet, Jacqueline or Joyce? 'No idea, all I know is you asked her to marry you while balancing a glass of whisky on your forehead, remember that?' says Dufresne, throwing a pillow at him from his bunk. Squatting on the floor and using copper pipes and a gas cylinder, Ferreiro is engrossed in building an alcohol distiller to secure the night's supply. Connolly twirls a wooden spoon around in a stainless steel cup filled with 'Irish lemonade', a repulsive concoction prescribed by the Rainbow Corner bartender and containing three fingers of hydrogen peroxide and two teaspoons of lemon powder. De

Stefano is asleep, puke on his shirt, piss on his trousers, still wearing his boots. Only Matías and Eugene Moore, who has returned from his morning run, are fit to attend the meeting called for noon. If Cousland were to make one of his periodic, unannounced inspections right now, they would all end up peeling onions in the kitchen. The downpour outside is no bad thing. The cloudy sky is so dark it could still be night. Cousland has decided that, until the bad weather clears, no one will board the planes.

Over the following weeks and months the missions continue, and the B-17s prove their effectiveness in a clear sky. They sink U-boats, knock out the electricity supply to military installations, pulverise factories. Yet, just as Moore had predicted that night, the daytime operations become steadily more demanding. In September, the U.S. bombers attack a twin-engine plant at Meaulte, in northern France, but the British escort fails to rendezvous with them at their intended coordinates and they are intercepted by fifty German fighters. Finding themselves unprotected, several planes abandon the mission, citing mechanical problems. The *All Americans* are horrified to see the neighbouring plane in the formation, the *Fancy Nancy*, with whose crew they had shared a long poker game the night before at the officers' club, go down, both wings peppered to bits by flak. Of the eleven crew, only three manage to parachute out. Two other B-17s are shot down by the Germans. On the next mission, attacking a steel mill at Lille on the Franco-Belgian border, the Spitfires arrive at the wrong time and the Luftwaffe fighters, flashing with hellish accuracy, take out five bombers. Watching in awe as these giants crash into flames and plunge into the water, Matías wonders if the *All Americans* will end up like this, submerged in the cemetery of rusting aircraft that is the English Channel. No one on the crew reacts. Captain Dave Hillard is frozen to the spot by muscular spasms in his neck and shoulders.

For the first time, fear consumes the airmen. Fear of being cut to pieces by the bursts from the fighters or shredded by a single flak shell. Fear of being left crippled. Fear of the plane being shot down and having to activate the parachute in the less than thirty seconds it takes a heavy bomber to smash itself into the ground. Fear of drowning in the frozen waters or getting lost in a remote region, wandering in the open like fugitives, having to ration the contents of their canteens to the brink of starvation, listening to the weak stomach gurgles of hunger, at the mercy of the untamed creatures of the night. Fear of landmines. Fear of dying in the middle of the woods, alone, without witnesses, with no one to vouch for or certify their determination to cling to life. But also fear of being ambushed by the enemy hordes, finding themselves face-to-face without a rifle, yet also fear of having one and being unable to shoot, because it's one thing to want to cut the necks of the Germans and another, very different, one to have the balls to pull the trigger point-blank, or even to cock their weapon in front of those leaden uniforms with eagle wings on the chest. Fear of getting used to killing men without mercy and sitting on a pile of bodies waiting for the rescue brigade. And of course, fear of being captured, roughly clothed in jackets with P.O.W. stitched on them, ostracised, or taken to one of those clandestine camps where the Nazis, in violation of the rules of war, savage their prisoners by pulling out their molars with pliers, flaying their scalps, or sawing off their toes one by one.

In October, during an operation against the Rotterdam dockyards, three German fighters attack the formation the *All Americans* is flying in, firing head-on at the noses of the B-17s. Matías sees a flurry of bullets from the silver planes hole the Plexiglas window and whistle past without scratching him. Behind him, Charlie Dufresne isn't so lucky. Matías hears him moaning, takes two steps along the gangway to help and sees his right kneecap shattered by the shrapnel. 'They got me, they got me,' stammers Dufresne. 'You're going to be fine, Charlie, take it easy,' Matías tells him, placing his handkerchief on the wound, pulling out the pieces of metal and tearing a strip of cloth from his uniform to make a tourniquet with two knots. He takes one of the navigator's pens to apply torsion and looks at his watch. 'I'm so cold, Matthew,' quivers the navigator, gripping him tightly by the wrist. 'We're on our way back, hang on in there, I'm with you, I'm not moving from here.' Matthew injects his companion's shoulder with a syringe of morphine, but Dufresne's face does not offer encouraging signs. As Matías lays him down to help him breathe more easily, he discovers with horror an injury in his friend's abdomen. He opens his jacket to find a dark, slippery handful of intestines there. He automatically pours some sulphamide powder on it to prevent gangrene. 'Keep this for me,' Dufresne mumbles, holding out the coin he uses to do magic tricks in the barracks. 'Charlie, look at me, talk to me, don't stop talking to me, brother, we're close to the base now, look at me,' Matías begs, but Dufresne's limp hand slips from his as if carried away by a gentle current of water. 'How are things going down there?' Connolly's voice comes over the open radio channel. 'Charlie's gone,' Matías announces. He doesn't know what else to add, nor has he been trained to watch a comrade die and act like it's nothing. He thinks to himself that it's the first time he's seen death at first hand, but then he remembers the young man who threw himself into the ocean from the steamship carrying him from Trujillo to New York. That time he saw the body in the distance, from the ship's bow, turning over in the water; now it is different, now the body is in his arms and he can feel it rapidly getting colder, see how the skin begins to tauten and go pale, like recently cut grass exposed to the sun. When later he climbs out of the

155

plane, with Dufresne's magic coin in his pocket, and makes his way without pausing through the ground staff and companions who seek to console him with futile offers of support, Matías is no longer the man who boarded the B-17 that morning: he is someone else, someone hurt, an officer already fed up with a war which – though he has no way of knowing it – is a long way from ending.

A few weeks later, Colonel Cousland advises his squadrons that they are to be transferred to the Mediterranean theatre, in order to operate over the North African coast. The recent losses, the stormy weather – which has prevented key missions from being carried out – and the fiasco of the most recent bombing raids have caused unease in the high command and under-mined morale. Discouraged or exhausted, some airmen are asking for extra leave, some to get married, others because their wives are about to give birth, and others to go to hospital with sudden indigestion, spontaneous mumps, unprecedented asthma attacks, symptom-free colds, and other imaginary complaints. The battle in the Mediterranean does not bring about the hoped-for recovery. At least not for the crew of the *All Americans*, who derail almost every mission by reporting technical deficiencies: if it's not the generators, brakes or hydraulic pressure failing, then it's the fuel pumps, the transfer valve, the hoses for the oxygen supply. One afternoon, Cornelius Cousland locks himself in his office with the captain, Dave Hillard, and Agustín Ferreiro, the flight engineer, to subject them to a gruelling interrogation.

'What are you two up to? Are you conspiring against me?' asks Cousland, a clenched fist on the desk, biting his tongue not to accuse them of sabotage from the off.

'No, sir,' reply Hillard and Ferreiro in unison, standing to attention.

'You want to oust me, is that it?'

Cousland's jaw is trembling. It's the first time they've seen him lose his cool.

'No, sir.'

'Do you take me for an idiot?'

'Not at all, sir.'

'Have you conspired with another crew to boycott the missions?'

'How can you say that, sir?'

'In that case, what the hell has happened to your performance?'

'We don't know what to say, sir.'

'Why have you aborted the last four missions?'

'For technical failures, sir.'

'Non-existent failures, admit it, for God's sake!'

'There were real failures, sir.'

'Are you suggesting I'm a liar?'

'Not at all, sir.'

'I could have you up before a military tribunal for insubordination!'

'We know that, sir.'

'So, are you admitting your responsibility?'

'Partially, sir.'

'For the love of God! What are you trying to do to me? Do you want me to piss blood?'

'Absolutely not, sir.'

In the face of these laconic, perhaps even sarcastic, yet apparently honest explanations, Cousland declares that the entire crew is to attend the office of Major Gregory Savage, chief medic for the base. After examining them one by one, Savage concludes in his report that the men are 'dangerously demoralised'. Not only because of the loss of Dufresne, but also because of what happened to Medina and Sosnowski: the former lost his sight and hearing over France when the rear turret exploded; and the second asked to be released from service after the first mission in Africa, when his machine guns jammed just as a horde of German fighter plans was attacking; he wasn't hit, but he swore on his life he wasn't going to go through that again. Doctor Savage indicates that several crews are already displaying a high level of physical and psycho-logical exhaustion: 'The men report extreme fatigue, they hardly sleep, they nod off during briefings; if they don't pull themselves together, it may lead to an unhealthy atmosphere in which animosities, malice, slander, and smear campaigns proliferate.' Cousland vacillates between sending them on leave or rotating them from base to break up some of the monotony. Dr Savage recommends ten day's rest under observation, but new orders, imperious and irrefutable, arrive from Washington: 'We must intensify the daylight bombardment of northern Europe and sap the German armaments industry regardless of the civilian cost. That is our stern duty.'

In early November 1942, Cousland decides to assign the crew of the *All Americans* to Bomber Group 303, stationed just thirty minutes away at Molesworth airbase. The day of the transfer, seated in the canvas-covered back of the truck, the men determine to recover their verve, their diligence; they need to regroup, to 'nucleate' as Kenny Doods likes to say, only in this way will they be able to complete the standard twenty-five missions and mark that number of bombs on the plane's fuselage.

In November and December they doggedly bombard France, with arduous missions to Saint-Nazaire, Lorient, Lille and Romilly. In-flight concussions, injuries and transfusions become routine. Accidents that once caused consternation are now assimilated as painful but unavoidable hazards of the job. One of the squadron's co-pilots has a twenty millimetre bullet explode in his eye, ripping it out entirely, leaving nerves and muscles outside the socket. Sosnowski is replaced by Scotty Larsen, a nineteen-year-old graduate from Wisconsin. When he is hit square in the forehead by a tracer round, he doesn't lose consciousness despite having his brain exposed: indeed, he continues to act as if nothing is wrong. But two minutes later he starts shouting like a madman, enters the cockpit dripping thick rivulets of blood, and collapses as he demands that Hillard and Connolly hand over the controls. During the operation over Romilly, a Heinkel blows off De Stefano's right arm; in agony, the gunner panics, picks up the mutilated arm from the floor of the turret and, hugging it to his chest as if it were a gun or a lifebelt, leaps out of the plane, hoping to land close to a French hospital where they can sew it back on, but the parachute doesn't open and the void swallows him like a stone.

'For those who are no longer with us,' says Morty Tooms in a breathy whisper as he leads the toast in the barracks at midnight on December 24. Hillard uncorks another bottle of champagne to raise their spirits. With his Wieden lighter, Matías lights the candles placed at the foot of the photos of Dufresne, De Stefano and Scotty Larsen on the altar that Ferreiro has improvised with the boots of the fallen comrades. The parents of these three will soon receive, together with the posthumous Purple Heart, an official letter informing them that their sons were killed in action. 'Merry Christmas, gentlemen,' Hillard proclaims, handing out condoms and copies of *Esquire* to anyone who wants one; dressed as Father Christmas, the captain laughs theatrically as he tries to prevent the lumpy white beard he has fashioned from cotton wool nabbed from the medicine box from falling off his chin. The new members of the crew – a navigator and two gunners – have been charged with decorating the pine tree they dragged in from the snow a few hours earlier. In place of baubles, they festoon it with grenades. After the exchange of hugs at midnight, Connolly rescues his harmonica from the bottom of his chest and begins to play 'Silent Night'. Eugene Moore is the first to sing, and the others join in, except for Kenny Doods, who prefers to isolate himself in a corner with his prayer book. At twelve-thirty a siren brings the celebrations to an end. Before the row of barracks goes dark, there are a few minutes for a final toast. 'To those of us who will return home,' says Morty as he tips back his glass, filled with an optimism very much akin to the faith he abjures. Everyone acclaims the sentiment. At times they act with the solemnity of veterans, which in some sense they are; the aircraft is like a time machine, especially after the toughest missions: they emerge from it older, hardened, as if in a few hours they had accumulated all the experiences the average man would acquire in a lifetime. Up there, life is turned upside down, changes happen faster, the limits of one's temperament expand. The non-smokers learn to smoke, the teetotallers learn to drink, the pragmatists who never thought about death learn to glimpse it, and the atheists who never believed in God, whether out of inertia or desperation, learn to believe and even − like the skinny Tooms − to cross themselves in private. The body, too, undergoes alteration. The alienating proximity to death weathers faces, hardens the features, changes the gait. Many of them have never fallen in love, nor seen prosperity or ruin, but with fewer than twenty-five years under their belt they consider themselves well-travelled men, both beaten and invincible. Yet at the same time, they're still − they can't stop being − kids and, like any kid, they have an urgent need to believe in the future. A belief that they nevertheless repress, keep to themselves. They fear that saying the word *future* aloud would cause it to vanish, condemning them to the endless present of the war; and so they only speak of *today*'s missions, of *tomorrow*'s operations, of the plans for *next week*. These are their maximum categories for time, they do not think, do not want to think, about what will come later, because they are almost sure that later there is nothing, perhaps only a little more of the same, something brief and finite in any case. They fear that the future is this, that old age has arrived for them before their time, before they had the chance to comprehend the fleeting nature of what they have lived. They fear that their store-house of memories will be limited to the war and will never hold, in some later epoch, different experiences to recount. Even the NCOs newly assigned to the base, who still behave with all the reservation of rookies, soon find themselves imbued with the mystique of the more seasoned, experience that same rapid maturing, and learn to treat the future with respectable caution.

In early 1942, most American cities feared a second Japanese attack as brutal as Pearl Harbor: schools taught children how to use gas masks, windows were covered with adhesive tape to prevent them shattering in a blast wave, and blackouts were imposed in major cities to disorient enemy pilots should they be flying overheard. Yet when no assault materialised, people gradually returned to their ordinary lives of shopping, dances, TV and radio comedy shows, chatting with their neighbours about hot topics such as the plane crash that killed Carol Lombard or the freezing over of Niagara Falls. It wasn't so much an attitude of apathy towards the war as a lack of appreciation of its magnitude. The general public was only interested in the naval campaign at Midway, the Pacific island battles against the Japanese, the decoration of Major James Doolittle by President Roosevelt for the first bombing raid on Tokyo, the new roles acquired by women in the army, the presence of African Americans in the armed forces, the sale of war bonds promoted by Bugs Bunny, the return of Babe Ruth to play exhibition games of baseball aimed at raising funds for munitions, and the neighbourhood campaigns to collect hoses, tyres, toys and anything else that could be recycled for the manufacture of war materiel.

This goes some way to explain why, thousands of miles away from Molesworth, these same Americans showed little concern for the fate of their compatriots on the distant European front. Only the families, partners and friends of the soldiers based in the United Kingdom – including the banker Gordon Clifford – follow the meagre news from England closely and stand at the news kiosks anxiously checking the lists of casualties published in the newspapers, hoping not to find any names they recognise. Even the letters sent home by recruits from British bases are not entirely reliable, as none of them want to pass on distress to their relatives, girlfriends or loved ones, so they give conflicting accounts, deliberately retouched with inaccuracies, far removed from the atrocities that have already begun to become the norm among the crews of the Eighth Air Force.

In Trujillo, meanwhile, Massimo Giurato shows a studied lack of interest in the fate of his son; on the handful of occasions he addresses the issue, almost always in response to an associate asking after Matías, he does so with a wary, displeased air. He completely fails to understand how his 'inept', 'thankless', 'good-for-nothing' son could have enlisted in the U.S. Air Force and become 'an enemy of Mussolini, of Italy and of Germany – of his own family!' He blames it on his 'stupid mother' for 'putting ideas into his head when he should be here studying law'. And he threatens to 'put him in line when he runs out of money and tries to set foot in this house again'.

Every fortnight, without her husband's knowledge, Edith Roeder goes to the editorial office of *La Industria* and asks to speak to the director to try and find out what is happening in Europe, even though the gentleman has little more to offer than a notebook with sparse and vague reports. One day she begs him to trace Matías' whereabouts for a sum of money, paying him an advance to begin right away; yet two weeks later she is left feeling confused, or even conned, by the words the director offers in his cracked voice: 'My sources, my dear lady, have been unable to gain access to the records of U.S. airmen in action in Europe, but they have, at least, confirmed that your son's name is not on the list of the fallen.'

Edith Roeder spends whole days re-reading Matías' most recent letters, but there is nothing to be gleaned from them about his location nor state of health. It is the missives from her father, old Karsten, however, that enable her to imagine, in the quietness of the hacienda, the fearful vortex that has dragged her son to the far side of the world. 'In Hamburg,' he tells her, 'the apartment block cellars have been reinforced to protect civilians from the Brits' explosive bombs. Before the war there were only eighty-eight public air raid shelters in the city, which he had thought far too many. Today, there are over two thousand.' He goes on to inform her that the ranks of the fire brigades have swollen, as the bombs are incendiary and can set whole districts alight: 'Your brother Klaus has been made an officer and is delegated to monitor incidents in our block.' In the port, the number of fire wardens has been doubled, and they have been raising the firebreaks that can be seen on street corners. Hundreds of sandbags fill the streets and squares, and each neighbourhood has tanks to maintain the water supply if the mains pipes fail. Meanwhile, an urban camouflage programme has been put in place to mislead the RAF planes. 'Wolfgang is thrilled as he always wanted to study architecture. He tells me that from the sky the train stations look like ordinary buildings, and that the oil tanks have been hidden in a way the English can't make them out. What I can't yet understand, my dear daughter, is how on earth they've been able to camouflage Lake Alster! According to Wolfgang, they have covered it over with a reproduction of the centre of Hamburg, isn't that marvellous?'

Against Matías' wishes, Edith Roeder sends him, care of the U.S. Air Force, handwritten letters extending to six or seven pages on both sides, accompanied by prayer cards showing the Virgin of Fatima and other pious charms. In addition to begging him to take care of himself, to remember to pray and to come home soon, Edith details her conversations with the Reverend Lizardo Carcelén in the parish church of La Merced, as well as reporting on the charitable activities carried out with the prim ladies of the German community, and the gossip from the dinners with which she continues to entertain illustrious visitors to Trujillo, get-togethers typically sprinkled with Rhine wines from their cellar and culminating in the infallible *Bratapfel*, great-grandmother Helga's recipe for delicious stuffed apples. 'For the love of God, how lonely my mother is!' Matías laments, reading these cliché-ridden letters in which Edith's life appears reduced to a merry-go-round of tragicomic situations in which she, with her graceful aura of self-sufficient womanhood and unwavering sweetness, continues to spin, enfolded in a veil of rampant mediocrity, unwilling to face the increasingly noisy complications of her deteriorating marriage. To Matías all those named characters and references to Peru, which in the early days of New York still awoke in him a certain nostalgia, now seem extraordinarily far away, as if they were indeed strangers, people he had never met, places he had never been, shifting silhouettes of a city and a country that long ago ceased to be his, if they ever really had been. Matías has no desire to write to his mother, but he does so. It is the other way around with Charlotte Harris: he longs to write to her, but doesn't dare to put pen to paper. He is overcome by arrogance, hiding behind childish reasoning. Only his correspondence with Gordon Clifford is real and regular, and in these missives, risking the wrath of the censors, Matías sets out the events of the war with the scrupulousness of one filling his personal diary. On January 2, 1943, shortly before air operations begin again in earnest, he writes to him:

> *Being up there for ten, eleven hours at a time is an eternity. There is no bravery in this, none at all. What we used to call bravery was little but a vague enthusiasm, full of ups and downs, the flipside of fear, and it vanishes the moment you think your plane might be shot down and that you won't see your loved ones again, or get to know the woman that might be your beloved. I believe I have become a cynic. I don't know how to explain it, but nothing causes me shame or disgust any longer. Not a week passes without me seeing my brothers-in-arms prostrate or agonising in tears, begging for their mothers – almost everyone begs for their mother when they're about to die, almost all of them to ask her forgiveness – but these scenes don't even move me any more. Many of these kids I know only by their Air Force nicknames, some are called after the states they are from, Wyoming, Idaho, Oklahoma, Texas, I know almost nothing of their pasts, but even so I consider them my brothers, the brothers I never had, men to whom I will be united unconditionally for life, for the mere fact of sharing this experience that is stealing all of our youths, and that with every passing day turns us harsher, more pitiless… and perhaps more unfeeling. It is aberrant how one gets used to living with degradation: you see it every day, it seems normal to you, sometimes you even justify it. War makes the repugnant the right thing to do – is there anything more inhuman than that?*

The first three weeks of the new year, on the orders of head of squadron Major General Peter Lewis, Group 303 intensified its bombing campaign in France, hitting Saint-Nazaire, Lille, Lorient and Brest. Numerous B-17s return to Molesworth with damage, and there are injured among practically all of the crews. The *All Americans*, despite their position in the lead squadron, emerge unscathed with the exception of Morty Tooms, who cracks three vertebrae and has to spend a week in hospital before rejoining for the next flight.

'Today's mission,' the Major General announces as he opens the curtain covering the blackboard in the briefing room on the morning of January 27, 'is to destroy the port of Wilhelmshaven'. The premature lines on Lewis' face, combined with his dark glasses and healthy skin, imbue him with a presence proportional to the degree of power he holds. The mere mention of Wilhelmshaven sends a shudder through those listening. It is the first time the U.S. Air Force will fly over German territory. The airmen look at each others' faces, seeking answers to questions they are barely beginning to formulate. They expected to continue dropping bombs on France, so this news brings concerns they cannot hide. 'If anyone has anything to say, now is the time to speak up,' Major General Lewis advises, gravely. Murmurs are heard around the room that crackle like sparks from burning coal. 'Silence!' Lewis orders, restoring quiet instantly. The respect he instils is notable, Matías thinks from his position in the third row, although he is more struck by the obedience with which he responds to any instruction from the mouths of his superiors. Having spent his childhood and adolescence rejecting all signs of authority due to the manner in which his father exercised it, he has come to understand that there are acceptable ways of imparting it.

The mission to attack the industrial warehouses

of Wilhelmshaven turns out to be just as arduous as anticipated, not only because of the one hundred German aircraft waiting like a shoal of piranhas, but because of the cold, which at 16,000 feet stiffens the joints and makes it impossible to handle the machine guns. Only fifty of the American planes release their bombs, yet it is enough to fulfil the objective. Tragically, three B-17s succumb to the anti-aircraft fire without their occupants being able to bail out in time.

Onslaughts on other German cities over the course of the winter and spring of 1943 – Osnabrück, Vegesack, Bremen, Essen, Kiel – bring with them the loss of more lives and craft. The crew of the *All Americans* are traumatised by the deaths of Agustín Ferreiro and Brandon Connolly on the mission over Vegesack: Ferreiro burnt when the oxygen pump he was inspecting exploded, Connolly killed by shrapnel from a Heinkel that literally shredded him, staining the glass cockpit panels red. German bullets also hit Jimmy Tucson, one of the new gunners; as his body was lowered from the plane, a photo of his pregnant wife fell out of one of his jacket pockets. It later transpired that their first child had been born the night before.

'What the hell are we doing here killing Nazis, Matthew?' says Eugene Moore one night in the Molesworth officers' club. 'Do you remember when we signed up? Wasn't it to shoot down Japs over the Pacific?' Matías is barely listening. Unlike Eugene, who says he'll get the hell out of there *any day now*, fearful that the higher-ups are looking to get rid of him by sending him to the slaughter without qualms, Matías is experiencing his moment of glory. He is now a first lieutenant and has received a written commendation from Washington for his actions in Bremen, where his bombs were instrumental in destroying an aircraft factory, a motorised transport plant and a synthetic oil refinery. Both General Carl Spaatz and Major General Lewis have let it be known that another action like this could earn him the Distinguished Service Medal. 'Did you hear that bastard Lord Haw-Haw last night?' Eugene Moore asks him, resting his elbows on the bar. Matías shakes his head. 'He made fun of our downed planes again, boasting that he knew the names of every crew member. On top of that, he said we'd have to train harder for tomorrow's mission because our losses would be very high. He's really in the know, that bastard, he's got better info than our own command.' 'Don't believe that idiot,' Matías counters. 'That's exactly what he wants us to do – take the bait.' Lord Haw-Haw is the pseudonym of a radio broadcaster of Irish origin, though born in New York. His real name is William Joyce. The minister of propaganda, Joseph Goebbels, has given him a slot on Germany Calling, where he peddles information, spouts bluster and cryptic messages, spreads incisive gossip, and parodies the Allies. 'Good night, my misguided friends,' he says sardonically, knowing that the Americans are listening.

The last letter that Matías sends to Gordon Clifford is dated Friday, July 23, 1943:

The other day they told me what happened to a young guy, a bombardier like myself, who went down to London to meet a girl. They'd spent the night chatting, dancing and kissing at a club. They were smitten with each other. He was going to propose to her. I'm sure you will think 'too soon', but, believe me, nothing is too soon with a war on. Two years of war is like twenty without it, someone would have to establish a table of equivalences. Anyway, the officer and his bride-to-be agreed to meet at a restaurant downtown. He was in a taxi, running late, when the air raid sirens began to sound. Luftwaffe planes were approaching. People rushed to safety inside any store they could find. The guy leapt out of the taxi and took refuge beneath mature trees in a park. There he remained, covering his head for the long minutes the bombardment lasted. Almost two hours later he reached the restaurant: or rather, what remained of it. A bomb had made a direct hit. He sneaked past the line of police and firemen, ran down the stairs and found nine bodies there, including the girl. They said he didn't sleep that night and returned to the base the next day dejected, asking to be relieved from his position on the aircraft. He requested to be transferred to the quartermaster's office or any other unit; he did not want to fly, let alone bomb. According to him, London had been an awakening, he'd discovered what happens in every operation and was no longer interested in being promoted to continue killing civilians he could now put a face to. He said that, up there in the air, you are capable of killing thousands of invisible, anonymous people you wouldn't dare lay a hand on if they were in front of you. He remarked that from the ground the tight formation of B-17s appeared at first as a constellation of little crucifixes, but gradually, as the craft approached in successive waves and the noise of their engines grew louder, the planes took on the appearance of a plague of immense, deafening metal fireflies. In just a few days his mood and his worldview underwent a radical transformation. He withdrew into himself. They told me he had renounced his religion, called God 'the great butcher', and discarded all the prayer cards he had pinned to the head of his bed. When I heard about him I felt I could identify with him a little, but you know what? A man's readiness to go to war is carried within or not at all; when it is there, you can tell in the way he looks at you, the way he walks and talks. That boy didn't have the right attitude, he hadn't internalised his sense of duty, he wasn't conscious of the fact that there's no way out of this: it's us or them. We are fighting over survival or annihilation, nothing less. Our task

169

is arduous, and it goes beyond tears, beyond good intentions, beyond faith, compassion or indulgence. And, of course, beyond free will, which does not exist, not here anyway. We have to take responsibility for what we do and to bear the painful consequences of our own mistakes, even if they are unintentional slips. I'm no idiot, I've known for a long time that the bombs kill defenceless civilians. It is an unavoidable collateral price. Within a few dozen feet of the workshops or military buildings we are there to destroy, there are often houses, schools, hospitals. No matter how accurate my shots are, even with my sights focused and the plane fully stabilised, it is not possible to hit the target and be sure I have not killed innocents. At first I refused to admit it, blindly trusting my aim and believing that technological advances allowed clean, accurate bombing. Now I know better. No one is willing to admit that machines are just as flawed and imperfect as the men who invented them. The press conveniently misrepresents what is happening here, but I tell you with full knowledge of the facts: men, women and children who did not choose to get involved in the war die on every single mission. Am I a murderer for that? I have no answer. It is part of the personal hell I will carry with me from the day this is over. But I know one thing. I know that with the power of bombs we can resolve this war sooner than we planned, and if so, if we can do that, millions of children will grow up safe in the world, less resentful than we are, and I will be very proud to have contributed.

FIVE

On the morning of Sunday July 25, the crew members of the three squadrons in Group 303 meet for breakfast at seven o'clock. They are served a double portion of boiled eggs and sausages. At eight o'clock they enter the briefing room. Matías notices for the first time the poster on the door, which reads 'Where Angels Fear to Tread'. He takes a seat next to Kenny Doods and Dave Hillard, behind Eugene Moore, and in front of Morty Tooms, the survivors of the original *All Americans* crew. 'What the fuck happened to your tail gunner,' Hillard asks Carson Baker, captain of the *Round Trip*, 'I heard they booted him back to the States.' 'You're not going to believe this, Dave,' replies the other. 'He was fifteen years old.' 'No way!' howls Moore. 'The sucker fooled us all,' Baker swears. 'How'd he get caught?' pipes up Doods. 'Someone tipped off command, and yesterday they sent us the report that he had falsified his details when he enlisted,' says the captain. 'And how many missions was he on?' asks Matías. 'He flew nine!' replies Baker. 'He was a crafty guy, he had confidence to burn, and he had an aim like the gods, he shot down four Messers.' 'What did the jerk say when he got caught?' asks Hillard. 'Nothing

171

very original: that he did it because he wanted to kill Nazis,' Baker relates, with a gesture of resignation. 'But before he was sent home he asked Dr Savage for crutches so his friends would think he'd come back from the war wounded.' A roar of laughter fills the room. For a long time the conversations continue without anyone interfering. Lewis should be here by now, he thinks, and he looks at the black curtain hiding the map.

'All rise! Attention!' a sergeant yells. Major General Peter Lewis enters flanked by two junior officers. The atmosphere quickly turns electric, as if a spirit had been summoned by a medium. There is a synchronised clatter of chairs and of heels being clicked together. From the dais, still looking at the men in front of him, Lewis signals to the sergeant to open the curtain and reveal the blackboard. Matías concentrates on the map. In a fraction of a second, a cascade of images passes through his mind, beginning with the letters from his grandfather, Karsten Roeder, the ones that enclosed maps of Hamburg, circling in red ink the places he would show Matías when he visited. That map, which Matías could draw from memory, is the same one that appears on the blackboard. 'Today's mission is to strike Hamburg,' Major General Lewis says, thumping his right fist into his left palm, over and over, and begins to point out the areas to be targeted by the B-17s. Matías hears without hearing, feeling in his stomach the churn of nausea, refusing to accept reality, the crudeness of reality. It can't be, he mutters to himself, his breath coming fast. He wants to leave the room, smoke a cigarette, and also to talk to Lewis, explain the inexplicable to him, ask him point-blank why Hamburg was chosen if it wasn't among the plans mooted the day before. Or, better, go to the chaplain for confession, but what for, he reasons, no prayer, no entreaty could really alter the course of things or contain the apprehension he feels spreading in every corner of his body; he cannot find a single gaze to take refuge in, or perhaps he avoids them all because he is afraid of being discovered. If they could unmask the fifteen-year-old who altered documents in order to get onto one of the planes, he thinks, then they could unmask him too, learn of his German heritage, accuse him of being *one of them*, a Boche, a Jerry, a Hun, they'll find out everything about his family, whom he loves without ever having met them, whom one day he swore to visit, something that seems more unlikely every day. He sees the Major General's lips move, but his voice is an indistinct, monotonous buzz. 'At last! We lead,' Morty Tooms exclaims, slapping him on the shoulder and jerking him from his stupor. He observes exuberant gestures of congratulation among his crew members and deduces that the *All Americans* has been designated as the flagship, that is, it will lead the attack ahead of the rest of the B-17s, meaning that he, the phoney Matías Giurato Roeder, turned Matthew Clifford Ryder, will be in charge of commencing the release of bombs that will probably take the lives of the only people he wants to meet in the world, those men and women for whom one day, back in Trujillo, in that past that now belongs to another dimension, he decided to undertake the journey that has brought him to where he is now. Unable to react, finding himself at a dead end, Matías wavers between giving up and moving on. He thinks about the letters from his grandfather; he thinks about the men he has seen die; about his mother's faint smile; about Gordon Clifford bidding farewell from the rear seat of the Pontiac; about the shadows of the black dogs the moon cast on the tall grass of the Chiclín hacienda; about the inseparable Steve Dávila and Billy Garnier, in the bowling alley of White Plains; about the coveted Distinguished Service Medal that could embellish his lapels to immortality; about the screeching of the seagulls in the port of Salaverry; about the sands of Coney Island at sunset; about the coffins carried by the huayco around the main square of Trujillo; about the woodworm-eaten window frames of Mrs Morris' boarding house; about the purple sockets of Dufresne's eyes as he breathed his last.

He finishes the briefing and, like an automaton, goes through the unchanging pre-flight routine without missing a single step: he picks up the bombscope from the quartermaster's, puts on his parachute harness, changes his boots, puts on his flak jacket, fills up two thermoses of coffee in the mess hall. He only slows down when, on the way to the airfield, he hears the cooks geeing him up, 'give those sons of bitches what for!', and he thinks about the hatred behind these invectives, which for the first time seem reprehensible to him.

It is not until noon that twenty-five aircraft take off from Molesworth. Within twenty minutes, they are joined by a further five groups arriving from other bases in England. One hundred and twenty-three American aluminium boxes crossing the sea on this sunny day. In his metal seat in the nose of the lead plane, Matías is unable to concentrate. The oxygen mask conceals his ghostly expression. On a normal day, he'd have approached the tense navigator Ryan Summers to calm him down, to stop him crumpling his maps as he tries to establish the location of the plane and curses his instruments as if they were deliberately hiding the coordinates. But this is no normal day. Once they enter enemy airspace, the thunderous anti-aircraft cannons begin to rumble, and smears of dust blur the pilots' vision. The turbulence begins once more, the lurching, the fighters streaking past, mercilessly pummelling the fuselage, the gunners spraying their ammunition in all directions. Captain

Hillard issues exasperated instructions to the squadron to keep the formation tight, not to lose position and to hold together against the German onslaught. But then come the first shoot-downs: the planes spiral, they plummet into the sea, the crews scream in horror, dizzy, howling, swearing. Over the radio the *All Americans* hear the pilots of other craft abort their mission. In their own B-17 too, there are wounded, viscera spattered on the windows. On the floor they see teeth, extremities torn off. They hear groans, gasps, and the shaking forces Hillard to straighten the rudder several times and rectify the course. Right then, beneath the black haze produced by the anti-aircraft batteries, past the last cloud bank, the mass of Hamburg emerges on the horizon. The planes descend at full speed like a flock of wild geese, and Matías cannot credit the cruel paradox of having finally arrived in the city where his mother was born with the abominable task of destroying it. And so he roars, not with sadness but with rage, or what passes for rage in such an indescribable situation. From his plexiglass bubble he identifies the Church of Saint Nicholas, Dammtor Station, the Altona commercial district, the Hagenbeck Zoo, the alleyways of the Reeperbahn and, to the south of the city, the inland port of Hamburger Hafen: the second largest port in Europe. The face of old Karsten occupies his thoughts. He recalls the wooden model aeroplane his grandfather sent as a gift to Trujillo and that he assembled and sent gliding over the cane fields on so many afternoons, and he suddenly believes, or rather feels, that he is inside that toy aircraft that swooped to the tragic designs of his imagination. He also remembers the Wieden lighter, with its red Saint James cross, whose tongue of flame he used to pass his index finger through, testing his ability to withstand pain. That was what the old man gave him: the plane, the lighter, the maps. Air, fire, earth. Is his grandfather now hiding in the cellar of the apartment building on Bernhard-Nocht Strasse, or in some dugout in the Blohm & Voss shipyard? And the others? Are they together in a bunker, crouched down, covering their ears, their heads between their shaking knees? Matías' questions are merely a prelude to tears that only deepen the confusion that assails him. He fantasises about refusing to follow orders, claiming lack of visibility, abandoning his post, asking for leave, deserting, leaping out of the plane in his parachute, faking unconsciousness. Now he thinks that everything he wrote to Gordon Clifford about the death of innocent civilians is not true, that this shouldn't be happening, that he isn't prepared for this outcome, that he feels no pride in anything he has done on this plane since he first boarded it.

'Ready, Matthew?' Hillard's voice returns him to himself. 'Matthew? All OK?' the captain asks again. 'Yes,' lies Matías. 'Two minutes out!' Ryan Summers yells. The gunners are going crazy back there, the rumble of the German batteries destroying their nerves. 'We're all depending on you, lieutenant,' Morty Tooms says over the radio. The priority objectives are the gas factories, the fuel storage tanks, the quays, the shipyards, the steel plants, the railway junctions, but Matías knows the bombs will raze the old fishermen's district, right where the Roeders live. He places an eye over the sight, clearly spies the concrete platforms of the port between the viewfinder crosshairs and, knowing that there are civilians down there running for their lives, places his finger on the switch that releases the bombs. He checks his watch: four twenty-five in the afternoon. He has less than sixty seconds to consider his next move. He spends it staring at his boots, his parachute harness, his woollen gloves, as if he suddenly felt ridiculous in this costume. And he reaches the conclusion, if it even means anything to catalogue the hotchpotch of primary thoughts that bubble up from the depths of his despair, that he can do nothing against the onward force of events. 'The aircraft is all yours,' Hillard advises. Matías frowns, expels twin streams of air through his nose, expanding his nostrils, grits his teeth for valour, and feels in his throat the emergence of a thick knot that, he senses, will never entirely disappear. He activates the switch, and the bomb bay doors open. 'Bombs away,' he says with the echoing bitterness of someone dictating an epitaph, and from his transparent fishbowl he watches the train of explosive bombs fall, followed by the train of incendiary bombs and, less than a minute later, he watches in terror the flashes of the first detonations, the smoke in the form of mushrooms, the craters on the surface of the harbour which, seen from the nose, suggest the shape and the depth of cavernous eyes that seem to look everywhere and nowhere. Unexpectedly he remembers the words of the priest who taught religion at the seminary school, his lesson about the corruption of bodies lacking in spirit, and he feels himself to be nothing more than that: a body lacking in spirit that conceals its rottenness by bearing the emblems of a country that is not his own. Suddenly the figure of the flaming angel that so impressed him as a child in the square in Trujillo comes to his mind, the sculpture by Edmund Moeller, the young man with one foot standing on the globe and a torch ready to subject it to the law of fire. As the plane sweeps over the city, releasing a second wave of bombs, hitting the neighbourhoods around the port, Matías senses the enigmatic features of that perverse angel surfacing on his face. Perhaps that is why he found the monument so disagreeable when he had it in front of him: it had revealed a prophecy that he was unable to decipher at the time. The one who was blind, he thinks, was not the angel, but him. It is as if he has become a winged emissary like those sent by

God to wipe out the towns of Sodom and Gomorrah, and he shudders as he recalls how that very morning Major General Peter Lewis christened the operation over Hamburg with precisely that name: 'This will be known as Operation Gomorrah,' Lewis announced, and then, seeking to imbue the airmen with courage, he read the passage from the Book of Genesis that Matías had obsessed over in his early adolescence:

> *Then the Lord rained brimstone and fire on Sodom and Gomorrah, from the Lord out of the heavens. So He overthrew those cities, all the plain, all the inhabitants of the cities, and what grew on the ground. But his wife looked back behind him, and she became a pillar of salt. And Abraham went early in the morning to the place where he had stood before the Lord. Then he looked toward Sodom and Gomorrah, and toward all the land of the plain; and he saw, and behold, the smoke of the land which went up like the smoke of a furnace.*

Beneath his feet, Hamburg is exactly that, a furnace, or rather a crematorium, the ineffable outcome of a new outbreak of God's wrath. 'Who are the reprisals directed at this time?' Matías curses silently, before inferring seconds later that they are against him, of course. And now he blames himself for having left his parents' home, for boarding that steamer to New York, for pausing to recover Gordon Clifford's lost belongings, for reuniting him with them. Undoing screws that had no reason to be moved comes at a high cost. He despises himself for having sought to escape a fate that, sooner or later – he now saw – was going to catch up with him. Sometimes fleeing only worsens things: the heroic gesture of marching into the sunset fails to have the lasting effect it invokes. To leave is to disobey, to resign, and all such resignation is penalised with a fate a thousand times more nefarious that takes time to materialise – but it does materialise. Leaving does not heal the wound, it only delays its becoming infected. Where do these voices come from? Are they his? What abyss returns them, from what realm do they emerge to settle fleetingly in the flimsy territory of life? Matías feels how certain scenes from the past become corporeal, take on meaning, generate repulsion. And so he realises at the wrong moment that he has not been transformed into the treacherous bronze angel that vomits fire on the world, but into an even more contemptible monster. Himself. Or the reverse of himself. The legitimate heir of Massimo Giurato, the Italian murderer who trained him to hurt defenceless animals, who instilled in him his astute ability to cause evil, a legacy that for years the son has tried to deny or silence in his head, yet that has progressively emerged over the course of the war and that now, in Hamburg, has reached its apogee. Matías has never told anyone how his father brutalised Edith Roeder – and perhaps continues to do so – how at night, drunk, brutish, he'd come for her, humiliate her bare-fisted, viciously calling her a whore, a German whore, a fucking German whore, swearing that one day he would kill her, and leaving her with wounds that she camouflaged with make-up. Matías remembers those violent phrases and thinks he understands what has just happened: he has tacitly complied with the paternal order, he has unconsciously followed the mandate of the family he hates in order to liquidate the family he consciously loves. He has passed the test of his criminal lineage with flying colours, and only by shattering his most cherished dream has he succeeded in going to meet his inexorable fate. In killing the Roeder family, however, he has also killed himself, or the person he thought he was and now will never be. He wonders if all his relatives have perished in the hecatomb of the bombs, of his bombs. He wonders if there will be any survivors left, just one who, in the future, will remember the fateful summer of 1943: memories that he will be unable to amend, that he will not want to shred, that he will seek to remove like gall stones or tumours. And what about him? Will he, too, remember this? Will he remember clearly what he has done, what he has committed, the sense of sacrilege that now devours him? Hopefully, he thinks, one day he will forget everything. Certain tragedies devour the memory of their victims, dismantle it, imposing a point zero from which everything begins to be told again. The mistake, the only colossal and unforgivable mistake, is to look back, because by digging into gloomy passages one runs the risk of being unable to close up the cracks again and being left at the mercy of the darkness. Matías thinks of Lot's wife and puts his face in his hands. The plane climbs above the black clouds and turns back towards England. They are out of danger now, above the German guns and the rubble of Hamburg. The operation, everyone on the radio agrees, has been a resounding success.

16

'It's going to be interesting living alone in this city again,' I told Antonio.

'I've never lived alone. At this point I'm not sure I could ever get used to it.'

'You can get used to anything,' I said, not entirely convinced by the homily.

'Tell that to my mother. She doesn't want to live alone. Since my dad died, she's applied for a passport for the first time.'

'She's alone? I thought you had siblings in Peru?'

'No... well, yes...'

The contradiction in his words was so jarring that Antonio felt obliged to expand without my needing to ask.

'I've got an older brother... but he lives in the States.'

'Ah, great. What does he do there?' I dug further.

'He's a concert cellist.'

'Oh really? From your mysterious tone I thought you were going to say he was a drug trafficker or, worse, an immigration officer.'

He didn't laugh. The cause of his discomfort soon became clear.

'Not long ago I found out that my brother is adopted.'

I bit my tongue again. Antonio started the engine, lurched forward the few metres that the traffic jam permitted, and continued the story.

'My mother says that one night in Lima, she opened the door to the neighbours' maid, a young lass from the provinces who'd sometimes lend her a hand, asking nothing in return. Her name was Anita. I'd met her once, she was dark-haired, petite. That night she was crying, shaking, covered in bruises. She had thrown herself down a flight of stairs. She was eight months pregnant, it was her sixth attempt at an abortion.'

'What did your mother do?' I asked.

'She took her to the police hospital. On the way there, my mother told the maid that if she didn't want the baby, she would keep it for her.'

'What about the baby's father? Did he show up?'

'That was the problem. Anita had been raped, I think more than once, by a friend of the neighbours' son, a real bastard, if you'll excuse the expression. His father was a politician from I don't remember what party. That's why Anita wanted rid of the baby. If that man happened to find out his son had left her with a bun in the oven, he'd be capable of doing away with her.'

'What a wretch, and how generous of your mother. Someone else might not even have taken her to hospital.'

'My mother was fond of her, but on top of that she'd had a miscarriage herself a couple of months earlier. She was very sensitive around the issue of pregnancy. She and Anita came to an agreement, without saying anything to my old man. He found out once the decision was taken.'

'And the papers? How did your mother manage to get the child registered as her son?'

'My cousin, the cop, spoke with the doctors and sorted it all out. You know what things are like over there, and back then it was even easier. I was born two years later, and grew up believing he was my older brother. His name is Félix.'

'And he knows himself?'

'They told him a few months back. My mother says he took it well. The only thing he said was: "All right, ma. I'd better go, I've got a rehearsal."'

'And why did they take so long to reveal the truth?' I asked, feeling like a predictable host on a TV chat show.

'My dad was opposed. He was worried the folk in the neighbourhood would find out and hassle my brother. It was a good thing Félix turned out a good student. He was constantly receiving scholarships for his high marks, and as soon as he could he went to California on one. He left Peru before I did.'

'How about you, do you play an instrument?'

Antonio laughed.

'Not even the doorbell, maestro. Félix on the other hand loved music since he was a lad. And not the salsa we played at home, but rock, ballads, classical music even. He spent his afternoons listening to cassettes on the player in the kitchen. He'd never come out to kick a ball around with the rest of us, we'd have to beg him to come stand under the goals a while – and then he'd bring his Walkman with him, tucked into his shorts. He played footie with headphones on, the nutter! One time he was almost run over by a truck because he couldn't hear the horn. And when we were a bit older, he didn't drink, he didn't like alcohol. The truth is that when my old lady told me he was adopted it made a lot of sense. Félix was always an outsider, a miracle in that barrio full of stoners and thugs. Look how far he got. My old man always said: Félix is going to be the pride of the Barracones. I hope he got his artistic vein from Anita and not from that bastard who fathered him.'

17

The morning after the divorce, leaving the apartment on Calle de Ferraz to go to Lima for two months, I was early enough to think about saying goodbye to Miguel before heading to the airport. The neighbourhood had become all the more familiar to me thanks to this man with a prodigious – or impaired – memory, whom many treated as if he had a screw loose. When I emerged from the entrance, I saw his red chair was empty. I went into the bakery for a coffee and took the opportunity to ask the owner if he'd seen our friend. He reported that he hadn't been in his usual spot for four days.

'He's never been away for so long,' he mused, passing me the hot cup on a minimalist-pattern saucer on whose chipped edge rested a complimentary biscuit.

'You don't happen to know where Don Miguel lives?' I wondered.

'In the building on the corner,' he indicated. 'He's moved around frequently, but he's always stayed nearby.'

'I thought he'd always lived on Leganitos, since he kept mentioning the street when he talked about the civil war.'

'Sure, but that's because of what happened to his father, didn't he tell you?'

'No, what happened?'

'His father was a fireman during the war years and in service during the bombardment of Madrid. In Leganitos, several buildings collapsed. His father had to recover a score of bodies. In one of the damaged buildings, a gynaecologist had his office; the patient who was there when the bombs began to fall was the girlfriend of Miguel's father, his first girlfriend.'

'She was pregnant,' I jumped the gun.

'That's right. But the father didn't know, so you can imagine how it hit him, first of all finding her dead; second, realising she was pregnant.'

'And how did he learn that?'

'The doctor survived, he told him. He also told him that when the alarms sounded that day, he and the girl ran for the stairs to the cellar, and that's where they were when the bombs hit, the whole building shook, the windows blew in and between the smoke and the commotion of people evacuating, he lost sight of her.'

'How awful for the father,' I surmised, finishing up my coffee.

'Yes, well, later he married another woman and they had Miguel, but, of course, the mother and child didn't get along.'

'Why on earth not?'

'Well, I reckon the mother despised the child for his illness.'

'What illness?'

'I don't know if it's a disability or a congenital disorder, but, you know, Miguel is a bit odd, it's enough to see him and listen to him for a while to realise he's had something his whole life; I don't mean to say there's anything bad about him, of course, he's a good guy, friendly, frank, but there's something a bit dysfunctional there, even if it doesn't justify what his mother did.'

'What did she do to him?'

'Well, Miguel says that as a child she'd beat him for any old thing, she'd give him cold baths, called him a *retard*, left him alone for hours, stuffed him with uncooked food. He's told me this standing right there where you are now, and not once or twice, but ten times at least. He'd say that his mother was an evil woman, that he wished his father's first girlfriend hadn't died in Leganitos, and that if the child she'd been carrying in her belly had been born, then his father, he said, would have been a happier man.'

I took a taxi to the airport, and as my local streets receded behind me I remembered something Miguel had told me one time I ran into him. He retained an intact record of the interventions made by the Madrid firemen in the bombing raid of November 1936. That notebook showed the date, time and place where each fire started, as well as their causes. The firemen noted whether the projectiles had been fired by enemy artillery from a military bastion, or from an aircraft. Without mentioning his father, he said that the firemen could spend days extracting not bodies but blackened body parts from the rubble.

Listening to Miguel, it was inevitable that I remember what I had seen in Lima on December 29, 2001, after the fire at Mesa Redonda, a central market with a succession of shabby arcades that at Christmas time becomes impassable. Days earlier I'd swapped shifts with a colleague at the newspaper in order to take the 31st off and spend New Year's at the beach. In the newsroom, the 29th had been a dreary night in journalistic terms, with scoops conspicuous by their absence, and we had to dig up insubstantial stories and apply the usual 'inflator' to them – finding an angle that gave them a significance they lacked. At 7:20 that evening, a Mesa Redonda stallholder set off a few pyrotechnic devices in a bid to demonstrate his wares. It quickly got out of control. The rockets shot in all directions, spraying sparks that lit other piles of fireworks. Flames began to climb the walls of the market, and by the time people realised what was happening the conflagration had spread to all sides. Minutes before, a watchman had blown the whistle that was used in the event of a looting attempt, so that many vendors, believing their goods might be stolen, instead of vacating the premises, lowered the metal shutters of their stalls and padlocked them, unaware that they were condemning themselves to certain death. Nearly three hundred people lost their lives that night, many of them young people and children who were trapped in the maze of alleys or trampled by the horrified crowd.

The newspaper offices were not far away, so from one of the balconies we were able to follow the flashes of fireworks emerging from a cloud of smoke that slowly began to envelop the neighbouring avenues. We soon realised the terrible scale of the incident. The chief editor ordered us to head over there immediately, without putting ourselves at too much risk, and gather whatever information we could about what would be the most devastating fire in the country's history. I arrived with two photographers, an editor and an intern. The fire brigade was already there, but they were far from being able to control the situation. Two blocks from the market, the first thing that hit us was the stench of burning meat. The worst, however, awaited us further on. A policeman allowed us access to an area where the fire had already been extinguished, but smoke was still billowing and the remains of the victims lay as they had been found. There, the smell was unbearable. The intern gagged when he saw inside one of the stores a tangle of charred people, most of them clinging to beams and columns with skeletal little arms that looked like black stalactites; and he began to vomit when a fireman warned us to watch our step because the floor was covered with a sticky fat produced by the cooked bodies. The flash from one of the photographer's cameras revealed to us how the iron shutters of the shops bore the claw marks and dents of people who had been trapped, unable to escape. After forty minutes, as we turned around to return to the newspaper, in the midst of a desolation unprecedented for any of us, we came upon a last macabre scene: a pile of skinned corpses that would be taken in trucks to the morgue. Some had no visible upper or lower limbs. The firemen dumped them there like sandbags and as they fell on top of each other we could hear the crunch of bones breaking.

I learned so much from Miguel. When Erika met him, she was captivated by his stories of the civil war, and even invited him over for dinner a couple of times, invitations that he graciously declined, making implausible excuses. In the years that followed, the years of my marriage, our chats became more sporadic, but I never stopped seeing him. Every time I listened to him I was left with the feeling that his life was governed by random forces comparable to those I myself had experienced, not only since my departure from Peru but perhaps throughout my entire existence. There was, of course, no equivalence between the catastrophes he had seen at close quarters and my own particular misfortunes, but I was pleased – and a little frightened – to note secret correspondences between the two.

Months after my return to Madrid, with the divorce concluded, I heard that Miguel was in hospital. The bakery owner told me over the phone. I didn't think twice and went to visit. As soon as I entered his ward and saw how much weight he had lost I knew something was very wrong. He claimed to feel absolutely fine, and ready to return home. It wasn't true. He had leukaemia. With this unequivocal diagnosis, the doctor opted not to offer him false hope, predicting he had three to six months left. It was shocking to see him in the bed – that is, out of his usual chair. The afternoons I went to spend with him we entertained ourselves answering the questions on culture, history and society that would come in the Spanish citizenship exam. I read them out loud and he answered them swiftly, not without a touch of sarcasm.

'Where is the festival of La Tomatina celebrated?'

'In Buñol, where else.'

'What is the largest river that empties into the Mediterranean?'

'That's the Ebro, darn it.'

'What is the capital of the Autonomous Community of Galicia?'

'Santiago de Compostela, where the wine resuscitates pilgrims.'

'How many reforms to the constitution have there been?'

'Two, the first and the second one.'

'Where are the Picos de Europa?'

'In Asturias.'

'What key event in Spanish history took place in 1704?'

'We lost the Rock of Gibraltar to Admiral Rooke. But it's less a key event than an Olympic-scale fuck-up!'

'What happened in Spain in 1868?'

'The Glorious Revolution that ended in the dethronement of Isabel II, queen of the three tragic destinies, as Pérez Galdós said.'

Miguel complained that there was nothing in the quiz about the bombardments of the Civil War. 'In this country people forget everything!' he grumbled, pushing his glasses up his nose, demanding that I write a letter of complaint to the authors of the test for failing to include a single question about these events: 'How can someone become Spanish if they've no idea what happened in Spain!' Until the end he maintained his spark. I know of many cases of terminally ill patients who have managed to overcome supposedly incurable ailments; unfortunately this was not to be for Miguel. Within a month of his hospitalisation, after two weeks in which the leukaemia aggressively reduced his energy to a minimum, my good friend expired. No relatives came forward, so I had no choice but to gather Miguel's meagre possessions, take care of the paperwork and deal with the solicitous undertaker who, like the vulture that sniffs out death, turned up within hours. I went to break the bad news to the baker on Calle de Ferraz and we agreed to go to the funeral together the next day. I was leaving when he said 'better take that away' and pointed to the street. He was referring to the rickety red chair still standing on the pavement, which had supported Miguel's body for who knows how many years, and which now, from a corner of the house, seems to watch over me as I write these words.

18

One fine day, not long after Miguel's death, I awoke resolved to move out of the flat on Calle de Ferraz and return the keys to the landlord. I felt ready in spirit, but also financially in need, as the costs of renting the two apartments were rapidly drawing down my savings. In the letterbox, beneath a pile of council notices and promotional leaflets from estate agencies, Thai restaurants, massage parlours and clinics specialising in invisible orthodontics, there was a letter with my name on it. I checked the date: it had been lying there for more than a week. It was from Erika. My first instinct was to toss it in the waste paper basket, but I stopped myself. If it had been an email, a mere click would have been enough to rid myself of the message, but holding the envelope in my hand made it harder not to give in to the temptation to find out the contents.

Entering the apartment, I was surprised by how tidy everything was. Without Erika's belongings it felt spacious once again – and also grey and cold. I missed the presence, on a corridor wall, of the *Portrait of an Artist* we bought in the Pompidou leaving a David Hockney exhibition; I realised that Erika considered the reproduction to be hers, though I had paid for it. I sat down on the sofa in the lounge and tore the envelope down one side. As soon as I unfolded the two handwritten sheets inside, three photographs slipped out onto the floor. I picked them up.

In the first, Erika and I were lying on a bed with purple sheets in a cabin we rented for my birthday, in the Madrid mountains. That was our first year together. I'd forgotten this photo, but on seeing it my memory reconstructed the moment with great clarity. We'd just made love with a fiery passion that left us exhausted. We showered together and she gave me her present: a pair of sunglasses (which I put on for the photo, horsing around). I paused the memory and stopped to observe certain details: the provocative side slit of Erika's dress, my unkempt beard, the ecstatic smiles we offered the camera, evidence of a happiness that I could not at the time ever imagine undone. In the next photo, taken two years later, we are wearing swimming costumes, standing on the deck of a yacht during a trip to Ibiza. It was a sweltering day. Erika leans in for a hug. I'm wearing the same dark glasses. That day we played several games of a dice game called *quispe* on board and we bet, with the captain as witness, that the loser would have to dive into the sea and then strip naked. I lost, but Erika, out of solidarity, or simply because she felt like it after downing four glasses of vodka with orange juice, jumped into the water, took off her bikini, scissored her legs to stay afloat, then braided them with mine and kissed me until we began to sink. In the final photo we are on the terrace of a restaurant on Calle de Orense, drinking beers with some Peruvian friends who've just moved to Madrid. It's a winter's day, judging by the shades of the sky and the coats the group are wearing. Earlier we had spent the day in the Parque del Oeste and, if memory serves me right, in the evening we went to the theatre to see a multi-award-winning musical that I found insultingly banal to the point of falling asleep at the interval.

I picked up the letter and observed Erika's handwriting: each word was separated from the next in good proportion, while the lines respected the margins. There hadn't been many occasions for me to appreciate her meticulous calligraphy, her error-free Spanish, her discipline in keeping sentences short. I held the sheets to my nose, wondering if I would detect an aroma that would remind me of her. And then I began to read.

Berlin, June 30

I don't know if you'll read this letter. I'm not sure if you're still living in the flat on Ferraz. I don't even know if you're still in Madrid. Or if you have the same phone number as before. I hope this letter meets with better luck than the emails I sent and you never replied to. You probably didn't even read them. Well, as you know, I don't like to beat around the bush, so I'll get straight to the point. I'm eight weeks pregnant. Can you believe it? I did two tests as soon as I noticed I was late, and they were both positive. I went to a clinic for a blood test, and that came out positive too. I waited a few days before I told my mother. She said she'd already realised, because she'd noticed that I was restless, nervous. Verdächtig nervös, she said. Obviously, I thought I should tell you, but since you unfriended me on Facebook I guessed you didn't want to know anything about me. I discussed it with my family. My mother reckoned it was my obligation to let you know, my father the opposite. Like (almost) always, I listened to my mum. And like (almost) always, my dad turned out to be right. 'He'll ignore you,' he said. Er wird dir nicht zuhören. I wrote you two emails with the news, but also to let off steam about all the lies from the Madrid doctors. Those idiots, dümmliche!, they assumed I had problems while barely examining me, and ignored the possibility it was a temporary blockage due to stress, as my current gynaecologist told me. That was all: a temporary blockage! Do you understand? All those years I thought the problem was with me – you thought the same – and each month, each time I bled, each of those stains, I felt like my body was reminding me of my error. I knew, inside, that I was capable of bearing a child, and if I opposed alternative methods it was because I didn't have much faith in those doctors. In any case, I didn't want to force maternity. So what did you do with those emails? Did you read them? Did you delete them? Since I never received a reply, I swore to myself I'd never get in touch again, no matter. Nie wieder. And here I am, contradicting myself. And I'm doing so for a very specific and delicate reason. I've decided not to go ahead with the pregnancy. I write that, and I still can't come to terms with it. I didn't decide alone, in case you think that. I thought about it a lot, I talked it over with my family, I read up on it, analysed the issue with a psychological consultant. I have an appointment for next Monday in a private clinic run by a doctor who's a friend of my mother. A discreet, clean place with a small team.

This hasn't been easy, as you might imagine. If anyone knows just how much I wanted to be a mother it's you. But not like this. So kann ich es nicht machen. This pregnancy comes along right when I'm alone and trying to start over both personally and professionally. I've been working for a month and a half at a Swiss-German company that designs office furniture, on a salary four times higher than what I was earning there. It's one of the best companies here. And the office is just five blocks from Alexanderplatz. I still haven't signed a full time contract, but they said it renews each six months if we complete our targets. I can't, I don't want to, let an opportunity like this go. Is that egoism? I prefer to call it honesty. Ehrlichkeit.

But that's not all. There are two basic reasons not to have a child right now: first, I don't think it growing up far away from its dad makes sense. I didn't just want to be a mother, I wanted to have a family, for us all to live under the same roof, for my children to grow up with both their parents, not their grandparents. Can you imagine how exhausting it would be for you to come to Berlin each month to see the baby if you had to? I don't know, it doesn't seem a good idea. And let's not even talk about the financial implications... I'm not sure you could cover these kind of costs.

The other reason has to do with the pregnancy in itself, in how it came about. Yes, I'm talking about that night. Have you ever thought about whether we really wanted me to get pregnant? Did we do it for that purpose? The answer for me is clear: no. We got carried away by our emotions, by the desire to recover something that was already lost. We weren't careful, I know, but it had been so long since we had taken precautions, remember, since we'd been told that I couldn't conceive.

I need you to know something: the time we spent together means a lot to me. I don't regret getting married, none of it. I learned a lot from you, we grew together, we fit each other, I think we were good allies. But in the past two years we changed. Or I changed. There was no specific reason. I began to feel stuck. I felt like I was drowning in a sea of doubt. Those ups and downs were turning me literally crazy. Verrückt! I lost my temper at the slightest thing. I never used to be so hysterical. Work didn't help. You lived in your world, absorbed in your own stuff, always on your computer. A point came when we barely spoke. You didn't even realise how much not being able to get pregnant affected me, you minded your own business. I remember once in the theatre I said to you: I just got my period. The play was about to start. And what did you do? You stood up and left, claiming claustrophobia. On another similar *occasion, you fell asleep. I'm not saying this to throw it in your face. It's just an example of how disconnected we were, and proof that maybe we had rushed into moving in together, getting married without knowing each other well enough. Wir kannten uns nicht gut.*

Could we have gone to therapy? Sure, we could, but it wouldn't have done us any good. That whole rarefied, tense atmosphere, for me it was already a clear sign that things weren't going well. Maybe I was too radical, but I needed to put my own peace of mind first. Someone had to put us out of our misery and it wasn't going to be you.

It wasn't easy. Nothing has been easy. Not the divorce, not the pregnancy, not kickstarting my career all over again – definitely not living with my parents again at the age of thirty-three. I wanted my return to Berlin to mark the beginning of a new, more orderly cycle. I wanted to start over, but not like this, not with ties, not with a pregnancy that prevents me from moving on. I know it sounds harsh, but I've got to accept it. And not only me: we both have to accept it. Wir müssen es akzeptieren.

I hope this doesn't open up more wounds and enables us to close existing ones. Why can't I have a civilised relationship with my ex-husband? Even if it's by post! The truth is that I don't know if this letter is a coherent act or mere foolishness. It doesn't matter. I trust you will appreciate my sincerity.

I send you a hug. Eine große Umarmung.

E.

PS: The photographs were inside a book you gave me. I thought you'd like to keep them.

At eight weeks, two pills are enough to end a pregnancy: one neutralises the production of progesterone, halting the progress of the gestation; the other causes cramping and bleeding until the uterus is empty. This is what a gynaecologist friend explained to me. I phoned him as soon as I finished reading the letter. The second thing I did was to read it again, more slowly, focusing on the lines that had annoyed me, which turned out to be most of them. The pregnancy thing had me perplexed. I recalled all the times we went to bed resolved to become parents, all that bureaucratic, procedural sex, devoid of all sensuality, and I saw her circling in her diary her period of ovulation, talking at breakfast, lunch and dinner of her 'fertility window', and I visualised both of us heading for the bathroom cabinet, night after night, she to take her folic acid tablets, me to take vitamins to increase my sperm quality. And I glimpsed our exhausting visits to the hospital, to the gynaecology department, the faces of the couples in the waiting room, some battered by anguish, others illuminated by joy. Erika would look sideways at the new mothers stroking their months-old bellies and I would mentally compare myself to their partners, wondering if I was in fact the impediment to fertilisation, but then the specialists would assure me otherwise and Erika would leave those white or pale blue or yellow offices devastated, while I would hug her, feeling stupidly virile. I also remembered the last time we made love, without protection, half-drunk, driven not by desire but by an anticipatory nostalgia which – that night – falsely supplanted desire.

As for the news of the abortion, what can I say. It's not every day that you find out in a single letter that you're going to be a father, and then that you're not. Checking the date, I deduced that the procedure must already have taken place, so my fatherhood had lasted a single paragraph. What hurt the most was not having been considered. I understand that Erika had reason to feel frightened, but it was too much to address me as if the conception of this child was none of my business. No question that it was up to her to make the final decision, but wasn't it my right to at least have an opinion, to say whether I wanted to be a father or not, wasn't it a little reckless, if not malicious, to leave me completely out of it? Even though she had zero faith in my possibilities, perhaps I could have worked things out to be able to travel to Berlin once a month; it would have been both sad and arduous to raise a child long-distance, to see it grow up in photos, hug it every thirty days, but I could have made the effort, could have given it a shot. The old Erika would have encouraged me. The old Erika wouldn't have rejected the pregnancy, on the contrary, she'd have said it was *a sign*, and that it was worth staying together because *things happen for a reason*, and I would have believed her and thrown myself into fatherhood with excitement. From what I could glean from the letter, however, esoterism was no longer pertinent to her new goals. For a moment I thought someone else must have written these lines. And what were the expressions in German about? She'd never done this with me before. Were they coded messages? What was she trying to tell me?

For all of these reasons the letter left me with an overriding feeling of ill will that I couldn't and perhaps didn't want to set aside. I was disappointed at Erika's pragmatism, and the – perhaps involuntary, yet nonetheless hurtful – condescendence with which she concluded her words. I could even imagine her haughty expression as she wrote that stuff about *I think we were good allies*. Allies? Could she really not find a better category? Or was she being ironic? But above all, what annoyed me was that, just a few months after the divorce, she was so clearly back on her feet, so in control of her emotions (and apparently of mine, too), while I, although significantly better, remained the one who hadn't got over it yet. I thought about how to reply, but excluded it altogether when I realised that this was exactly what she was after, an answer that would bring her story with me to a neat close, an ending, an epilogue. I retaliated by keeping silent once again. Was it immaturity? Like her, I prefer to call it *honesty*. Two days later I looked for the letter in the drawer where I had banished it and did the only dignified thing I could think of: set fire to it. I flicked the lighter and watched with secret delight as the flame gnawed at the paper, with a voracity matched only by that of the foaming sea on the sand at the nebulous hour of sunset. I also got rid of the photos, not wanting to risk finding them again in the future and suffering a self-destructive melancholy impulse that might lead me to commit some senseless action. On top of that, I'm not one for keeping old photos, at least not these kind of timeless pictures that eternalise or seek to eternalise the moments of fullness experienced by two people who, a while later, having passed through all the stages of grief, end up behaving like strangers who pretend to ignore their shared past.

19

'If you leave, come back,' my dad urged me the day I told him I wanted to study in Spain. I didn't dare to tell him that what I really wanted was to stay there indefinitely. A one-way trip.

'Go on, then,' he said. 'But come back and put into practice what you learn over there.'

He must have suspected my intentions because, right away, trying to make me hesitate, he brought up the name of my grandfather, who had died a year earlier.

'That's what he would have wanted, for you to come back. He'd have told you the same.'

It was the crudest kind of last ditch effort. He knew how much I'd loved my grandfather, how much I admired and respected him. He'd been a spirited military pilot. In 1941 he was sent north to fight in the war with Ecuador and took part in the decisive bombardment of Quebrada Seca, piloting one of the U.S.-made planes they called 'little bulls', from which he saw the celebrated José Abelardo Quiñones, the Peruvian ace, go down in flames. 'Quiñones was a real man! Alone he shot down something like twenty patrols,' the old man would say, proffering figures that differed noticeably from those in the history books, but with a conviction that made them seem all the more real. I don't remember a single lunch in his house that didn't involve anecdotes about the conflict with Ecuador. It was his actions during that war that earned him official honours at his funeral.

'Your grandfather was a real patriot, and you should follow his example,' my dad reiterated.

Playing the patriotism card was another predictable piece of blackmail. My father has always boasted that he has never lived outside Peru. If he goes abroad, it is exclusively as a tourist. Not even in the country's worst periods – the first government of Alan García, the Fujimori dictatorship – did he consider leaving. Despite having experienced episodes of discrimination in the past, he loves Peru, or claims to love it, in a manner that weaves together conviction and fetishism. My sisters and I grew up inducted into this bottomless love, repeating to the point of exhaustion that 'we treat our country with respect and sacrifice' and other such self-invented maxims. More than a chauvinistic sermon, it was the preaching – rather naïve, it is true – of an unshakeable idealist. His perorations did not place so much emphasis on patriotic symbols – to this day he raises the flag on July 28 only because it is obligatory – but spoke continually of giving back. That was the lesson to be internalised: we had to return to Peru *all that it had given us*. A somewhat controversial lesson, because, to give just one example, it was my father – thanks to my mother's supervision – who paid for our school and university education in private institutions that were not at all cheap, and he did so without skimping, with money that did not exactly come out of the state's coffers. But I understand or used to understand the meaning of his words when he lectured us:

'We've got to help this country get ahead, son. We must contribute to its progress. There are many who are getting rich at its expense. Not us. We have to do the patriotic work.'

The day I announced my trip, he again used that abstract figure that seemed to sum up his philosophy of national prosperity. *Patriotic work.* My mother joined in. She liked the idea of having a son studying in Madrid, but not so much the idea of a son who would stay there forever. For her, living abroad was not a symptom of curiosity, but of alienation.

'It suits you to come back,' she cajoled me. 'This is your country, here so many people know you, love you. Here you're someone, you have a name. It would be sheer stubbornness to go and starve in another country when here you've got everything you need to live well.'

In the eyes of both, however, these unquestionable orders felt more like pleas, which represented an extra heavy burden to overcome, because parental orders, after all, are meant to be disobeyed: there is a certain heroism in refusing them. Yet what can be done with parental entreaties but to heed them as far as possible?

My sisters didn't make it any easier for me, either.

'You're going to come back, aren't you?' the younger one implored me.

'Look, the most likely thing is I'll not get used to Spain, and I'll be back before you know it,' I said, knowing it was a lie. I was determined that the plan would work.

'Don't beg him,' my older sister said. 'Don't give him the idea we want to force him to live with us.' She stretched out her arm to flick through the channels on the TV with the remote control. She spoke without taking her eyes off the screen. She was the kind of girl capable of reproaching you for their own indifference, to the point of making you doubt you were even alive. She halted her search on a Turkish soap opera, and would have turned up the volume if it hadn't been for the fact that the button had become unusable from having been mashed for so many years.

'I'm going for a while, not forever,' I said, seeking to head off any possible confrontation with them.

'So work isn't going well, then?' asked my younger sister.

'On the contrary, it's going really well. It's just that… I want a change of air,' I said.

'Oh, give me a break!' chided my other sister. 'Don't give her that. If you want a "change of air" then you go to Cieneguilla, not Madrid.'

'I'm not lying…'

'Then tell her the truth! Tell her that you can't stand Peru, that you're sick of home, that you'd prefer to spend your secret savings traveling round Europe.'

'Traveling? I'm going there to study!'

'Are you really sick of home?' my younger sister asked, her eyes filling up.

'Ha. *Study*,' the other one chipped in.

'It burns you up that it's me who's leaving, doesn't it? You'd love to be in my place, you'd give anything, that's why you get so upset.'

'Look, kid brother, here the only one who doesn't know what the fuck they want from their lives is you, don't get me mixed up in your mess.'

'Do you remember when you were about to go to Australia on a scholarship and you changed your mind because it was "too far away"?'

'I didn't go because I'd already decided to study here!'

'Liar! You gave in cos you're a softie.'

'Stop it! Shut up, both of you!' interrupted my younger sister.

The Turkish soap opera seemed to be taking place on the other side of the screen.

Despite our differences, on the morning I flew to Spain, my older sister was the one who gave me the most heartfelt hug. My younger one gave me a box with playing cards, photos, Peruvian candies and a USB stick with a playlist of songs she'd prepared 'for the plane'. My parents said farewell to me exactly the way they still do each time I return to Madrid after visiting them: with disappointment rather than sorrow. My father's hugs, in particular, have never been able to disguise his unhappiness.

My reasons never persuaded them. When I talk to them for the nth time of how safe the district I live in is, of the free medical care or the enviable public transport system, they remain silent, as if awaiting more decisive arguments to justify my decision to settle so far away. They'd never say it, but I know that I have disappointed them. For them, and for my sisters, leaving Peru amounts to deserting, to betraying their trust, to wasting the education they gave me. They feel that I failed them, that I wasn't with the programme, or that I threw it all away. Up to a certain point, I understand them; my grandparents migrated to the capital, my parents settled in Lima; therefore my sisters and I have to fulfil the responsibility of the third generation: to honour the patrimony bequeathed to us, and to expand it. It was down to us to unite, not to separate. We all assumed that's the way it would be. Until I left.

The last time we all saw each other in Lima, despite the fact my sisters for the most part proved sympathetic to my state of emotional shipwreck, in some of their comments Erika, far from being the driver of the divorce, became, as if by magic, the principal victim of the separation.

'She was the one who left me!' I reiterated, as if it were necessary.

'All I said was that perhaps she's suffering as much as you,' the younger one defended herself.

'You didn't say *perhaps*, you said *for sure*,' I pointed out, hurt.

'But it's natural that we should think of her too,' argued my older sister. 'She's our sister-in-law. Don't expect us to start hating her from one day to the next.'

'But you've seen her all of twice since we got married.'

'Three times,' clarified my younger sister.

'You should put yourselves in my shoes, not in hers.'

'Let's not talk about *should*, eh? You don't come out well,' my older sister retorted.

'Can we change the subject?' I suggested. Now I was the one flicking through the TV channels. It was midday, but I was still in pyjamas. I came to a halt on a news bulletin: the presenter was talking about the recent elections. The images showed the president-elect, beneath his hat, greeting his supporters from a balcony. The electoral authority had just officially declared him the winner.

'These communists are going to bring ruin to the country!' muttered my elder sister, agitated. She seemed to have forgotten the days when she marched against the Fujimori dictatorship in her university years, and knelt down to wash red-and-white flags in the Plaza de Armas alongside her bearded friends from the law faculty at the Catholic university.

'My parents say we're going to turn into Venezuela,' the younger one said, timidly. 'And the currency will crash.'

'This is your first election, right? Who did you vote for then?' I inquired.

'For Keiko,' she said, making a face.

'And you? the elder shot back at me. 'Could you vote from over there?'

'Yes, I did.'

'Knowing you, you're capable of voting for these left-wingers.'

'You clearly don't know me, then. I didn't vote for anyone, I left it blank.'

'That's so irresponsible! Those votes are what have left us with this lowlife. I don't get you. Or do you want the country to turn into Cuba or Nicaragua?'

'I had no idea you were so into international politics.'

'You're just irresponsible,' echoed my younger sister.

'Please, listen to the guy for a minute!' I raised my voice, gesturing at the screen with the remote. 'Do you seriously think this guy is capable of a revolution?'

I snorted in disbelief.

'Well, it's easy to talk about what's going on here from your comfortable spot in Spain,' said my older sister, launching a dart she'd been keeping back.

'What do you think?' I shot back, turning to stare at her. 'That I spend all my time hanging out on pavement cafés, drinking beer and eating tapas?'

'No, I'm talking about…'

'What you really mean to say is that living in Europe is a synonym of luxury for you, right? Don't you read the news? Don't you ever see beyond your nose? You think that in Spain no one has challenges or problems? Do you want to know what I earn each month? Or do you simply assume that people, because they "live in Europe", can't be badly off too?'

'What I think,' persisted my older sister, 'is that you live in a different world. You're going back to Madrid in a few weeks' time, while the four of us are stuck here suffering with these clowns, watching Peru go to the dogs. Putting things like that, little bro, I think that yes, you are far better off.'

I was about to make clear to the two of them exactly in how many ways I did in fact enjoy a lot more 'comforts' when I lived in Lima, but at this point I threw in the towel. It wouldn't have done any good. They've no idea what I'm talking about. They'd have to live abroad to understand it. No immigrant, regardless of having chosen to leave of their own accord, is ever wholly comfortable. You can feel accepted, valued, you can have money, you can even be happy, happier than you were back home – you can feel all that and yet, at the same time, you can perceive the discomfort of uprootedness like a splinter under the skin, something you can never remove however hard you try.

'To top it all, you spend your time on Facebook criticising Peruvians who are here, defending our democracy,' said my older sister, returning to the fray. She had me by the throat.

'So now it turns out that criticism isn't allowed? Is that kind of intolerance what you mean by democracy?'

'Writing that kind of thing from over there seems unwise. And you're just asking for trouble. My friends have been asking me: what the hell happened to your brother?'

'I couldn't care less about such comments. I don't write to be liked by everyone.'

'So then why do you do it?' piped up my younger sister.

I couldn't find an answer to that.

Perhaps the real question was – and remains – why I can't stop doing it, why I feel compelled to put down on paper my opinions about a country I'm no longer sure I belong to. Perhaps writing about Peru is the only way I have to hold on to it, even if this entails an intrinsic paradox, an ambiguity I cannot swerve, since at bottom, however considered my interpretation of what happens there, the country I am speaking of is the one where my childhood, youth and early adulthood took place, it is the country of a man I no longer am. A country I left almost ten years ago and that perhaps only exists in my memory.

'Sometimes there's a certain sense of guilt about living away,' I said.

'You went of your own accord, no one kicked you out,' shrugged my younger sister. She was determined to rub it in.

'What's more, you hardly get in touch,' added the older one. 'Weeks can pass without our knowing anything about you. If we hadn't called you that time, perhaps we wouldn't even have known you and Erika had split up.'

'Just like when we were kids. We had to beg you to come out and play with us.'

In a book somewhere I read a theory that the middle sibling is the one that tends to flee, to stray from the flock, to slip away and complicate their life more than the other members of the cast: they are the independent, unbound, conflicted kid, the claustrophobic one who fights for air, the solitary one who marks out their territory, the neurotic one who feels imprisoned between two others (or between two countries).

After I came to Spain my relationship with my sisters changed, cooled. Without the everyday contact, we only have the past left to us, that is the only link we share. I came to realise this in Lima: our heated discussions, about politics or about whatever, turned increasingly bitter, and the only way to bridge them was to retreat into the memories of the time when we all depended on our parents – the lavish Sunday breakfasts, the stories and songs our grandparents taught us, the carnivals at a resort in the South, our garage sales where we offered any old piece of junk to pedestrians in exchange for coins we spent on pieces of ice dipped in dye called 'Martians', the games in which I suffered early, bloody deaths, the tasteless school shows, the trips and, inevitably, the mythical holidays in Paucarbamba at the Trinidads' house. These well-cemented memories still succeed in counteracting the present nastiness. Without them, the bond with my sisters would be untenable. It's the same with my parents: the best time together is over, we've lived through it, it would be foolish to deny it, everything that once seemed unbreakable has withered away. And if there is one thing to be said about the family fabric, it is that it does not regenerate when it is damaged, it only continues to deteriorate.

'This whole thing will help you to grow up, you'll see,' said my older sister, and patted me on the back.

'Maybe it'll even make you want to come back,' the other one suggested with a mock smile.

I humoured them for a while, but I was overcome with an irrepressible urge to confess right there and then that, despite all the regrets that were eating away at me, with every day that went by my stubborn desire never to live in Peru again was growing stronger. I wondered how they would react.

'Can you change the channel?' asked my younger sister. 'I'm sick of the news.'

20

Antonio was a compendium of stories, both those of others and his own. True or not, each was more fascinating than the last. Not at all like those garrulous taxi drivers who bore you with an insufferable monologue, dragging you into a conversation you have no desire to keep up, and that usually leads to fruitless debates about the future of humanity or other such tiresome matters. Antonio was the very opposite. Like a jukebox that plays songs when you insert a coin into the slot, he would dish out stories as the conversation demanded. He told me that one day he'd had in his cab a short Ecuadorian who, years earlier, had travelled to Japan to seek his fortune and tried his luck in different business ventures. One day he came across an employment agency in the city of Nara, whose owner, a private man who kept a low profile and took care not to be seen in public, entrusted him with the premises and moved to another province. The Ecuadorian ran the agency with the greatest of ease, unaware that the Latin American girls he assigned to different houses to provide domestic service were actually being surreptitiously paid for sexual services. Some middle-ranking members of the Yakuza, the Japanese mafia, were among his clients. The Ecuadorian answered the phone without the least idea that he was conversing with bloody-handed hitmen, merciless drug traffickers, in short, criminals of the worst kind. A neighbour alerted the police to the presence of 'a South American who traffics in women and is in cahoots with gangsters'. The cops descended on the office, handcuffed him without even asking his name, and three days later a summary court sentenced him to twelve years in prison for pimping and trafficking in women. Everything happened so quickly that before the Ecuadorian could even protest, he was already sitting in a cell, wearing nothing but a blue jumpsuit, in Nagoya prison, notorious for housing the biggest names in the Japanese underworld and for the bestial violence with which the old lags greet the newbies. One night he saw an inmate slash another's face open with a screwdriver for no reason. 'It was the baptism,' he told Antonio. The drama did not end there. On the very same day he had been admitted to prison, his wife had been admitted to a hospital in Nara to give birth to their son. Six years later, his sentence having been reduced for good behaviour, the Ecuadorian was released on condition that he leave Japan immediately and never set foot there again. He didn't even have time to say goodbye to his family. He moved to Spain and started a new life. When he told Antonio his story, his son was already thirteen years old, and he'd never seen him in person.

Another time, a Colombian passenger with a distinct limp told him how he'd survived being shot in the back. He was the youngest of seven children of a wealthy Bogotan businessman, whose wife had died years earlier. On the day in question, the young man and his father were alone at home, a mansion that occupied half a block in the Macarena neighbourhood. A squad of six masked men broke down the door and forced them into the basement, where the safe was kept. The businessman, handcuffed to a chair, refused to give them the code, and they beat him with their rifle butts. After a few minutes, frustrated at the delay, the criminals started to bicker: three of them were in favour of killing the two hostages and getting the hell out of there, while the other three wanted to continue torturing the millionaire until he revealed the combination. Suddenly, the son was able to escape his restraints, and amidst the confusion got up and ran for the door. One of the assailants, who appeared to be the leader, ordered his second-in-command to shoot the boy, but the subordinate challenged him, saying: 'Why don't you do it yourself?' At that point the lad, the youngest son, skidded to a halt, recognising the plaintive voice of his eldest brother, who had been estranged from the family for months because his father had refused to provide his son with a large sum of money, fearing that he was involved in drugs. The younger son turned around, identified his older brother's eyes through the balaclava and shouted his name, exposing him. The father turned pale. 'Is that you, you bastard, is that you?' he shouted, not quite believing or accepting that his own son was one of his executioners. The boss pulled his gun from his belt, fired a first shot into the hooded brother's head and another into the businessman's heart. Both were killed instantly. When the younger son tried to make a break for it, two bullets knocked him to the ground. The first bullet pierced one of his lungs from the back, exiting through the armpit; the second severely bruised his left leg. The criminals thought he was dead and dashed out of the house before the neighbours arrived, alerted by the shooting. Seconds earlier, one of the robbers had managed to open the safe: it was empty. To avoid being robbed, the old man cautiously hid his wads of dollars inside the stuffing of the upholstered living room and dining room chairs. The news was widely reported in the tabloids and on television. The boy never fully recovered and was sent to Spain by his family, given the risk of reprisals. Some years later it was revealed that the assailants were members of a division of the federal police. By then, the son had already changed his identity.

SIX

Gordon Clifford and Matías met for the third time on November 4, 1943, almost three months after the events of Operation Gomorrah. Prostrated on a bunk bed in the psychiatric ward of Lake Placid Hospital in New York, under the effects of sedatives, Matías did not register his friend's presence. It was Lieutenant Colonel Robert Ellsworth who had contacted Clifford to update him on the boy's whereabouts. He got lucky. Earlier, in the last days of July, he had telephoned him without success when Matías returned from Hamburg in the state of shock that had so worried his colleagues and superiors at the Molesworth base. Ellsworth had failed to reach the banker when he wanted to inform him that Matías, now supposedly recovered, had applied to Major General Peter Lewis to be discharged on the grounds of 'moral unfitness' to continue in the service. On both occasions Gordon Clifford's phone rang but went unanswered. Clifford had left it off the hook, not wanting to be inter-rupted while he cared for his wife, Manuela Altamirano, who had contracted bacterial meningitis in the Long Island hospital where she had been hospitalised for years. In the early hours of the eighth day of her illness, at the

end of a long night of vomiting, convulsions and excruci-
ating neck pains that not even the most powerful antibi-
otics could cure, Manuela died in her husband's arms.
Two nights after her death, despite still having no wish
to talk to anyone, Clifford reluctantly put the telephone
receiver back in its place. Twenty minutes later it rang. It
was Ellsworth.

The following morning, entering Matías' room,
Clifford found him still under sedation. He spent some
time contemplating his friend's cadaverous face, the
forehead criss-crossed by furrows, the prominent cheekbones, the parched lips. When after half an hour Matías
finally opened his eyes, he recognised the black bracelet
on the right sleeve of Gordon Clifford's jacket, and this
was enough for him to understand that Clifford was
recently widowed. He said nothing, and nor did the
banker really expect him to do so; indeed, he wasn't sure
what to expect at all from this sick young man whose
appearance bore no relation to the vigorous Matías he
had persuaded to enlist for the war two years earlier.
Clifford sat on the edge of the bed, sought a gap between
the white sheets and took the boy's head in his arms, as if
in a Renaissance painting. As he embraced Matías, he felt
as if he were receiving an injured bird. Injured, and caged.
But he had wept so many tears over the death of Manuela
Altamirano that he could only react to the physical transformation of Matías with an arid melancholy.

The attending physician, Dr Bernard Larkin, made
an appearance, but Clifford could only fix him with an
incriminating look, as if to ask him what had been done
to Matías, and to assure him that no argument, however
scientific, could appease his indignation. Dr Larkin, who
had been following the airman's progress since his arrival
at Lake Placid, asked Clifford to accompany him to the
corridor 'to discuss the patient's condition in private'.

With a gesture, Clifford let Matías know he'd be back right away, and received a crooked smile in response. Clifford spoke with Larkin for around forty minutes. This was only the first of the testimonies he would gather to reconstruct what had happened and understand how his dear friend, his adopted son, had turned into this wreck of a man.

On the evening of July 25, emerging from the B-17 on its return from the bombing mission over Hamburg, Matías was immediately taken to the Molesworth base infirmary by order of the *All Americans* captain, Dave Hillard. The lieutenant was trembling violently and sweating profusely as he berated himself, calling himself 'murderer, murderer' while at the same time stammering out the excuse that he was 'just following orders'. The conflicting voices left him gasping for air. As the orderlies undressed him, they noticed that his skin was grey, as if his body was coated with a dense layer of dust. The base doctor, Gregory Savage, concluded that he was suffering from shell shock and prescribed sleep treatment. It took him a week and a half to wake up, shortly after Operation Gomorrah had concluded. Three-quarters of Hamburg had been reduced to rubble by the U.S. Eighth Air Force and the Royal Air Force, killing 45,000 people (although the initial rumours spoke of more than 200,000). Matías remembered none of it. Little by little, flashbacks began to appear, at first as single images in isolation, but then woven together until they formed a nightmare narrative that played constantly, like a film on a loop. He was haunted not only by the macabre memories of the thirty-seven minutes of his participation in the mission, but by the terrible foreboding of what had happened next, what he did not see.

By the summer of 1943, the inhabitants of Hamburg had got used to seeing enemy planes overhead, but felt secure in their belief that they would carry on their way to Lübeck, Kiel or Rostock. Most continued to follow the safety precautions, but many no longer ran to the public bunkers when they heard the air raid sirens, instead remaining where they were and carrying on with their work. The authorities had predicted that, were a bombardment to occur, it would be at night and would be led by the British Lancasters; they hadn't counted on a daytime raid by the U.S. bombers. An obligatory blackout was imposed after 7 p.m. On the roads, drivers passed each other like shadows, their headlights covered with hoods that only let the light through a tiny opening. Residents had to switch off their lights when the alarm sounded. Smoking in the street was not permitted. However, this very darkness, rather than functioning as a camouflage shield, became an invitation to indiscriminate bombing.

Over nine days and nine nights, between July 25 and August 3, the Americans and British released thousands bombs over Hamburg – a calculated mix of explosive and incendiary shells – triggering fires that, combined with the effects of an unseasonably dry summer, acquired such strength that a conflagration on a previously unimaginable scale was unleashed. The centre of the firestorm reached temperatures up to 1,400 degrees Fahrenheit, and the flames grew to such a height that the pilots could feel their heat. The firemen were unable to contain so many simultaneous fires, and in any case the water plant feeding the mains pipes was the first site to be hit; in addition, reaching the worst-hit areas became impossible as rubble filled the streets. By the time the fire engines and hoses came into action, it was too late: a voracious red tide was advancing out of control, feeding on the inflammable material in the building roofs. As it ran up against the walls, the tornado of fire would change course, spreading to other districts, the winds tearing up trees by their roots, flattening billboards, shattering cornices as if they were papier-mâché, causing cars to explode, and turning people into human torches. In just fifteen minutes the districts of Hammerbrook, Hamm, Billwerder Ausschlag, Sankt Georg, Borgfelde and Rothenburgsort were razed, together with a number of residential areas in Eilbek, Barmbek and Wandsbek. In the mansions in the two or three more distant neighbourhoods that the flames did not reach, parents turned up the Wagnerian operas on the radio, and made their children read *Alice in Wonderland* or *The Happy Prince* to distract them from the howling of the air raid sirens, while they drank coffee on their summer balconies, their gazes fixed on the horizon from where the terrifying glare was coming, not yet reckoning with the fact they would have to explain to their children, as they grew older, why this had happened.

The second wave of bombs shook the buildings to their very foundations: doors were blown off and windows torn from their frames, enabling the winds to carry the flames deeper inside the homes. There, the red tide shattered the brick walls, exploded glass bottles and, if it reached the cellars that served as bomb shelters, which fatefully happened in almost all the buildings affected, it set alight the coal stored there, cooking alive the dozens of men, women and children huddled on their blankets on the floor.

In the port, old Karsten risked leaving the dockyard despite the exhortations of his companions. He had shut himself up with them, assuming that the bombardment would last fifteen or twenty minutes, but when he saw that there was no let up, he did not think twice: he opened the door, and left, saying he had to protect his family. Once outside, he was shocked to see the sky filled with red and black clouds from end to end, without a single crack of light. He watched open-mouthed as warehouses and sheds burned, as bridges collapsed, as trains sank into the docks as if swallowed up by an underwater creature. He was afraid, hesitated, almost retreated, but finally slipped through a narrow exit from the loading area. Once on the promenade he heard the monotonous roar of anti-aircraft batteries firing on planes and saw a plane hurtling into the river with the speed of a comet, leaving behind a curved wake that was slow to dissipate. Clusters of bombs began to explode around him, like a chain of brief but intense earthquakes. Old Karsten eventually reached the battered Sankt Pauli district, and climbed to the top of a mound of debris to try to get a better idea of what was happening. He was presented with a panoramic view that chilled his blood. Matías' grandfather could not believe his eyes. He had thought that the bombardment was confined to the port area, but now he discovered that the whole city was in flames. Everywhere he turned, his eyes were greeted by a hellish spectacle. Ash was falling everywhere. In the window openings of the very few buildings still standing, the curtains were burning, swaying in the gale-force winds. Men were breaking down doors to flee from their homes, carrying leather suitcases in their hands: some were instantly swallowed up by the red tide; others, wrapped in wet towels, managed to reach the street, but then became trapped in the bubbling asphalt and began to flounder and melt. He saw people running wildly through the dust with their hair scorched, their clothes torn off by the fire-induced gusts, refusing to let go of the aluminium buckets in which they carried provisions, and succumbing to the storm in moments. He saw men mutilated, covered in phosphorus, begging for water. He saw crazed women grab their children by the hair and throw them into the ponds, even if they could not swim, for that was preferable to seeing them scorched by the whirlpools of fire. He saw living men who resembled dead ones, and dead men who seemed to be alive. He saw two horses on fire, bolting from a transport yard, whinnying in pain or madness in the dark. He saw three baby's prams fly through the air as they turned to ash. Looking over towards the Trostbrücke, he saw a Bösendorfer piano cross the skies and crash against the pedestal of the statue of Count Adolphus III. He saw fragments of gravestones from the Ohlsdorf cemetery, now pockmarked with craters. He heard the desperate cries of people trapped in bunkers that, their entrances blocked by rubble, had become scalding prisons. Those who managed to escape melted into the boiling pavements, converted in minutes into pools of human fat. The cataclysmic scenes were so atrocious, so grotesque, that old Karsten, disoriented as he was, felt his strength leave him altogether. Gradually, the explosions came from further and further away and the fire had begun to turn towards Altona, having consumed the densely populated district of Sankt Pauli. He slid down the pile of rubble and walked for a long time on a zigzag path, avoiding the flames, striving to divine amidst the towers of smoke the former pattern of the streets. On the lintel of a pair of doorposts that had not yet collapsed, he saw plaques with numbering that now made no sense. All around him the ground was burning, in the middle distance he could hear cries, pleas, creaking, objects, perhaps signs, detaching from their structures and crashing to the ground. He inadvertently kicked a can of lard and only then did he remember that he had not eaten for two days, as he had not been able to make use of his weekly ration card. He was not hungry, however. He inhaled a smell of burning tar that made him screw up his nose. A cluster of arching trees and the outlines of half-ruined yet identifiable façades told him he was on Bernhard-Nocht, his own street. He carried on, a void in his chest that grew bigger with every step. His heart was beating frantically, but when he turned into what he assumed was the last block and found a mountain of rubble where only hours before his building had stood, in whose basement his family had taken shelter from the bombing, his heart stopped, as if it had been abruptly replaced by a piece of ice on the verge of cracking. A fireman in a gas mask from the fire protection police stood in his way. Karsten was ready to fight to get inside and look for his family. Then he saw a second fireman emerge from the ruinous depths, smeared with soot, walking wearily, as if he were carrying an intolerable weight. Old Karsten recognised him and started waving his arms. 'Hey, Walther, over here, over here!' It was Walther Berger, the eldest son of Alfred Berger, a colleague from the dockyard who lived in the outskirts. The lad approached, snorting through his mask, steel helmet under his arm, gloves smeared with grime. 'Did you see them, were they in the cellar?' he asked Walther Berger as soon as he was near enough. The other lowered his head, not wanting to meet the old man's trembling eyes. 'Tell me you've seen them,' he begged, 'tell me they're alive!' The young fireman looked up, wiped his mouth with the sleeve of his uniform and spat out the only expression he could formulate: 'I'm sorry, Mr Roeder, I'm really sorry.' Karsten's dumbstruck face contracted into a stunned grimace. 'I have to see them, let me through, I have to see them,' he grunted. Walther Berger dropped his helmet and caught him in his arms. Old Karsten tried to break free, and almost succeeded, his muscles, although tired, still responding. Soon two more officers rushed over, and only between the three of them did they manage to contain him. Then he collapsed and began to cry out uselessly to his wife Ingeborg, his children; his grandchildren; his ageing mother, Helga. His howls were unintelligible. 'They're dead, sir!' Walther Berger told him. 'I have to see them, do you understand?' the old man groaned. 'Let me see them!' he bellowed, incredulous, beside himself. 'There's nothing to see there, do you understand, they're dead, they're charred,' Walther blurted out. Grandfather Karsten started, left off his whimpering, shook his shoulders vigorously to free himself and looked at them, perplexed. Walther Berger guessed his thoughts exactly and lowered his brow again before finishing: 'They weren't killed by the collapse, Herr Roeder, it was the fire... their bodies are... unrecognisable.' The combination of the fireman's words, or the parsimony with which they were uttered, devastated him. For the remainder of the day he stood at one end of the street, stranded on a pile of rubble, watching the emergency brigades at work, waiting irrationally for a sign that would disprove the version of events he had received. He thought of Edith, his only living daughter. He thought of Matías, his Peruvian grandson, and shivered as he realised that he would no longer have any relatives to introduce him to, no house to welcome him into, no town to walk through together the day he came, if he came at all. That was the last thought to occupy his mind before it emptied out altogether. The chaos and whorls of scalding clouds were growing closer. No one noticed the grandfather's absence when he left three hours later, silent and incomplete. No one was interested in the identity of his body when it washed up two days later, floating in the waters of the Elbe, close to the wreck of the Blohm & Voss shipyard, his eyes eaten out by fish. And naturally there was no one to miss him, no one to enquire about him in hospitals, infirmaries or convents, and no one to lift a finger to give him a Christian burial.

Matías emerged from the sleep cure in the base infirmary without knowing any of this, yet he somehow intuited it, as if his grandfather had telepathically shared with him a blurry vision of what he had seen. What old Karsten had borne witness to, however, was only a fraction of the damage caused to Hamburg. Once Operation Gomorrah was over, it was difficult to know when it was dawn and when it was dusk, because for a couple of weeks afterwards so much of the sky was covered by a thick, unmoving black cloud, which further hampered the rescue efforts and worsened the odyssey of the survivors as they struggled to recover their belongings. Old Karsten was no longer there to see any of that. Nor did he see the men and women with faces swollen from their burns who criss-crossed the avenue like wraiths, shooing away the sparks that thronged in the air, calling out loud for their family members, still trying to believe they'd find them alive. He didn't see the piles of naked bodies with blackened feet, so stiffened they seemed to be stacks of articulated mannequins. He didn't see the dead as they began to decompose, their fetid stench attracting repugnant hordes of rats scurrying among the distended bodies, and the slow swarms of thick-winged green flies copulating on the rotting skin of these lifeless beings. He didn't see the roasted children on their twisted bicycles. Nor the men asphyxiated inside the metal remains of their cars, their rigid, purple hands still clinging to the wheel. Nor the woman without a head who, seated on a bench on Hammer Park, continued to breastfeed the baby that survived in her arms. He didn't see the police officers in green uniforms administering the coup de grâce to the dying who lay groaning in the streets. He didn't see the stopped clock on the disfigured tower of St. Michael's Church, nor the enormous bronze bells tumbled in a heap at the foot of St. Nicholas' Church, turned into a great smoking pyre. Both churches had burned with the grandeur with which such temples burn, as if the faith, the sacred rituals, and the words pronounced by the thousands of faithful who over the centuries gathered there seeking relief or some immaterial form of redemption had gone up in smoke with them. He didn't see the thousands of thin strips of aluminium foil, blackened on one side, that littered the parks erased by the firestorm: the English Lancasters had released them together with the bombs in order to neutralise Nazi radar, creating magnetic fields that prevented the German radar from intercepting the Allied aircraft. The survivors believed these strips could be toxic and took care not to touch them. The planes also dropped leaflets printed with figures showing why Germany would lose the war. But old Karsten didn't see any of this. He didn't see the kids no older than the war itself out of their minds cleaning the inside of a three-storey building without a roof, windows or walls, all its piping exposed like the skeleton of a doll's house. He didn't see the black crosses that indicated the spots where human remains had been buried. He didn't see the chimneystacks emerging bizarrely from an under-ground metropolis populated by the dead. He didn't see the bandaged women scavenging voraciously through the weeds and piles of rubbish for any reusable item to trade on the black market for potatoes, a bowl of soup, a bundle of firewood, a bunch of dirty vegetables or a bar of soap. For many of them there was no alternative but to prostitute themselves in exchange for a slice of stale bread and margarine or a handful of roasted chestnuts to take home to their children. He didn't see the execution of the looters and of all the other outlaws who, seeking to profit from the generalised misfortune, stole other people's coats, cases of wine, radios or household goods. He didn't see his lifelong neighbours, the Biermanns and the Görings, join the diaspora of a million people who in the months that followed had to move along deserted roads through barren countryside, unable to explain how their prosperous city had become, in the blink of an eye, an inhospitable no-man's-land. It was not only that they had lost their place in the world, but that, even if Hamburg could be restored in the future, brick by brick, with or without the help of the British, it would never again be the same city where most of them had been born, grown up and achieved a reasonable standard of living. Old Karsten did not see these men and women walking barefoot, in rags, in the same clothes as they had been wearing the night the air raids began. They were leaving with their children in their arms, their honour sullied, yet cursing not the Allies but Hitler, certain that the collapse of the Third Reich was now inevitable, and wondering whether his defeat was not, in a sense, also their own. They did not believe they deserved such a harsh punishment, and they were aggrieved by the precarious situation they now faced, but nor would they allow anyone to treat them as victims. On the day they boarded the army trains bound for exile in Bavaria, they did not have to wait for the locomotives to start running to feel that their exile had begun. Huddled in those filthy carriages, they caught their last glimpse of Hamburg's ruined skyline and, although they no longer felt any sense of belonging to what they saw around them, they said goodbye to it with the surrendered and absent eyes of those whose homes have been destroyed.

Old Karsten didn't see them go. Nor did he see how the prisoners of the Neuengamme concentration camp were taken from their captivity and set, day and night, to clearing the disaster area with picks and shovels. In addition to lifting concrete blocks under which corpses and unexploded bombs could be found, they were responsible for cutting down hedges and anything else that might encourage the spread of fire. He didn't see them enter the basements and bomb shelters, where they would vomit as they stumbled over pieces of rotting flesh, heaps of maggots or pools of human fat, and had to cover their faces as they raked up the ashes of countless dead which they would later toss into the embers of the final bonfires. Matías' grandfather never saw what happened to his family. When the fireman Walther Berger entered the building's cellars he found the Roeders burnt to a crisp. The corpses were tightly embraced, and he shuddered at the thought of their last moments alive, deprived of the oxygen that the storm had sucked out of the cellar. Some bodies were prematurely mummified, others terribly deformed, shrunken to a third of their original size, and, worst of all, three or four of them made up a lumpy, mineral-hard, ochre mass in which it was impossible to discern who was who.

Nor did Matías' grandfather see how, after a few months, the redstarts and jays began to chirp again in the musty gardens of Jenischpark. He didn't see how the moss sprouted, how the ivy climbed the walls again, how the bulbous buttercups, the blue-leaved chickweed and the dwarf mallows bloomed out of the warm ashes of the unforgettable dead. He didn't see how the citizens of Hamburg returned to saying good morning and good evening to each other using the *moin*, that typical northern greeting which, since 1933, had been dropped from the German vocabulary to make room for the 'Heil Hitler!' And nor did he see the British soldiers, the Tommies, occupy the city following the inexorable collapse of the National Socialist regime, taking over the manor houses of the better-off Germans and applying to the residents the *Fragebogen*, a list of 133 questions designed to determine the degree to which they collaborated with the regime, and thus to 'denazify' them. He didn't see the families of the newly arrived British officers reading and memorising the humiliating manual on how to deal with the Germans, which contained warnings such as: 'Germans are to be avoided', 'do not walk next to them, do not enter their houses', 'do not play sports with them or attend any social event they attend', 'do not be polite, this will be seen as a weakness', 'do not show hatred, they will be flattered', 'express yourself sharply to them and keep a correct, dignified distance', 'do not fraternise with them'.

Doctor Gregory Savage wanted to send Matías to a psychiatric hospital in London but he refused. He wanted to be medically discharged, then discharged from the forces, to return to New York and never hear from the Air Force again. Despite the severity of his mental state, he had long intervals of lucidity, and in one of them he blackmailed Dr Savage into discharging him if he did not want Major Lewis to learn of the booming business he had built up dealing in morphine and drugs seized from German prisoners, methamphetamine-derived substances that the Nazis gave their younger soldiers to keep them awake, to stop them feeling hungry, and to make them believe they were invincible. At first, Savage proclaimed his innocence – 'that's slander!' – but after a few minutes, seeing Matías so determined to turn him in, he hastily signed the papers.

When he presented his discharge request, Major Lewis sought to dissuade him, reminding him that he might be in line for a Distinguished Service Medal together with a promotion, a command position that would keep him away from flights. However, Matías not only felt immune to this genre of military vanities, but actively despised them. 'Wearing this badge on your lapel, lieutenant, is tantamount to being a hero for posterity,' said Lewis, believing that this argument would tilt the conversation in his favour. Matías was calm enough not to tell him to go to hell and, remaining polite, asked him to expedite his resignation from the service. 'It's a pity, we're losing our best bomber,' Lewis emphasised, shaking his hand, and those apparently complimentary words only confirmed his decision to get out of there as soon as possible, even if he didn't know where to go, or what to do, or where to start. He dismissed out of hand the option of becoming a commercial pilot, which Gordon Clifford had spoken to him excitedly about in that bar on Baxter Street the night he had encouraged him to join the Air Force. He didn't want to get on a plane ever again, let alone wear another uniform. Nor did he want to seek out Gordon Clifford, not right now at least: a part of him laid the responsibility at the banker's door for everything that he had experienced in Germany and, as long as this feeling lasted he preferred to avoid a reunion. He also discarded the option of taking a boat back to Peru, to Trujillo, to the hacienda in Chiclín: he couldn't look at his mother without feeling like a criminal, and even if he did look at her and managed to put into words what had happened in Hamburg, what could he expect from her but utter repudiation? He did not even want to see his father; in fact, he did not want to see anybody, or to be seen by anybody, or to explain his behaviour, or to outline a plan for the future, or to set himself any deadlines.

He returned to New York and, although he now had enough money to stay in a comfortable hotel, he chose to go back to the boarding house on Madison Street in the Lower East Side. Mrs Morris was perturbed by his changed appearance and his attitude, which oscillated between petulant and apathetic. It was him, but he seemed like someone else. Even so, she was glad to host him again, though her joy would soon meet with serious impediments. At first, the signs of Matías' pathological trauma only manifested themselves at night, in nightmares from which he awoke screaming profanities. Frightened residents of the boarding house would turn on their bedside lamps, believing there had been a robbery in the neighbourhood. Then followed the endless episodes of weeping, at all hours. Matías would hardly leave his bedroom, saying that his life was in danger out there. Some tenants began to complain to Mrs Morris that the locks to their rooms had been broken and the clothes in their wardrobes had been rifled. The feeling of impending disaster drove Matías to act in this way. He was suspicious of strangers, believing that a government spy sent by the high command lurked among them, bent on taking him back to the airfields and forcing him to climb back into a B-17 and drop bombs and kill people until the end of the war. This led him to rummage through other people's belongings to see if he could find any hard evidence to support his suspicions. Sometimes, returning from shopping, visiting the doctor or attending church, Mrs Morris would find him in the entry, and she would be startled by the bewildered expression on his face, and much more so by his interrogating her about where she had been and who she had seen. However, there were better days, when his apprehension would fade, and then Matías would go out to look for work, or say that's what he was doing, and when he returned he would share his supposed advances with Mrs Morris, and she would take advantage of the moment of ease to prepare a meal, open a bottle of wine, turn on the radio, put on some music, some Bing Crosby, or an episode of *The Right to Happiness*, and though she saw Matías as a son, a son she might have given birth to at fifteen or sixteen, on some of those evenings, since the boy had quickly grown into a vigorous man, Mrs Morris would succumb to the passing temptation to fantasise about him in intimate

situations, and wait up for him, lipstick on, hair flirta-
tiously loose, dressed in girlish nightgowns she bought
with the excuse they were a wedding present for a niece,
but after a time she would give up, return to her room to
change into her baggy flannel pyjamas and remove her
make-up, feeling foolish.

Little by little Matías got used to going out more. At
first he would walk only a few blocks in the mornings,
either to Seward Park or Corlears Hook Park. Nodding
tersely in response to the greetings of passers-by was the
limit of his socialising. Then he started spending whole
days in the tumultuous streets of Chinatown, and after
that he began to lose himself late into the night in the
bustling clubs of Delancey Street. It took him longer to
return to the run-down pubs of the Bowery, not to throw
darts and bowl, as he used to do in the past with Steve
Dávila and Billy Garnier, but to play poker, take another
drag on the cigarette, chat with the barmen, or drink a
couple of beers, rapidly growing to seven or eight, and
then the glasses of gin, the shots of bourbon, and a bit
of cocaine provided by a local, and then the mood in
the boarding house would turn grim as he would return
drunk, swaying, and the alcohol and the drugs unleashed
fits of anxiety with ever more unpredictable effects. More
than one resident left, telling the landlady it was impossible to live with someone so out of kilter. She would
lecture him, telling him that if he continued to cause her
trouble he would have to find himself a hole to live in,
but Matías would soften her up with grovelling apologies
and promises of good behaviour. Then after two weeks
he would relapse, losing himself for days on end in those
same pubs and decrepit bars, also frequented by prostitutes from the neighbouring brothels who saw in him
not only a generous client who would flatter them with
a drink, but also a highly entertaining raconteur who

would dazzle them with his stories about the war, because Matías only talked about the war when he drank, and the more he drank, the more he talked, and he spoke to the point of tears with this audience of whores and drunks who, in the middle of the night, no longer knew if all these dramatic accounts of bombs, collapsing buildings, fires, dead civilians and destroyed cities were true or if they were just the delirious, if rather well-spun, tales of the neighbourhood madman. Several of these prostitutes were turned on listening to the ex-lieutenant recount his adventures up there, and did not hesitate to seduce and service him in the sordid compartments of the toilets, the poorly lit alleys nearby, or behind the bushes in a suburban park. This was an irresistible novelty for Matías, because during the war, whether out of respect for Charlotte Harris or just to avoid emulating Massimo Giurato's adulterous practices with the whores of Trujillo on Jirón Sosiego, he had never gone with the airmen who headed off to London some Fridays to visit brothels of all kinds, from the most select to the most ordinary, where they mounted legendary bacchanalia from which they emerged with a placid smile that remained fixed to their faces until they returned to base the following morning. On such nights he would remain with Kenny Dodds, playing rounds of cards in the barracks.

One of the prostitutes listened to Matías with particular interest: Helen Anker, daughter of a Dutch father and Dominican mother, who knew how to put men who got cocky with her in their place. Not only that, but she stayed with him until he fell asleep on the bar with a half-drained drink at his elbow, and sent him off with trustworthy taxi drivers who took him back to Mrs Morris's boarding house. They began to see each other outside of the bars, and to both of their surprise the mutual attraction flowed as well by day as by night, in light as much as in darkness. From one day to the next, Helen Anker began to visit him at the boarding-house, and, far from going unnoticed, her presence attracted the accusing – even envious – glances of the whole neighbourhood, especially of the prudish neighbours, including Mrs Morris, who, from the window ledge observed Helen cross the threshold with far too deep a cleavage for her taste, and then followed through the walls the clacking of her heels on each step, until after a few hours, hearing the creaking of the bed springs and the eloquent moans of the girl, instead of getting angry and reprimanding the lovers, she would run to put on her youthful nightgowns again, return to bed, imagine herself sitting astride her tireless twenty-three-year-old lodger, caressing her pale nipples, touching herself unashamedly beneath the sheets, heatedly murmuring vulgar and sinful phrases she would never have dared to say in public, and got moist feeling like a sinner herself, a harlot, and she prayed, contrite, wishing that Matías would soon suffer the nightmares and nervous disorders again, for if there was a greater torture than to hear him cry at night, it was to hear him fornicate with 'that indecent woman who has brought dishonour to this house'.

And so it came to pass: Matías' exhausting dreams returned, and with them the tremors, frayed nerves, incessant migraines and stubborn belief that someone was out to do him harm. In the dreams he was assailed by livid faces lacerated by fire, monsters that emerged with bewildering precision and that he was unable to banish, however many sedatives he ingested or however hard he covered his head with the pillow. This led him to drink as much as three or four cups of coffee at night to avoid sleep altogether. His insomnia and wakefulness, however, were worse, because they were filled with macabre visions not of the future but of the past, visions in which all kinds of barbarities occurred and he would wickedly unleash his own, then weep, curse himself, break objects, tear his knuckles against the wall. 'My head is broken, it's like a city that no one will rebuild, a city that must be abandoned,' he would say to Helen Anker on nights when the crises granted him a respite. 'Memories of horror can fade, but not the horror itself. In England, a major once told me that horror leaves men on the brink of either cynicism or unreason: I feel I am on the brink of both.' This is how Matías rambled on. Helen Anker consoled him by urging him to find a doctor, words that triggered in him a rage she found unforgiveable. One night she became so insistent, threatening to knock on Mrs Morris' door and call an ambulance, that Matías, beside himself, grabbed her by the shoulders and slapped her across the face so hard that he cut open her cheek and bruised her upper lip. Blood spattered the floor. If Helen hadn't fled immediately, he would doubtless have continued with a second and a third blow.

That marked an irrevocable break. He sought her desperately in bars, clubs, parks, the attic she rented, ready to beg her forgiveness on his knees. In the past few months she had become the closest thing to a girlfriend he had ever had. She continued working the brothels, but Matías didn't care about that. He valued her company, her stories, her extravagant beauty, her dedication in bed. It excited him that Helen slept with him for her own pleasure or out of a peculiar variety of love, and that she gave him packs of Camels, magazines, shoes and shirts paid for with the same bills that her clients paid to spend twenty minutes with her. Not even when Helen Anker passed syphilis onto him did he reproach her for continuing to prostitute herself. That's how he'd met her, and he accepted her that way. In any case, she cured the disease with extracts of guava, garlic and green tea, washing his genitals with a care, diligence and thoroughness which, Matías reckoned, very few women could claim. That honeymoon period was soured by the violent slap and there was no way to repair what had been ruined. Helen left the boarding house in a fury and it would be no exaggeration to say that she erased herself from the map. After a few weeks, Matías returned to his routine of tangling with the affectionate whores who approached him in the Bowery bars, drinking himself into a stupor, and trying the patience of the bartenders, who, sick of listening to his rantings about the war but above all tired of having to force him to pay for the nine, ten, eleven glasses of whisky he tended to drink, rolled him into the first taxi that would agree to take him. Some nights, Matías reacted to these offers of assistance by lashing out, punching anyone who came too close, which earned him a night in the gutter, jabbering incoherently to vagabonds and drug addicts whose unshaven faces and deleterious habits gradually became familiar to him. If he was lucky, he woke up in the same spot, spread-eagled among cardboard boxes with the first light of day peeling at his drooping eyelids; if he wasn't, he'd wake up on the cold floor of the drunk tank in the Bronx. Just as they were about to let him ago, he'd rebel, start to insult the guards wildly, winning himself another twenty-four hours in the cells. He pursued these rampages wilfully, as if he were begging to be punished, as if he wanted to make clear that he was no honourably discharged military man but a contemptible murderer who deserved chastisement to match his crimes. The cops looked at him with scorn, dismissing his insults and, except for a couple of whacks on the legs to shut him up, sent him back out onto the street without sanction, restoring to him a freedom that was becoming more and more unbearable by the day.

It was on one of these bad nights that the incident occurred that would first send him to prison and then, a month later, to the psychiatric ward at the Lake Placid hospital. He entered a bar, sat down on a stool and started on the whiskies. He hadn't forgotten Helen, but no longer spent so much time looking for her. He drank six shots, spat out four anecdotes, exchanged anodyne remarks with the barman, left under his own steam, climbed into a taxi and gave an address to the driver. Half way there, the driver heard him mumbling a string of phrases that seemed to be spoken in another language. In the rear-view mirror the driver saw him perspiring as if he were running a fever of a hundred and four; he looked tense, in a trance. 'Are you feeling all right?' the driver asked. 'Whassat?' replied Matías, pretending not to have heard. 'Just asking if you're feeling all right, pal.' 'Do I look like I'm feeling bad, *pal*?' 'You look a little upset, that's all.' 'If you don't step on the fucking gas and shut your face, then you'll see me upset and you're not gonna like it.' The taxi driver carried on driving while slowly withdrawing his left hand from the wheel to feel for the metal pipe concealed under his seat. When they arrived, the man held onto the wheel with his right hand and kept a firm grip on the weapon with the other, hoping not to have to use it. In the mirror he scrutinised every movement in the back seat. As he climbed out of the car, Matías tossed him a few dollars dismissively and then, once he was a few feet away, emitting a cynical or demented laugh, yelled triumphantly: 'And stick that tube up your ass!' The driver sat still, watching him without letting go of the metal bar.

'You're telling me he raped a young woman?' Gordon Clifford quizzed Bernard Larkin, unable to believe what the doctor had just told him. Two weeks earlier, Matías had been transferred to the hospital from the federal prison in Brooklyn, where he had been detained for sexual assault. The victim's allegations and the medical evidence were so compelling that the matter had to be settled in court. To prevent Matías from serving eight to ten years, but more importantly to keep the case from coming to light and creating a scandal to the detriment of the U.S. Air Force, the institution hired a New York lawyer, Ed Kupferman, whose reputation for successfully pulling off tricks on the margins of the rules more than justified his taking on the defence. Five minutes were enough for Kupferman to corroborate that Matías was not in his right mind and that he would be able to save him a severe sentence. His first strategic move was to write to the doctor at Molesworth base, Dr Gregory Savage, asking him to testify that months earlier he had signed off on a spurious medical discharge claiming that Lt Matthew Ryder was suffering from 'exhaustion' when in fact he was suffering from 'shell shock'. This testimony, together with that of Mrs Morris, a waiter from one of the Midtown bars, and that of Helen Anker herself, who providentially reappeared to show the scar on her cheek, all served to underpin Kupferman's argument and persuade the judge that Matías was not in possession of his critical faculties at the time of the assault. Instead of sending him to an ordinary jail, the magistrate resolved that he should be treated in a rehabilitation centre. The victim protested emphatically upon learning of the verdict and threatened to go to the press, but Kupferman disarmed her by offering her a handsome civil reparation, which the Air Force was obliged to cough up.

'Where was he caught?' Gordon Clifford asked the lawyer at the conclusion of their only conversation.

'No one caught him,' Kupferman explained. 'Matías handed himself in at a police station, asking them to arrest him for abusing a young woman.'

'He handed himself in.'

'That's what I'm telling you. The complainant didn't take long to press charges and presented medical evidence that backed her up, but by then Matías was already in a cell.'

'And what was the motive? Robbery?'

'No, everything suggests that it was an act of reprisal.'

'But why? Who is she? I mean, what is her name?'

'You will understand, Mr Clifford, that I can't share confidential information; despite the judge's ruling this remains classified.'

'Come on, Kupferman, you know very well who you are talking to.'

'I know, I know, but the law doesn't allow me...'

'I will be discreet. You have my word as a banker.'

'And you, my silence as a lawyer.'

They both grinned broadly.

'Her name is Harris, Mr Clifford, Charlotte Harris, she is twenty-four years old, single, sales manager at a second-hand car dealership, she lives with two friends, but on the night in question she was home alone.'

'Charlotte Harris,' repeated Clifford, and weighing these syllables on his tongue triggered a blurred memory of the day he heard her name for the first time.

'That's right,' said Kupferman.

On the night in question, after he got out of the taxi, Matías rang the bell on Charlotte's building. He wasn't wholly sure she still lived there, but decided to try his luck. The young woman opened the door a crack, surprised to see him – astonished, rather. Not sure she was doing the right thing, she invited him to come in and sit down. They both immediately realised they were not the same people they'd been two years earlier. They remembered perfectly the last time they'd seen each other, in the home of Charlotte's fiancé Paul, but they said nothing of that tumultuous night – not in those first minutes. She acted prudently as he made exaggerated efforts to conceal his state of drunkenness. He asked Charlotte to turn on the radio, and to give him a glass of whisky. She nodded and, as she filled his glass, thought to herself that it would be a good idea to clarify things at last and – why not – go back to being friends, like they'd been in the old days when they worked together. She was sure Matías would be in agreement. For the next few minutes Matías stammered out disjointed ramblings about what he had seen and experienced in England: the training, the flying, the omnipresent fear, the bombings, the deaths of his comrades, the horrible scenes every time they had to attack a city. Just as he began to stray into digressions that led nowhere, Charlotte asked him to stop and listen to her. She reprimanded him for not having written her a letter in almost two years, but made it clear that she didn't bear him a grudge. After a pause, she mentioned Paul's name, spoke of how much better he was doing, and told Matías tactfully, moderately, in a kindly tone, that they had indeed got married. Hearing this drove him out of his wits. He stood up, took a few directionless strides, retraced his steps, shook his head. He walked over to the radio, turned the volume up and walked briskly into the kitchen. Charlotte thought about following him, but was daunted by the sound of the cutlery drawers opening and closing with a clatter. From where she sat she begged him to calm down, to come back to the living room, to continue talking, but Matías silenced her with a sharp yell. When he returned abruptly, she saw that his fists were clenched in fury. Out of pure instinct she grabbed a cushion from the sofa and pulled it to her chest. He berated her for her lack of transparency, told her he hadn't thought her capable of such disloyalty, and when he referred to Paul as 'that paralysed piece of shit', Charlotte stood up and demanded he leave. Not only did he not leave, but he grabbed her by the wrists, telling her they had an agreement from before he signed up, that she couldn't come out with these ruses now, this nonsense of a regretful girlfriend, let alone reject him as if he were a common bum. 'Get out, you're drunk, you're on drugs, you need a doctor!' she yelled, and he pulled her towards him, trying to kiss her by force. Charlotte tried to pull away, 'You're hurting me,' she warned him, and he, possessed by demons he knew were his but did not know how to forswear, assured her he would not leave without finishing what two years earlier they had left unfinished. She instantly understood what he meant, and when she turned around to call for help, Matías grabbed her by the throat with one hand and gagged her with the other. Charlotte was unable to resist when he pushed her face down on the floor, threw his bodyweight on her, forced up her dress, pulled apart her legs with a primitive violence, tugged down her underwear, not entirely but enough to penetrate her from behind with vehemence, as if guided by an imperative need for vengeance and, calling her a slut in a voice so changed she wouldn't have recognised him, whispering in her ear how much he enjoyed being inside her at last, he continued to thrust into her until he had had his fill. During that trance, the din of the music was all that could be heard in the rest of the building. Matías left her passed out, smeared with semen and blood, left the apartment without bothering to hide his fingerprints, zigzagged for about six blocks and presented himself, impassive, with his hands in his pockets, at the first police station that appeared in his path.

After the trial, as soon as he entered the hospital at Lake Placid he underwent a detoxification process to alleviate the cumulative effects of his alcohol, tobacco and cocaine consumption. Simultaneously, he received a series of therapies, such as hypnosis to reverse his amnesia and narcosynthesis to bring out repressed emotions. He also underwent electroencephalograms to locate possible organic alterations in his brain, and was given intravenous injections of Trapanal to stimulate his subconscious. If he had a seizure at night and the palliatives did not work, he was put in a straitjacket to keep him from hurting himself; he had not attempted suicide, but Dr Larkin did not rule out the possibility that he might do so. Doctors often resorted to electroshocks to cure his psychosis, but Matías came back from these shocks shaking, alienated, a spectre, and spent most of the day in a room with high, ash-coloured walls that suffocated him, going from bed to table, from table to toilet, from toilet to bed, struggling to erase from his mind the dead of the war, the booming of the anti-aircraft guns, the whimpering of Charlotte. In his periods of calm, they led him to a room where he could practise gymnastics, make wooden toys, paint still lifes, use a sewing machine, listen to records, or sit together with other patients to hear talks aimed at helping them to discover the source of so much rage or insecurity. There he met guys like Norman Wouters and Trevor Meishner, young men of twenty-six and twenty-four respectively, navy seamen who had fought in the Pacific, having grown up in peace, taught by their parents to hate war, but who one day decided to enlist and go to the front unaware that what they would find there would destroy them emotionally. In the good moments, they learned to play guitar, ate vanilla ice cream, listened to radio comedies; but a relapse was all it took for them to become gruff, irascible and start speaking obscurely of their desire to die. Everyone there bore their own terrible story, some painful to hear, but none so much as that of Isak Karlin, a young Norwegian photographer, son of a Swedish father and Romanian mother, taken prisoner when the Germans invaded his hometown of Rennebu, near Trondheim, in early May 1940. When they learned he knew about cameras, the Nazis recruited him. Karlin's task was to accompany the mass annihilation squads, peering into the freshly dug mass graves where hundreds of corpses lay ready to be cremated, activating his flashbulb camera, and then, usually at night, developing the negatives and handing the images to the officers of the invading army. One night, as he approached one of the developed plates to pore over the details, he identified, at the base of a mountain of previously amputated dead, the unmistakable faces of his father, mother and three siblings, whom he had not heard from since his arrest but had presumed to be alive, probably hiding in a farmhouse somewhere. He covered his mouth in horror and contained his tears. That night he escaped from the German encampment carrying the negatives inside his jacket and wandered through the forests and hills, which he knew by heart, until after two days he came across a column of partisans who were beginning to organise the Norwegian resistance. He told them about the evidence he was carrying and, with two of their number, fled across the North Sea to the United Kingdom to denounce the butchery he had witnessed over these first weeks of the invasion. In England, he entered into contact with a Norwegian brigade receiving training from the Allies and joined their ranks, but his insomnia and anguish sidelined him. He was first referred to a London hospital where there was no psychiatric department and he was treated with basic hydrotherapies; there, placed in a module of crippled patients wearing bandages, splints, plaster casts, patches and using crutches or wheelchairs, Karlin seemed the least seriously ill of the lot. No one could tell him what was wrong with him; one doctor went so far as to say that his symptoms were 'after-effects of malaria'. It wasn't long before, learning that he had relatives living in the area, the hospital director recommended his transfer to Lake Placid Hospital in New York, where, he certified, his 'abnormalities' would be better treated.

Like most of the other patients there, Isak Karlin was capable of forming sentences in his mind, but found himself unable to utter them. He wanted to tell the others what it had been like to survive by the disreputable subterfuge of photographing bodies. To carry on living, he needed there to be more deaths. The more deaths there were, the safer he was. Karlin knew that the day there were no more dead bodies to photograph, he would be next. When he discovered the image of his family executed, naked, he was shocked that he had not recognised them in the moment of taking the photo. He was so worried about his own fate that he didn't stop to think about them, about what might have happened to them; he assumed they were safe, but who could be safe when his people were being ravaged by the Nazi hordes. He was spared at the cost of his family's death, but was condemned to live with a perpetual sense of ingratitude and betrayal. When he thought of those abrupt deaths, Karlin was broken not by the deaths themselves, irreparable after all, but by everything that those dead had left half-finished: their most precious projects, their solitary or collective plans, the existential turns they hoped to take, their elemental need to one day become different to the person they had been up until then. That was the real tragedy of dying suddenly, something so personal, something that urgently needed to see the light and be shouted out to the world was left truncated, confined in a drawer, laid out in a manner that no one would know how to interpret accurately, but would be irremediably distorted.

Karlin wanted to speak bluntly and confess truths that hurt like daggers. But it was physically impossible for him. All he managed to say one day was: 'I never want to shoot a camera again.' Matías seemed to understand. He too wanted nothing to do with the devices he had operated months before. Karlin's words brought to his mind not only the names of each of the Roeders lying dead under the rubble of Hamburg, but everything that could have outlived them and that had been suddenly, brutally taken away from them: their dreams, their works, their legacy, everything they so ardently desired to achieve and that was now lost in an inaccessible limbo.

Matías received his final sleep cure on November 3. Hours earlier, following his encounter with Karlin, he suffered a crisis that might have been just the same as the previous ones if it weren't for the fact that this time he made two cuts to the veins and arteries of his wrists with a pair of scissors. The following day, when Gordon Clifford entered his room and approached his bed, what he saw there was an emaciated, sick man who, on top of having spent two full months self-destructing with all sorts of substances, and a third month on pills and injections – which cured him in one sense but in another only damaged him further – had just seen his first and last attempt at suicide thwarted. 'I know his appearance may suggest otherwise, but, believe me, we've made progress, you should have seen him when they brought him in, he was... in very bad shape,' Dr Larkin said, pulling his white coat closed, during their conversation in the adjacent corridor. There he told Clifford about Matías' alcoholism, drug use, depression, paranoia, the failed attempt to take his own life. He left the subject of rape to the end. Clifford reacted with scepticism: 'You're telling me he raped a young woman?' When he wanted to talk to Matías, Dr Larkin suggested he should leave. 'The lad needs to rest,' he said.

Gordon Clifford left the hospital determined to corroborate what the doctor had told him. He went to the police station where Matías had handed himself in, to Mrs Morris' boarding house to find out what he could (in passing, he settled the outstanding debt for overdue rent), he sought out Kupferman in his office, and was even able to track down Helen Anker. She had a perfect recollection of the night Matías had transformed into a 'disgusting beast' and hit her so hard that her cheek required six stitches. With the testimony of each, he formed a picture of Matías' life over the past months and soon concluded that his friend should not remain a moment longer in Lake Placid nor in any other hospital. He was further persuaded when, five days after concluding his investigation, as soon as they were alone, Matías himself, haggard as ever, trembling but aware of his surroundings, begged him in a choking voice: 'Get me out of this madhouse, Mr Clifford, get me out of here, get me out.' These were the same words that Clifford had heard from the other side of the door of the basement in the New York house the day that Samuel was trapped by the fire that would end up consuming him. 'Get me out of here, daddy, get me out of here!' That spine-chilling scene was vividly reawakened, a fragment of a time that he had doggedly kept apart from his daily life. Gordon Clifford squeezed Matías' bony hands and promised to get him out of there any way he could.

Over the following days, he deployed his influences at the highest level, with a view to securing, first of all, an order from the magistrate to change Matías' detention regime to house arrest, and second, to obtain a medical discharge from the director of Lake Placid. The latter was the most difficult to obtain, as Dr Bernard Larkin was

247

determined to keep Matías in hospital as his psychiatric treatment had not yet been completed. 'The patient is a latent social danger,' he asserted, waving papers that he claimed were proof of Matías' mental disorders. Caught in a bind, the judge at first appeared reluctant to grant the appeal, but changed his mind after receiving timely telephone calls from two Supreme Court offices, and eventually ruled in favour of the patient's transfer. Gordon Clifford's efforts had paid off. The only objection from the magistrate was the risk of flight. 'Can you guarantee to me that the detainee will not flee?' he asked. The banker informed him that he would personally undertake to maintain the conditions of detention. 'Does your home have adequate security measures?' inquired the judge. 'He won't be living with me,' clarified Clifford. 'In that case,' objected the former, 'where?'

Over the past five years, Gordon Clifford had advised the archdiocese of New York on the acquisition of several plots of land and the management of their accounts, establishing close ties with a number of bishops, most notably archbishop Francis Stillman. He wasn't his spiritual guide, exactly, but Clifford often sought him out in his parish office with its plush brown leather armchairs adjacent to St. Patrick's Church to converse or hear his confession at times when the archbishop was not busy with anyone else. In return, Stillman would telephone him, no matter the day or time, whenever he had questions about the archdiocese's finances and property portfolio. On this basis, Clifford felt confident enough to tell him about Matías and to ask if he would consider finding a suitable place for him. The archbishop suggested that St. Joseph's Seminary in the Yonkers neighbourhood was the right place 'for the young man's recovery', and gave the banker to understand that he would personally oversee his admission.

The judge, who was a devout attendee at masses led by Father Stillman, consented when Gordon Clifford informed him of Matías' new whereabouts. Twenty-four hours later, the banker went to collect his young friend. He was convalescent, his muscles weak, but he could get around on his own and speak without faltering. He dropped into the passenger seat of the Pontiac and watched as Clifford, before turning on the engine, unfolded a map over the steering wheel and studied the route with his right index finger. A while later, on the highway, with the windows down, enjoying the wind, moved by the green fields growing up close on both sides of the road and the gleams off the lakes that appeared like inter-mittent mirages, Matías tried to find some enthusiasm for what awaited him. He knew he would have to make an effort to get used to the seminary, but it would always be preferable to remaining in the hospital, where the fruitless experimental procedure was tugging at the frayed ends of his sanity. He did not mind confinement, he had to assume his position as a sentenced man, a detainee, but he wanted to be able to face the torments of his isolation consciously and sit down to read books or write letters to, for example, the grieving Edith Roeder, his mother, who must be on tenterhooks, begging to know what had happened to her son in the war against the Nazis. He told Gordon Clifford that he would get in touch with her, he thought he was ready to put into words the unhappy feelings he had been unable to name or process for months. 'When something has no name it is more frightening,' he said, his gaze fixed on the windscreen. Clifford let him explain without interrupting, but as soon as he saw an exit on the highway, he took it, slowed down, and pulled the car over where he could.

Matías felt the engine rumble to a halt, glanced at his friend as if asking why they were stopping, and when he saw him sigh hesitantly, wipe a handkerchief across his lined forehead and make an awkward gesture of rummaging in his jacket pockets for his pipe, he knew at once what he was about to tell him. Days later, once he was in the seminary, during one of the daily visits he was permitted to the chapel to pray alone before the image of Jesus Christ, he collapsed and wept disconsolately over the death of his mother. He spent many nights cursing himself for not having insisted that she accompany him on the steamer that took him to New York; for failing to persuade her that her life was at risk at the hands of that man who even then Matías refused to call his father; and for having remained immobile in his room all those nights, doing nothing to prevent the furious beatings that Massimo dealt her. 'They found her body in the hacienda, near a riverbank, the perpetrators are unknown,' Gordon Clifford had told him, but he had no doubts about their identity.

To a certain extent he was comforted to have arrived at the monastery, for only there, only in that precinct, only enclosed by walls like those, could he eradicate or at least mitigate his visceral desire to return to Peru, to Trujillo, to Chiclín, with the sole intention of putting an end to the scum who went by the name of Massimo Giurato and his wretched brothers. Only in that purgatory could he clear his mind, alleviate his grief, and even find a quiet relief in the fortuitous fact that his mother had never had to hear from him what had happened to the Roeder family in Hamburg. He found it hard to admit but Edith's death, with all the grief it brought, also lifted a great weight off his shoulders.

Built in the early nineteenth century, the architecture of the St. Joseph seminary harked back to the early Renaissance, with arches, vaults, turrets and stained-glass windows. The ground floor contained the chapel, auditorium, offices and refectory; the other three floors, which were more restricted, alternated between the dormitories of the priests and those of the seminarists. The room assigned to Matías was in the quietest part of the top floor. It was a gloomy, austere space; a canopy bed, a chair, a desk, a basin and a gas heater. A feeble-looking deacon brought him three meals a day, together with his medicines, the books he asked for, followed him to chapel and waited for him to complete his prayers, without ever speaking to him or answering any questions he might have. The only person outside of St. Joseph's who was permitted to visit him was the court official who each month attested to the discipline of his confinement; yet even these inspections became more and more infrequent until by the eighth month he gave up coming altogether and Matías lost all contact with the outside world. This turn of events did not trouble him. As an only child, he had always been an expert in finding diversions: it was just a matter of finding the right materials to come up with a pastime. With no windows to open, he entertained himself with the oil painting hanging over the bed, a portrait of Cardinal John Henry Newman, a distinguished Anglican priest who converted to Catholicism. Cardinal Newman's lethargic features reminded him of the chaplain at the Polebrook base, that poor twenty-nine-year-old priest who would impart blessings to the airmen as they boarded their planes, even though he knew it would not spare them from death.

From his bedroom, Matías could hear the faint bustle of the seminary and could infer the time of day just by the urgency or apathy with which the soles of the seminarians' rubber shoes squeaked on the tiles of the corridors on their way to and from classes. He imagined them young, hairless, dressed entirely in black.

He nicknamed them the 'crows'. 'There go the crows again, flapping about,' he murmured, one ear glued to the door, alert to the slightest sign that might provide a clue from the outside. One day, the seminary's director, Monsignor Joseph Harrington, after asking Archbishop Stillman for permission, sent him a note inviting him to join the community's activities. Little by little, as the months went by, Matías overcame his lethargy and began to win the sympathy of the aspirants and the respect of the clergy. Watching him wash the stacked dishes with his sleeves rolled up, recite the prayers before the frugal breakfast, attend ceremonies punctually, or decorate the wooden slats of the chapel pews when the doors were opened to the local people of Yonkers on Sundays, anyone would think he was cut out for this life. No one asked why he was there, or even inquired after his real name; ever since one of the seminarians spontaneously called him Brother Matt, that became his distinctive moniker. The days were monotonous and unvarying, but Matías was going through a phase in which any repetition was considered a welcome boon. After spending two years in a never-ending back-and-forth, uncertain what would happen next, he was grateful not to be subjected to any more shocks. Sometimes he had the impression that the period with the bomber crew, which he euphemistically referred to as 'his English period', had been in a previous life, and were it not for the episodic nightmares that still reminded him of it, part of him would swear he had never taken part in a war.

On the day of his first anniversary in the seminary, Monsignor Harrington announced to him that from now on he would be allowed to use the telephone. Matías thanked him warmly, but within seconds realised that, apart from Gordon Clifford, he had no one to call. Harrington also told him that he was looking for volunteers to provide listening services for the vulnerable of the city.

'It is a question of listening to people who have had a chaotic, earthly life, been near to perdition and now want to get on the straight and narrow,' the priest explained.

'That description fits me perfectly, monsignor,' Matías reflected.

'Fits who you were in the past, you mean to say.'

'Don't you believe that we always carry with us the people we once were?'

'Not when there is sincere contrition. If one is conscious of having offended God and seeks forgiveness, the past no longer perturbs you.'

'But sometimes repentance is not enough, monsignor.'

'Do not worry, Matt, we considered you for your honesty, not for your past: that is what we most appreciate about you,' Harrington said.

The evening meetings were held once a week in one of the seminary courtyards. They were attended by chronic drinkers, hardened addicts, wife-beaters, ex-convicts, but also mothers who had unjustly lost custody of their children, widowers, beggars, and destitute people of all kinds. Under the guidance of the 'crows', the participants were grouped in circles of eight or ten people. For the first two weeks, Matías attended only as a listener, and wandered among the groups listening to testimonies. In the third and fourth weeks, he was encouraged to get involved by offering a few comments of his own. From the second month onwards, he was already in charge of a section. He felt useful, offering his attention to these men and women who had lost their way, speaking to them as pupils, the way he would have liked someone to talk to him over that series of nights he lost control altogether. Matías avoided giving predictable advice, or lessons based on parables, and limited himself to sharing his own experience, even as he avoided alluding to its military character.

One evening, a scruffy guy showed up who stared at him persistently. Matías recognised him at once: he was one of the homeless men with whom he spent those nights on the streets after being kicked out of the last bar to close. Neither acknowledged the other. He wasn't so discreet the day a young woman who bore an uncanny resemblance to Helen Anker burst into one of these sessions. His heart skipped a beat when she appeared in front of him. He found it hard to carry on, sure that he was being watched by the others, as if everyone there knew the details of his story with Helen. The woman declared that she was a prostitute and had been disenchanted with men for years. 'Because of your clients?' asked a lady in the group who, minutes before, had confessed, in addition to a recent tarot addiction, that unrequited love had led to attempts to kill herself. 'Because of men, in general,' replied the woman. 'And why is that?' probed the lady. 'Because they're liars, possessive, selfish, the worst are the violent ones,' she said, and turned her gaze on Matías with the unhurried certainty of someone returning a lost object to its place. The tarot lady nodded her head, agreeing with those words laden with disappointment or resentment. Matías swallowed hard and began to scratch his elbows as if to check that he was awake. He listened or pretended to listen to the rest of the testimonies, scrutinising the clock on the wall, clinging to the hands in his imagination to see if he could move them forward. 'Could you hear my confession, father?' the woman abruptly asked him before anyone could leave. Matías glimpsed in the question, or in the way it had been phrased, an air of pantomime, defiance and provocation. 'I'm just a lay brother, I can't confess you,' he excused himself, overacting in response. 'Could you make an exception,' she pressed, 'I won't be long.' 'Come on, brother, don't be insensitive, attend to her!' demanded the superstitious woman with the tarot addiction. Matías gasped and prayed that the granite building would soon collapse so that this martyrdom would end. 'Follow me this way,' he said, extending an arm with a complete lack of conviction. They walked to the most distant of the columns in the cloistered garden. The fading light of day illuminated the girl's face. The lips, the eyelashes and the nose were identical to Helen's. It's her, he said to himself. 'Do you really wish to leave your line of work?' asked Matías, failing to hide his nerves. 'Yes,' she answered. 'I want to study, learn. We can all change, can't we, brother?' To Matías' ears this sounded like a sarcastic, even malicious insinuation. 'I have not changed,' he resisted. 'What's that, brother? Are you all right?' Matías distracted her by asking her to begin her confession. As he heard her recite her sins, he dared to pass the back of his hand over her cheek, paused at her rounded chin, slipped down her neck and came to rest on her forearm. She lowered her head easily and he felt that those eyes hid irrefutable truths that were struggling to be revealed. 'Is there anything else you want to tell me, Miss?' he said, anxious. 'I'm finished,' she said. They were breathing at the same pace. Matías took advantage of the fact that the woman had let her guard down and he told her what had happened with his mother. In the good old days of their relationship, they had talked about Edith Roeder so many times, always at Helen's request, and the news of the crime seemed to genuinely sadden this woman too. Or so Matías thought he sensed. 'I knew something bad was going to happen to her and I did nothing, nothing,' he muttered. And now it was this new woman who was caressing his face, patting his shoulders and holding his hands. From a corridor on the upper floor, Monsignor Harrington was observing the scene in silence. Matías sensed his steely, reproachful gaze and quickly took a step back. 'Come back soon,' he whispered to the woman, desiring the excitement of the days when he and Helen had seen each other frequently. She responded with a languid embrace and pulled from her handbag an enigmatic prayer card that she furtively snuck into his shirt pocket as if entrusting a secret to him; only then did she leave through the door she had entered two hours earlier. Watching her go, Matías longed for her company, the sensuality of her body, and in his mind he altered the course of the past, erasing from his memory the night of the slap, and was able to glimpse in retrospect a long period of happiness with that ethereal woman who, he now realised, would never come back. If she had come, Matías imagined, it was not because she wanted to change her life, even less because she was short of spiritual guidance, but because she wanted to see him, to speak to him directly and endow the time they had spent together with a fairer or more harmonious ending. That conclusion left him floundering. He took the prayer card out of his pocket and saw the image of a lit candle accompanied by a caption that read: 'It is better to light a candle than to curse the darkness'.

Questions swirled abruptly in his head, questions about what he was looking for, if he was still looking for anything, and about his role in this place. He looked resentfully at his loafers, his white linen trousers, his cotton shirt: more than an outsider, he felt like an imposter. He realised that it was discipline or perseverance, not faith, that had allowed him to fit into the seminary with such ease; perhaps something similar would have happened in any other kind of organisation, whether it be a pagan sect, a gang of smugglers or a counterfeiting mafia, as long as there was a hierarchy involved. He was still good at taking orders, doing his homework, obediently carrying out his duties as a military man. Was that enough for him to dedicate himself to the priesthood? Was that truly his vocation or merely a temporary escape valve? He wasn't sure, but he was determined to take all the time he needed to find out. Sometimes he would linger in the garden, smoking in the sun by the waterfalls, exhaling the smoke at his leisure, and out of the blue there returned to his mind, no longer with apprehension, clear memories of the war: he would revisit the hard days of training at Westover airfield, the names and aliases of each of his crewmates, his brothers, the jokes that enlivened the evenings in the barracks, the laughter, the riotous nights in London; but then he saw himself in the fishbowl of the B-17, suspended in the void, hazards on all sides, dropping bombs and more bombs on so many cities until he arrived unfailingly at the sequence of Hamburg, the impossible choice, and at that he would abruptly cut off these musings, finding them degrading, crush the cigarette under his heel, and resume his work. One afternoon he sought out Harrington to confess, and for the first time, sober, with no whisky in front of him, and without sacrificing details, he spoke of his time in Europe, the aerial victories, the massacres, the desire to desert, as well as the impossibility of ever redeeming that lasting sensation of guilt and failure that 'thanks to you' – that's how he put it – 'thanks to you' he had learned to master. The monsignor was also interested in 'the girl from the other day', and Matías admitted the truth of his daydreams: he said her name was Helen Anker, confessed that she was a harlot, that they had been lovers, and unashamedly admitted that some nights he masturbated thinking about her. Harrington advised him of the impurity of lust, dictated a benevolent penance and told him to go in peace, reciting the formula for the absolution of sins. Although these solemn words could not erase his crimes nor cauterise the cracks in his memory, Matías found that they had a favourable effect on his mood, freeing him, even if only briefly, from the extenuating prison of his bitter doubts.

One morning he understood that it made no sense to continue to ponder the dilemma of his stay at the seminary. What else could he do? He had no alternative. He chose to lead this monastic life in the most cordial manner, trying to make the best of the situation. By the end of 1944, he was just another member of St. Joseph's. He was not given specific duties, but he continued to take care of a range of different tasks: he updated the calendar of extracurricular activities for the seminarians, inventoried the books and magazines that the senior deacons used for the students' entertainment, gave ideas to the priests on how to increase attendance of the faithful at the parish's Saturday events. The bishops often asked for his opinion as a former military man concerning the optimisation of resources and the security of the cloister, and on certain occasions he was even asked to assume the deciding voice in the usual community discord. Matías interacted with everyone without distinction. On Thanksgiving Day he volunteered to roast the turkey and taught the hidebound cooks the recipe for *Bratapfel*, his great-grandmother Helga's stuffed apples, and a month later, at Christmas Eve mass, he was able to sit in the deacons' choir, alongside the taciturn young man who for months had attended to him in decorous silence. That night he discovered that this man had prodigious vocal chords, and hearing him sing the universal Christmas hymns he felt comforted and near to the sense of devotion that radiated from the architecture of the chapel.

Early on May 8, 1945, having read the newspapers that proclaimed the victory of the Allies following the formal surrender signed the previous day by General

Alfred Jodl, Chief of the Operations Staff of the Wehrmacht, Matías ran to bring the news to Monsignor Harrington. He found him seated at his desk, shaving over a porcelain basin filled with water and foam. A sleeveless shirt revealed his barrel chest, somewhat undermining his usual clerical authority. When Harrington heard the good news he dropped the razor and stood up, embracing Matías and smearing shaving foam over one cheek. 'Don't move!' he said, excited. He dried himself off with a towel, turned around and with three quick steps reached the built-in cabinet where, behind a few old chalices and reliquaries, he kept hidden a bottle of triple sec for such moments. Days earlier the newspapers had been filled with speculation over the suicide of Hitler and took it for granted that the German army's days were numbered; but only now was the Nazi defeat sealed with the signing in Reims of the unconditional surrender, requiring a complete ceasefire within twenty-four hours. The monsignor, now wearing his cassock, ordered one of the deacons to ring the bells twelve times and to raise the flag over the building, as if it were a fortress rather than a seminary, and offered a mass in honour of the fallen of the war, especially the U.S. soldiers. After this mass, Matías was asked to say a few words.

'I've been thinking of going.'

At the other end of the telephone, Clifford played the innocent.

'Going where, my lad?'

'Hamburg. Where else?'

'Matías, it's been over two years, don't you think it's time to…'

'To forget? No. I want to go now more than ever and continue with the work that I've been doing here: speak with those who lost their homes and their families, hear their needs, read them lessons from the Bible, offer them tools to get back on their feet.'

'Or in other words, you want to stop your conscience eating away at you?'

'When you put it like that it sounds like a bad thing.'

'No, not at all. It's laudable on your part, but I thought you would focus on your health first.'

'I owe myself this voyage, and even more important, I think that I owe it to my mother, my grandfather, the day that I finally go I can…'

'Son, enough, stop torturing yourself thinking that you…'

'You don't know what I'm thinking!'

'Matías, do you really believe that someone needs you right now in Hamburg?'

'Me! I need to be there!'

'Are you sure about that?'

'I've rarely been surer of anything recently.'

'All right, all right, don't get overexcited. Let me talk to Stillman. I don't know if his archdiocese maintains contact with any congregations in Germany. In any case, we'd have to talk with the judge again, ask for a special dispensation, in short, I'd have to pull some strings. In a week I should have news.'

The phone call from Gordon Clifford that Matías was waiting for took not one but three weeks. As soon as he heard there was a call for him he leapt down the stairs two at a time, leaning on the banister, and shot into the telephone room.

'I've good news and bad,' said Gordon Clifford, 'Which do you want to hear first?'

'The bad news,' mumbled Matías.

'The bad news is that you can't go to Germany.'

'There aren't any sister churches there?'

'Yes, there are, but Stillman refuses to sanction it.'

'What does that mean?'

'Stillman thinks that it's not a good time, it's too soon.'

'Too soon? That's absurd! I should be the one to decide that, don't you think?'

'Stillman sees things differently.'

'Stillman! Stillman! What the hell does he know about what I feel or need?'

'Matías, please calm down, and remember that if it weren't for the intervention of the archbishop you'd still be in the asylum.'

The line went quiet. Matías could sense the flashing anger in the banker's eyes at the other end.

'I'm sorry, my impatience gets ahead of me.'

'Your problem isn't impatience, Matías, it's foolishness, stupidity, caprice.'

'Are you going to tell me what the good news is or not?'

'The good news is that Stillman has been receptive to the idea, and proposes to send you temporarily to a church in Foggia, in Apulia, about three hours from Rome.'

'And why there?' said Matías.

'Because there were bombings there too. There are a lot of people living in misery, with nothing to eat and no hope for the future... I think that may be the experience you're looking for.'

Monsignor Harrington and a police officer accompanied Matías to the port of New York, where for the second and last time in his life he boarded a steamship. The voyage lasted sixteen days. He disembarked in Messina and from there caught an overnight bus to Foggia, and made his way to the basilica of San Giovanni Battista, where he presented himself to the priests in a mixture of Spanish and English, and to which his hosts replied in Italian. Thanks to his letters of recommendation, the priests afforded him a privileged treatment that did not match his situation as a condemned criminal, of which they appeared to be unaware. 'Ha bisogno di qualcosa di più?' asked Father Angelo Pallotti, the priest who oversaw the parish house attached to the basilica, showing Matías to a cramped and ill-lit chamber. 'Voglio una ventana,' Matías replied, attempting to ask for a window, in the forlorn hope that the Spanish and Italian words would be the same. 'Una fontana? Qui?' the priest looked confused at what he took to be Matías' request for a fountain. 'Una ven-tana, Padre,' Matías repeated, enunci- ating the syllables and tracing a square in the air with the forefingers of each hand. 'Ma certo, una finestra!' replied Pallotti, finally understanding what Matías wanted, and promptly relocated him to a chamber overlooking a tree-lined garden on the Via San Lazzaro.

From the outset, he did all he could to earn the friendship of the religious fraternity living there, who numbered no more than ten. The arrival of the impetuous, charismatic 'Brother Matt', with his jovial readiness to reach out to the population traumatised by the aerial bombardment and to help in any way he could, was a balm for them, a rare motivating presence. Every morning in the courtyard, Matías led a routine of calisthenics and gymnastics, which the other members of the house successively joined in, including the three overweight friars who were normally firm adherents of the law of minimum physical effort, but who now demanded the exercises with childlike enthusiasm.

The faithful began to see him on their weekend parish days, as well as at Sunday masses, particularly the midday mass, where Matías was part of the group of acolytes that assisted in the celebration of the liturgy, whether accompanying communion, passing along the pews the velvet bag in which the alms were collected, or swinging the censer in the entrance procession. He was always the most helpful in fulfilling these and other tasks until someone asked him to light the candles of a candelabra or build a fire to warm his hands. Then he would refuse with a delicate gesture of apology. The slightest proximity to fire still caused him horror. He never carried matches, and it had been a long time since he had carried the Wieden lighter. Yet his aversions were not only related to fire. He was also left dazed by the ringing of the alarm clock, the growl of engines, the detonation of the smallest firework, or the repeated use of expressions containing words such as 'bomb', 'fire', 'smoke' or 'ash'. Sometimes he averted his eyes from the image of Christ in the church, since the wooden cross reminded him of the crosshairs seen through the bombsight in the nose of the B-17, and even gazing up at the open sky carried a risk of bringing back ominous shapes or visions of the past, leading to a paralysis that wrought havoc with his mood. 'Everything changes its appearance except the sky,' Matías would declare when he was distracted by migrating birds, shifting clouds, unusually bright stars, or one of the phases of twilight. He said it as if he saw hostile messages behind these phenomena, inaccessible to the understanding of others. In later years, with every reference to 'charming Brother Matt', the friars would repeat that dull but accurate phrase: 'Everything changes its appearance except the sky.'

By day, together with three of the novice priests, he would tour the villages inhabited by the survivors of the Allied raids, bringing them sustenance, blankets, hearing their stories of suffering, taking note of their requests, resolving their doubts. The nine aerial attacks on Foggia, which were aimed at the transport network, killed over 20,000 civilians and left hundreds of homes in ruins, as well as the railway station. 'The most pitiless bombing of all came on July 22 of '43, just three days after Mussolini's arrest,' recounted a skeletal, stooped man who looked older than his years, as he sipped despondently at a spoonful of the warm soup brought by the visitors. The date did not leave Matías indifferent: Operation Gomorrah in Hamburg was about to take place in those days.

With the efforts at repairs to the city, Foggia had regained some of its battered beauty; however, from the top of the region's steep hills or on the edge of its foliage-clad cliffs, the unmistakable signs of devastation were clear, together with a ghostly halo that still hung over the city. Every morning for three months in a row, often on an empty stomach, Matías spent hours at a time with these wretched men, women and children whose condition, in every possible way, was impoverished. The more fortunate had occupied half-ruined buildings; groups of ten or twelve people lived crammed into a single room whose windows were covered only with greaseproof paper. Others managed to hide in stinking concrete tunnels and there, amid the filth of garbage dumps and latrines, they organised temporary burrows. The shortages were such that young and old brushed their teeth with sand; the day Matías brought them tooth-brushes, toothpaste and bottles of water, in addition to a few other utensils that were donated to the church, the expressions of gratitude were indescribable. Some days, as he followed these ragged men through the lonely waste-lands that their former neighbourhoods had become, as he listened to their stories of how peaceful life had been in that astonishingly fertile region before the advent of the war, and as he saw them set on rebirth after having been stripped of everything they owned, Matias felt he was contributing in some way to the recovery of a town that had been smashed to pieces by heavy craft similar to the one in which he had flown. 'Forget the past,' he told the inhabitants of Foggia, 'forget tomorrow too: your whole life is concentrated in this one moment, this is the moment you must survive, there will be time to worry about the next one.'

Four months after his arrival, just when he was seriously beginning to contemplate settling down in Foggia, the mishap occurred that would lead him to abandon it altogether. It was early Thursday morning. Matías woke up, went out into the courtyard to do his exercises and was surprised not to see any of the brothers. Then he remembered: they had gone on an excursion, they would not be back until after midday. He looked for Father Angelo Pallotti in his office, but he was not there either. After a few minutes, someone rang the doorbell. Matías opened the door without looking to see who it was and found a woman in her twenties standing there with a baby in her arms. He thought he might have noticed her before, when still pregnant, on his first forays into the bombed villages. In her haggard face her black pupils shone like jet spheres. The young woman wanted to baptise her child, and he told her there was no one present to perform the sacrament and that she should come back later. She was so insistent, however, that Matías considered improvising the ceremony himself. He knew it like the back of his hand and it wouldn't take more than twenty minutes. Hadn't Father Palloti told him he could do whatever he believed appropriate in the house? 'Come with me,' he told her, half-closing the door, imbued with a sense of euphoria. They walked the fifty paces to the rear entrance to the basilica, crossed the gloomy rooms of the sacristy and entered the sumptuous central nave. Even though the light of Foggia filtered through the half-open shutters of the church windows, Matías lit a few lamps. He took the Bible from the pulpit and approached the font, where the woman was waiting.

Matías looked at the boy, whose sulky expression he found amusing. 'And the father?' he ventured. 'He's a soldier, he's already back in Rome,' the girl mumbled, losing her black eyes in the geometric figures of the tiles. With no one else there but the three of them, the basilica was even more imposing than usual. Matías raised his voice, declaring that baptism was synonymous with salvation, for it purified original sin and turned men into children of God. He read a few verses from the book of Exodus and began to pour the holy water. He hadn't finished when he asked her for the name the child would bear. 'Carlo Giurato,' replied the mother. Matías shivered, and let a big splash of water fall on the baby's head. Hearing his Italian surname after so many years was worse than heresy. Finally, unsettled, suspecting a conspiracy between this woman and his father or one of his uncles, and at the same time fearing that the child was his own reincarnation, the new recipient of the ancestral curse of his paternal family, he fearfully repeated the ritual words, 'I baptise you in the name of the Father, and of the Son and of the Holy Spirit,' poured out the last drops, watched them fall as the bombs fell, in clusters, and continued their course until they exploded, one by one, on the newborn's unclouded forehead.

21

The day I returned to Madrid, it wasn't until eight in the evening that we got past the obstruction caused by the overturned truck at Ciudad Lineal. Once we'd left the accident behind, the taxi snaked along the A-2 highway in the direction of La Castellana and continued its route through the San Bernardo neighbourhood. The journey from the airport, which should have taken thirty-five minutes at most, had lasted more than twice that. Despite the late hour, the early September light meant the outline of the city's largest buildings could still be distinguished.

'Are you going to go back to your ex-wife?' ventured Antonio. At this point, after everything we'd told each other, his curiosity seemed wholly reasonable.

'No,' I told him. 'It's time to be alone for a while.'

'Not alone – single,' he corrected me, mischievously.

'Right,' I thanked him, half-smiling. 'Better to be defined by your marital status than your mood.'

'Look on the bright side: you can meet girls, flirt, play the field.'

His peroration made me think of the useless nights when I went out in search of adventure only to return home empty-handed.

'It's not good to be alone,' he added.

At that, there flashed into my mind what the saleswoman had said about Fritz in the aquarium shop: 'That fish died of loneliness.' I wondered if humans could die of the same cause.

'Nah, sometimes it's better to be alone,' I said, trying to sound resolute.

'There I disagree. When is it better?'

'I don't know, when it's indispensable.'

'And how do you know when that moment arrives?'

'You feel it, I guess. Of course, if it's a solitude imposed by someone else, that makes everything more difficult,' I digressed.

'You're thinking about your wife.'

'How did you guess.'

'I know what you're talking about, all I'm saying is it's not a good thing to get old without company.'

'I fear neither old age nor solitude,' I claimed. It wasn't true.

'If you run into her, I hope it will be a civilised encounter.'

'I'm not going to run into her, I can assure you of that. She returned to her parents' house in Germany. Did I tell you Erika is German? Did I tell you her name is Erika?'

'No, but it doesn't matter. I didn't tell you my wife's name is Bertha, either.'

'Right. That's fair. We're square.'

'And which city is Erika from?'

'From Berlin.'

'Did you learn any German from her?'

'Very little. Erika's mother is from Argentina, so her Spanish is perfect. We met, lived, married and divorced in Spanish.'

'The only German city I know is Hamburg.'

'Hamburg. In the north, right?'

'Yes, up top, three hours by car from Denmark. The climate is awful, the city spectacular.'

'Doesn't sound very touristic. Did you go for work?'

'I went with my wife to visit an uncle of hers, a guy from Trujillo. My wife's from there. Do you know Trujillo?'

'Sure, I've been a few times. Great climate. Better food. I can't imagine it's anything like Hamburg.'

'My wife's uncle is a journalist, like yourself, but older, retired. He worked for *La Industria*, do you know it?'

'Of course, the biggest paper in north Peru.'

'He travelled to Hamburg for an article, but ended up falling in love with a German girl, just like you, and stayed there.'

'Another one who didn't come back.'

'He told us it was a story he really wanted to write. He only published a short piece in the end.'

'What was it about?'

'Something that happened to a kid who studied at the same college as him in Trujillo.'

'What period are we talking about?'

'Second world war. The kid took part in the bombings.'

'He participated in the war? He was a pilot?'

'Something like that.'

'You mean to say a Peruvian dropped bombs on Hamburg?' I exclaimed.

The car braked abruptly. For several minutes now we'd been driving through the Malasaña district.

'Sorry, I think I've passed the address. You told me Calle de la Palma 59, right?'

'That's the one,' I confirmed.

Antonio turned on his warning lights and reversed a

few dozen metres until we were in front of the building.

'Here it is. Is this good for you?' he asked. 'This your home?'

'Yup.' I didn't say any more. The word *home* caused me to hesitate.

We got out. As he got my suitcase out of the boot, I scanned the neighbouring businesses: a call shop, a tile shop, a flower shop with flower pots outside, a restaurant with a faded Italian flag on the façade, a bar with glass doors, a pub that had apparently closed down. Antonio shut the boot and when I was about to take out my wallet to pay him, as if he could read my mind, he uttered the sentence I was longing to hear:

'If you're not in a hurry, I'll tell you the story of the Peruvian bombardier.'

The owner of the flat had told me to pick up the keys from the adjacent call shop. I asked Antonio to wait a moment while I went in, and when I came back with the keys I had a proposal for him.

'Tell me the story, but let me invite you for a beer,' I offered, signalling the bar opposite, whose name was spelled out in green and red neon.

'I'll accept a Coca-Cola, maestro,' he replied.

We sat down, face to face for the first time. I ordered the drinks.

'Go on then, I'm listening,' I said, once they were brought.

And so he began.

Madrid, May 2023

CHARCO PRESS

Director & Editor: Carolina Orloff
Director: Samuel McDowell

www.charcopress.com

The World We Saw Burning was printed on
Munken Cream 80gsm paper.

The text was designed using Bembo 11.5 and ITC Galliard.

Printed in January 2025 by Bell and Bain Ltd.
303 Burnfield Road, Thornliebank, Glasgow G46 7UQ
using responsibly sourced paper.

MIX
Paper | Supporting
responsible forestry
FSC
www.fsc.org   FSC® C007785

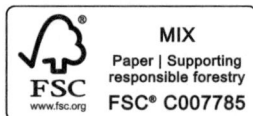